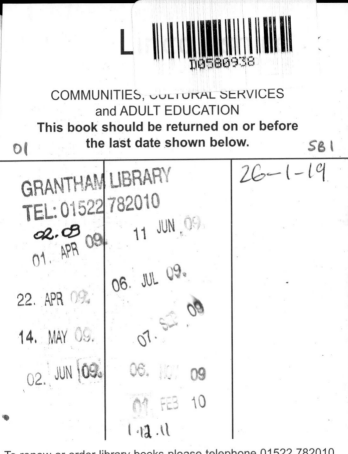

'Clio!' he growled, his icy calm **cking at last. He dropped the ms, his hands curling into fists.**

And Clio felt a stirring of some strange satisfaction.

'You are the most obstinate woman I have ever seen,' he muttered. 'Why can you not just listen to me for once in your life?'

'Just listen to you? Quietly do what you want, just as everyone does with the exalted Duke? Well, I'm sorry, Your Grace, but I am too busy o stand here arguing with you any longer.' She rode past him, not sure where she was going, ly knowing that she had to get away. Had to cape from those crackling bonds before she ploded!

he gave Averton a wide berth, yet not quite vide enough. Before she had even seen him nove, he caught her by the wrists, pulling er close to him. Startled, she dropped her lagger. It landed mere inches from his booted foot, yet he did not glance at it at all. He only watched her.

Author Note

When I was a child, my parents had a photo-filled book about 'Ancient Places'. I loved that book, and it made me fascinated with archaeology! I even tore up freshly planted grass in the garden, looking for Viking treasure. It all seemed so adventurous and romantic.

The three Chase sisters share my fascination, and they are lucky enough to exist in the Regency period where interest in the ancient world is strong. They can spend their time studying artefacts, digging on archaeological sites—and finding love with gorgeous and dashing men!

When I first met Clio and her Duke, in TO CATCH A ROGUE, I didn't see how they could overcome their many differences. The fact that Clio knocked him down with a marble statue seemed the least of their troubles! Yet they obviously belonged together; they shared a very powerful attraction, an unusual way of looking at the world. But would that be enough? I had a wonderful time 'visiting' Sicily with them, and finding the answer to that question. I hope you enjoy their tale, too!

TO DECEIVE
A DUKE

Amanda McCabe

MILLS & BOON®

Pure reading pleasure™

All the characters in this book have no existence outside the imagination of the author, and have no relation whatsoever to anyone bearing the same name or names. They are not even distantly inspired by any individual known or unknown to the author, and all the incidents are pure invention.

First published in Great Britain 2008
Paperback edition 2009
Harlequin Mills & Boon Limited,
Eton House, 18-24 Paradise Road, Richmond, Surrey TW9 1SR

© Amanda McCabe 2008

ISBN: 978 0 263 86763 3

Set in Times Roman 10½ on 12¼ pt.
04-0209-76349

Printed and bound in Spain
by Litografia Rosés S.A., Barcelona

Amanda McCabe wrote her first romance at the age of sixteen—a vast epic, starring all her friends as the characters, written secretly during algebra class. She's never since used algebra, but her books have been nominated for many awards, including the RITA® Award, the *Romantic Times BOOKreviews* Reviewers' Choice Award, the Booksellers Best, the National Readers' Choice Award, and the Holt Medallion. She lives in Oklahoma, with a menagerie of two cats, a pug and a bossy miniature poodle, and loves dance classes, collecting cheesy travel souvenirs, and watching the Food Network—even though she doesn't cook. Visit her at http://ammandamccabe.tripod.com and http://www.riskyregencies.blogspot.com

A recent novel by the same author:

TO CATCH A ROGUE*
Linked to TO DECEIVE A DUKE

Prologue

Queen of fragrant Eleusis,
Giver of earth's good gifts,
Give me your grace, O Demeter.
You, too, Persephone, fairest,
Maiden of all lovely, I offer
Song for your favor.

Clio Chase glanced back over her shoulder as she tiptoed along the narrow corridor of Acropolis House, the labyrinthine London home of the Duke of Averton. No one followed her. Probably they did not even notice her absence from the ballroom, not in such a crush as the Duke's Grecian masked ball.

Perfect.

It was silent here, unlike the roar of music and shallow conversation. So quiet it was almost like a cave, lit only by a few lamps built to resemble flickering torches. The shifting light touched the dark panelled walls, the low, carved ceiling and the gilt-framed paintings, making them glitter and waver as if alive.

She paused to slip off her heeled green satin shoes, hurrying on stocking feet to the end of the corridor where there was a small, winding staircase, a miniature of the grand one soaring up from the foyer. She held up the heavy green-and-gold silk skirts of her Medusa costume as she hurried up the steps. The Duke was being very cagey about the statue's whereabouts tonight. But his servants were not all so secretive. Clio had been able to persuade a footman to tell her where Artemis, the Alabaster Goddess, waited.

At the top of the stairs ran a gallery, almost the entire length of the front of the house. Its bank of windows, uncovered, looked out at the front garden and the street beyond, the open gates that still admitted latecomers to the ball.

The gallery was dotted with more lamps, most of them unlit. No doubt waiting for the 'grand reveal' of the statue after supper, when they would spring to life as if by magic. Right now the light was dim, falling only in shimmering, narrow bars on some of the treasures displayed there, leaving others in darkness.

Clio found herself holding her breath as she crept along the gallery, peering right and left at all the wonders jumbled together. Her father and his friends were all great collectors and loved to show off their prizes, so she had grown up surrounded by beautiful antiquities. But this—this was something else entirely. A cabinet of curiosities such as she had never seen before.

The gallery almost resembled a warehouse, it was so thick with objects. Ancient stone kouros, stiff and precise, their empty eyes staring back at her. Bronze warriors, marble gods; cases full of Etruscan gold jewellery, lapis scarabs, jewelled perfume bottles. Steles propped against the walls. Shelves of vases, kraters and amphorae. All jumbled together, just to serve one man's vanity, his lust for collecting.

Clio frowned as she thought of Averton. So handsome that half the women in town were in love with him—but so mysterious. That strange light in his green eyes when he looked at her…

She shook her head, the satin snakes of her headdress trembling. She couldn't think about *him* now. She had a task to do.

At the end of the gallery, alone in a pool of candle-light, was an object covered in a sheet of black satin. Only a bit of the separate coral-coloured marble base was visible. Clio approached it carefully, half-expecting some sort of trap, some alarm. All was silent, except for the whining hum of the wind past the windows. She reached out and carefully lifted the sheet, peering beneath.

'Oh.' She sighed. It was really her. The Alabaster Goddess. Artemis in all her solitary glory.

The statue was not large. It was easily dwarfed by many of the more elaborate creations in the gallery. But she was so perfectly beautiful, so graceful and elegant, that Clio could understand why she had become such a sensation. Why ladies wanted 'Artemis' coiffures and 'Artemis' sandals.

Why the Duke hid her away.

Carved of an alabaster so white it seemed to glisten, almost silver, like a first snowfall, she stood poised with her bow raised, a lost arrow set to fly. Her pleated tunic flowed over the curves of her slender body as if caught in a breeze, ending at mid-thigh to reveal strong legs, tensed to run. Her sandals, those ribbon-laced shoes every lady copied this Season, still bore bits of gold leaf, as did the bandeau that held back her curled hair. A crescent moon was attached to the band, proclaiming her to be truly the Goddess of the Moon. Her gaze was focused intently on her prey; she cared nothing for mortal adulation.

Clio stared up at her, enthralled, as she imagined the Delian temple where this goddess once resided, where she once received her worship from true acolytes. Not just *ton* ladies and their 'Artemis' shoes.

'How beautiful you are,' she whispered. 'And how sad.'

Much like the Duke himself.

She reached out to gently touch Artemis's foot in a gesture of silent sympathy. As she did, she noticed that the goddess stood on a wooden base, a thick block with a thin crack running along its centre. She leaned closer, trying to see if that crack was a fault or deliberate. It seemed such a strange perch for a beautiful goddess.

'Ah, Miss Chase. Clio. I see you have discovered the whereabouts of my treasure,' a voice said quietly.

Clio ducked away from Artemis, spinning around to find the Duke himself standing halfway along the gallery. Watching her intently.

Even in the dim light, his eyes gleamed like the snakes in her headdress. He smiled at her gently, deceptively, shrugging the leopard pelt of his Dionysus costume back from his shoulders. He moved closer, light and silent, as if he was a leopard himself.

'She is beautiful, is she not?' he said, still so quiet. 'I knew you would be drawn to her, as I was. She is quite—irresistible, in her mystery and solitude.'

Clio edged back against the goddess. She had indeed

found Artemis irresistible. So much so that she had let her guard down, and that was not like her. As the Duke came closer, she reached behind her, her fingers just touching Artemis's cold sandal. She slid her touch down, finding that crack in the wooden base. She curled her hand around it, as if Artemis could protect her from Averton, from the dark confusion she always felt when he was near.

Just as it was now. He drew ever closer, slow but inescapable, like a leopard in the jungle. He watched her carefully, as if he expected her to bolt like a frightened gazelle. As if he could see all the secrets of her heart.

Clio stiffened her shoulders, tightening her fingers around the base. Suddenly, that silence she had craved in the crowded ballroom seemed oppressive. All the jumbled treasures of the room loomed higher, narrowing on just Artemis and her white glow.

It was like this whenever they met, she and Averton. He impeded her work as the Lily Thief, her mission. Yet they were bound together by invisible, unbreakable cords. They could not stay away from each other.

She would not give him the satisfaction of running now. Not yet.

He finally reached her side, and Clio held her breath. He touched the hem of Artemis's tunic, his jewelled fingers just inches from Clio's green silk sleeve. She could feel the warmth of his skin, the bright light of his gaze on her.

That tension between them grew, stretched taut until Clio thought she would scream with it.

'I cannot let you take her, Clio,' he said. So gentle. So implacable.

Clio tried to laugh. 'Oh? Do you think I could just

tuck her under my skirt and spirit her out of here? Past all your guards?'

His gaze flickered almost imperceptibly over her green silk skirts. 'I would not be surprised at anything you did.'

'I *would* like to give her a finer home than this,' Clio said. 'But I am not such a fool as to try such a thing.'

'Not tonight, anyway.'

'As you say.'

His touch slid from Artemis's stone tunic to Clio's draped sleeve. Their skin did not even brush, but Clio felt the spark of his caress none the less. She swayed towards him as if spellbound. The crowded ball, the vast city outside—it all vanished. There was only him. Them, together.

And that scared her as nothing else ever had.

'I know what you're up to, Clio Chase,' he murmured, deep and seductive as a lover. 'And I cannot let you continue. For your own sake.'

Clio reared back from his sorcerer's caress, the lure of his voice. 'My sake? Oh, no, your Grace. Everything you do is surely for yourself alone.'

His hand tightened on her arm, not letting her go. 'There are things you do not know.'

'About you?'

'Me—and what is happening here. With the Alabaster Goddess.'

'I fear I know more about you than I wish to!' Clio cried. 'About your greed, your—'

'Clio!' He gave her a little shake, pulling her closer to him. So close there was not even a whisper between them.

He played the indolent, careless duke so well, but Clio could feel the iron strength of him next to her. The shift of his muscles. She wanted closer, ever closer.

And *that* frightened her even more.

'Why do you never listen to me?' he growled, his eyes like emerald embers burning into her.

'Because you never talk to me,' she whispered. 'Not really.'

'How can I talk to someone who so mistrusts me?' His touch convulsed on her arms, crushing the silk. 'Oh, Clio. What are you doing to me?'

His lips touched hers, a kiss that was utterly irresistible, like a summer thunderstorm. She tasted her own anger, her own frustration in that kiss, the desperate need of an impossible attraction.

Suddenly, the kiss, the nearness of him, her own heightened emotions—it was all too much. Something snapped inside her, and she had to escape. She pushed the Alabaster Goddess towards him, intending only to put a barrier between them. To remind them who, what, they really were.

Instead, Artemis's marble elbow connected sharply with his head. Both he and the statue crashed to the floor in a tangle of marble, leopard skin and drops of blood.

Clio gasped to see the red gash on his brow, his closed eyes. 'Edward!' she cried, dropping to her knees beside him.

She reached for his wrist, feeling the pulse beating there with a surge of absurd relief. She had not killed him.

Not yet.

'Stay here,' she whispered. 'I must fetch help!'

With that, she dashed away, past all the antiquities, the shadows, not sure what she ran toward—or away from.

She did not even notice the scrap of green silk caught in his hand…

Chapter One

❧

Enna Province, Sicily—six months later

"'**T**hou grave, my bridal chamber! Dwelling-place hollowed in earth, the everlasting prison whither I bend my steps, to join the band of kindred, whose more numerous host already Persephone hath counted with the dead…'"

Clio Chase turned her spyglass toward the ruined amphitheatre, where her sister Thalia rehearsed the lines of *Antigone*. The crumbling stage was far from Clio's perch atop a rocky hill, yet she could glimpse Thalia's golden hair glinting in the morning sunlight, could hear the despairing words of Sophocles' princess as she was led to her death.

That eternal struggle of life and death, beauty and fate, seemed to belong to this bright day, this land. Ancient Sicily, where so many conquerors had overrun the rocky hills and dusty plains, yet none had ever fully possessed it. It belonged to old gods, far older than even the Greeks and Romans could have imagined. A wild place, slave to no master.

Clio turned her glass, purchased from their ship's captain on the voyage here from Naples, past her sister to the landscape beyond. No London stage director could have imagined such a glorious backdrop! Beyond the steps and stage of the amphitheatre were only mountains, a vast swathe of blue sky. The hills rolled on like a hazy sea, green and brown and purple, until they reached the flat, snow-dusted peak of Etna, cloaked in clouds.

Off in the other direction, just barely seen, were the calm, silvery waters of Lake Pergusa, where Hades had snatched Persephone away to his underworld kingdom.

Between were olive groves, orchards of lemons, limes and oranges, stands of wild fennel, the large prickly pears brought in by the Saracens. Carpets of flowers, yellow, white and dark purple, spread like bright blankets over the meadows, announcing that spring had truly arrived.

"'Enna—where Nature decks herself in all her varied hues, where the ground is beauteous, carpeted with flowers of many tints,'" Clio murmured, an Ovid quote she now truly understood. Enna had once been considered the heart of Sicily, the crossroads of the Trinacria, the three provinces, a sacred spot. The home of Demeter and her daughter.

And now it had been invaded by the Chase family, or part of the family anyway. Clio had come here with her father and two of her sisters, Thalia and Terpsichore, after they had seen their eldest sister Calliope off on her honeymoon. Sir Walter Chase had long heard of the archeological wonders to be found in Enna, just waiting to be discovered by a dedicated scholar like himself. His friend Lady Rushworth had followed, having equally heard of the excellent English society to be found in the town of Santa Lucia, high in the dramatic hills. Society of a most intellectual and stimulating sort, escapees from the endless shallow parties in Naples.

Clio lowered her glass, her eyes narrowed as she thought of Santa Lucia. It was certainly a pretty enough town, with its baroque cathedral and old palazzos, with the ruined medieval castle guarding its town walls. But so often when she was there, except for their Sicilian servants and the shopkeepers of the town, it felt as if she had never left England at all. Receiving callers at their rented house, going to card parties at Lady Rushworth's or dances at Viscountess Riverton's and the Elliotts'—it was all so London-like.

And she did not want to think about England. About what had happened there, what she had left behind.

Clio drew her knees up to her chest, hugging them close, her old brown muslin work dress like a protective tent around her. The warm breeze, scented with scrubby pine trees and fading almond blossoms, ruffled the auburn hair pinned loosely atop her head. She heard the echo of Thalia's voice as she went down to her lingering death, felt the hot sun against her skin.

This was where she belonged, in this wild, ancient spot, alone. Not really in Santa Lucia, definitely not in London. Not the Duke of Averton's castle, so full of its dark, twisting corridors, where secrets and dangers lurked in every corner. Just like the unhappy shades of Hades' kingdom…

Averton. Clio hugged her legs tighter, pressing her forehead to her knees. Could there ever be one day when she did not think of that blasted man? Did not remember what it felt like when he touched her? When he looked at her with those golden-green eyes and whispered her name. *Clio*...

'He is miles away,' she muttered. 'Eons! You will probably never see him again.'

Yet even as she tried to reassure herself, she knew, deep down inside, that was not true. He might be far away, hidden in his castle, the famously reclusive yet always much sought-after Duke of 'Avarice', but he was never entirely apart from her. The way he looked at her, as if she was yet another Greek vase or marble statue he wanted, needed, to possess.

Well, he still had the Alabaster Goddess, that glorious figure of Artemis stolen from Delos, locked away in his castle. He would never do the same to *her*! Not even if she had to hide here in the wilds of Sicily for the rest of her days. The Duke was gone, he was past. Just like the Lily Thief.

For yes, once even she, Clio, had held her secrets. Had been the notorious Lily Thief for a few glorious months.

Clio unfolded her legs and stood up, stretching her limbs in the sunlight. How lovely it was to be alone, to be herself with no one to watch her, judge her. To just be Clio, not one of the 'Chase Muses'. Now that Calliope was wed, everyone looked to her to be next. To marry as well as her sister had—an earl!—and to start her own family, her own conventional life as chatelaine of a household, as a society hostess; to take her place in her family's scholarly, aristocratic world.

But Calliope loved her new husband, was happy in the life she had chosen. Clio had certainly never found anyone she could esteem as Cal did her earl. Clio did not belong in such a life. Maybe she didn't belong anywhere at all. Except here.

She lifted her spyglass again, training it on the valley below her rocky perch, the stretch of land between her and Thalia's theatre. It was really this valley that had brought them to Enna in the first place, an ancient Graeco-Roman site buried in a twelfth-century mudslide and only recently uncovered. Much of the site was still hidden beneath hazelnut orchards, but her father and his friends were working hard at exploring what was revealed: the theatre; part of the *agora*, or market place; some crumbling walls delineating shops and small houses; a great villa with almost intact mosaic floors in the atrium, which was Sir Walter's pet project; and a small, roofless temple, probably devoted to Demeter, with its *bothros*, or well-altar, still ready to accept sacrifices even if the grand silver altar set was long gone.

She could see them through the oval of her glass, her father sweeping off more of the mosaic floor as her fourteen-year-old sister Terpsichore—Cory—sketched the tile scenes of tritons and mermaids. Lady Rushworth, shielded by a giant straw hat, examined some newly found pottery fragments, sorting them into baskets. Other friends and servants scurried around like busy ants. They would not miss her when she crept away. They never did.

Clio snapped the glass shut and tucked it inside her knapsack. Slipping the strap over her shoulder, she turned and made her way up the steep stairs cut into the stony hillside.

When she reached a fork in the steps, with one way leading to Santa Lucia, she glanced up, raising her hand to shield her spectacles from the glare of the sun. The crumbling crenellations of the medieval castle's tower stood starkly against the bright sky, eternally vigilant as it stared out over the valley. She was again reminded of the Duke, of his Yorkshire castle that matched his strangely archaic, handsome appearance, his long red-gold hair, his strong hands that gripped her own so tightly, holding her prisoner to that intense light in his beautiful green eyes.

Clio frowned at the memory, unconsciously flexing her wrists. He could so easily have been one of the crusaders who had built that tower, standing between the crenellations, surveying his conquered land while his banners whipped in the wind behind him. Secure in the knowledge that his money, his exalted title, his fine looks would always gain him anything he wanted. The world was his.

But not her. Never her.

Clio turned away from the castle, from the safety of Santa Lucia and its old walls, and hurried up a second, even steeper set of stairs. They wound up and around the hill, and she soon left the noise and bustle of the valley behind. Even the sun grew dimmer here, the shadows longer, deeper, colder.

On the other side of the hill, the stairs suddenly switched back, taking her downwards again. Unlike the sunny valley where her family worked, this place still slumbered. It was a meadow, covered with a blanket of white clover, seemingly undisturbed except for the hum of bees, the distant tinkle of goats' bells in the hills.

She knew people must come here. There was rich fodder for those herds of goats, and wild fennel and oregano for the cooking pots. But she never saw anyone at all. The cook at their hired house, Rosa, had told her this was a sacred spot, a spot where once there had been an altar to Demeter. A crude sheaf of wheat carved into the trunk of a towering hawthorn tree, where offerings of flowers and fruit were often left at its base, seemed to confirm that. As did mysterious holes she found in the ground when she had first arrived, which seemed to indicate previous, illegal excavations.

Demeter never disturbed Clio when she was there. Nor did Persephone and her dark husband. They seemed to know Clio was one of them, that she did their work to bring them back to life.

She passed the tree, giving it a respectful nod. There were fresh lemons piled in a basket in its shade. There was a wide road nearby, a way for horses to get to the village, but she ignored it. Along another path, barely marked in the clover, she hurried her steps until she found what she sought. Her own perfect place.

While her father worked on the villa, once the dwelling place of rich men, and Thalia revived *Antigone* in the theatre, Clio looked for less exalted remains. Her explorations had brought her here, to this quiet little meadow, where she had found her farmhouse.

She paused at the edge of the site, as she always did when she arrived, drinking in the peaceful, quiet vision. It was not the ancient holiday house of a wealthy family, as the villa was. The people here had been prosperous, but they also worked for their coin. Lived off the fruit of their labour and their land. Once, this clover-covered valley had been fields of wheat and barley, with fruit orchards and groves of olives.

Until it all came to an end, one violent day in the second century BC. Now there were just some waist-high walls of small, uneven pieces of tan-coloured limestone, weatherbeaten and crumbling, to mark where their house once stood. But Clio intended to find more. Much more.

She hurried to the walls, pulling out her stash of tools wrapped in oilcloth and tucked into a sheltered niche. The wooden handle of the small spade fit perfectly into her hand, as a soldier's sword hilt would in battle. Maybe she did *not* belong in London, not really, but she did belong here. When she worked, she forgot the world outside. She even forgot Averton—for a time.

All the passion she had once poured into the Lily Thief was now given to her farmhouse. To finding the voices of the people who once lived here.

She went to work.

Chapter Two

'Is it quite satisfactory, your Grace?' the agent asked, his voice quivering slightly. 'Truly, it is the finest palazzo to be had in all of Santa Lucia. The views are most exquisite, and it is quite near the cathedral and the village square. And there is a hunting cottage, too, in the hills, if you require it. The baroness is usually very reluctant to leave her furnishings for the tenants, but for you, of course, she is only *too* happy…'

Only too happy to have an English ducal arse touch her couches? Edward Radcliffe, the Duke of Averton, examined the flaking, worn gilt of the apricot velvet chairs with some amusement. They looked as if the slightest touch would reduce them to a pile of splinters and shredded upholstery. The baroque flourishes of the place, plaster cherubs peering down from the ceilings and faded apricot-coloured silk wallpaper, seemed no better. Chipped and crumbling away, like an abandoned wedding cake.

It could certainly use a thorough cleaning, as well, for the scuffed marble floor was covered with a fine layer of silvery dust. Cobwebs spun from the elaborate frames of old portraits, where the baroness's exalted Sicilian forebears gazed down at him in disapproval.

Well, they were not the only ones who *disapproved*, to be sure. Old Italian barons and their long-nosed wives had nothing on one Englishwoman's contempt-filled emerald eyes.

Edward turned away from them, away from that cool green gaze that haunted him everywhere he went. He leaned his palms on a chipped marble windowsill, peering down at the scene below. The baroness's palazzo perched at the edge of the hilltop where the village of Santa Lucia gazed out over the valley. The tall, narrow windows, curtained in dusty gold satin and tarnished tassels, stared right at Etna in the distance, to Lake Pergusa and eventually even to the sea.

The palazzo's small garden, wild and overgrown, seemed to drop off into sheer space. As if an eagle could launch itself into space and go wheeling out over the amphitheatre and into the mist beyond, right from this garden.

The front of the palazzo, on the other hand, sported a much more respectable-looking courtyard, paved and neatly planted with myrtle trees, with tall limestone walls and wrought-iron gates that opened to the narrow street beyond. Its cobblestone length was silent, and seemed rather little travelled, but it did lead right to the village square with its shops and cathedral, its view of the whole village and everyone in it.

Perfect.

'Tell me,' Edward said, not turning his gaze from the theatre, 'where is the house the Chase family rents?'

'The Chases?' the agent said, sounding a bit confused. His mind was obviously slow to turn from views and furnishings to the other inhabitants of Santa Lucia. 'Ah, yes, the family with the daughters! Their home is on the other side of the square, just beyond the cathedral. They are often seen on walks in the evenings.'

So, not far from here. Edward closed his eyes, and it was as if he felt her very presence beside him. The wilful Muse.

'I will take the palazzo,' he said, opening his eyes again to the dazzle of the Sicilian sunlight. 'It is perfect.'

By the next morning, Edward's battalions of servants had removed the baroness's dour-painted ancestors and the worst of the gilt furniture and replaced them with choice selections of the Averton antiquities collection. Graceful red-figure amphorae rested on stands under the shocked stares of the plaster angels. A few marble statues took up places in the newly dusted corners, touches of austere elegance amid all the wedding-cake flourishes.

Edward's own chamber overlooked the front court-yard and the street beyond. The largest bedroom, which was obviously the baroness's own to judge from the bedhangings draped from a huge family coat-of-arms, looked upon the grand view of garden and hills. But he preferred this smaller space, where he could watch the town and passers-by.

He examined the arrangements as the servants deposited the last of his trunks and crates. Gilded mouldings carved in the shape of roses, wheat sheaves and arrows garlanded the windows and doors, matching the white-and-gold bed and armoire. The blue-and-red carpet was faded and threadbare, as were the coverlets and bedhangings of blue watered silk. It all lacked the medieval grandeur of his Yorkshire castle, the Gothicism of Acropolis House in London. But the mattress was aired, the room spacious enough—and he could see almost the entire town from the window.

Including the edge of the Chase house.

'It will all do very well,' he murmured, watching closely as the footmen carried in the last of the antiquities so carefully shipped from London. A statue of Artemis with her bow raised. The famous 'Alabaster Goddess'. They placed her next to the fireplace, where she looked as if she was about to shoot down a row of simpering porcelain shepherds and shepherdesses on the mantel. Along her base, barely visible in the veined marble, was a scratch mark from a thief's lever.

Edward traced it lightly with his fingertip, the tiny groove that was the only reminder of that night in the gallery of his London house. Artemis's cool fierceness always reminded him of Clio. The goddess of the moon, of the hunt—she never let any mortal man stand in the way of what she wanted, what she believed to be right. She never shied away from any danger.

But Artemis was immortal, the favourite child of all-powerful Zeus, who would never let harm come to her. Clio, despite her daring, was all too human. One day her gallant recklessness would surely catch up with her, and she would tumble heedlessly into the danger. Foolish girl.

Edward turned away from Artemis and her bow, and found himself facing a full-length mirror. What a strange vision he was, framed in the gilt flourishes and ribbons of that rented glass! The shoulder-length fall of reddish-blond hair his valet so often hinted he should cut, for the sake of fashion, was tied back. As stark as his black wool coat and white cravat, skewered with a stickpin carved with a cameo head of Medusa. As stark as the sharp cheekbones and square jaw that was the legacy of all the Radcliffes, handed down from some distant Viking ancestor.

Yes, he *looked* like a true Radcliffe, the heir to the old dukedom, but he was flawed. His nose, thin and straight as a knife blade in the faces of his late father and older brother, was marred by a badly healed break across the bridge. The legacy of a boyish, long-ago brawl with the man who was now Clio's brother-in-law.

And, a gift from the Muse herself, a jagged scar on his forehead. Healed to a white line now, it was the exact shape of Artemis's stone elbow.

Edward laid his fingertips lightly on the mark, feeling its slight roughness. Feeling again the fire of her kiss.

Yet he did not let her go then. He could not. It was as if there was a devil inside him, a dark demon that dwelled there, hidden, from the time he was a boy. A part of him that desired Clio Chase no matter what she did—now matter what *he* did. But he could not let her stand in the way of his work in Santa Lucia.

Edward reached out and tilted the swinging mirror between its hinges until it faced the faded blue wallpaper, and he was hidden from himself. He took off his coat and tossed it over the foot of the bed, rolling up his shirt-sleeves to reveal the glint of his ruby-and-emerald rings. His forearms were well muscled and sun-bronzed, the arms of a man who had been working on archeological sites under the southern sun for many of his years. The frilled sleeves hid those signs of un-ducal labour, just as the rings hid the white calluses at the base of his fingers.

It would never do for anyone to see what he was really up to. What the famously reclusive, famously louche 'Duke of Avarice' was truly like.

He unlocked the small, iron-bound box on the dressing table. Stacked in there were letters and papers, bags of coins, but beneath was a false bottom, which had stayed neatly in place ever since the box had left England. Edward levered it upwards and drew out two objects. A tiny silver bowl, Grecian to judge by its decorations, second century BC perhaps. It was exquisite, hammered with a pattern of acorns and beechnuts, etched with rough Greek letters spelling out 'This belongs to the gods'. A warning, and a promise.

Beside it was a scrap of green-and-gold silk, torn along a seam, edged with sparkling green glass beads.

He laid them both carefully aside, the bowl and the silk. They were the symbols of all that brought him to this place. All that brought him again to Clio's side— even as he fought against that desire.

But fate, it seemed, always had other plans when it came to him and Clio Chase.

Chapter Three

'**A**h, another invitation from Lady Riverton!' Clio's father announced over the breakfast table. He waved the embossed card in the air before depositing it with the rest of the post.

'Again?' Clio said, only half-listening as she buttered her toast. Her head was still full of the farmhouse, of her plans for the day. It looked as if it might rain, as it so often did here in the mornings. The sky outside the windows was ominously grey, and she had to cover up yesterday's work before the house's cellar filled up with water. 'We were just at her palazzo last week. Weren't we?'

'But this is different,' Sir Walter said. 'An evening of amateur theatricals, it says. And her refreshments are usually quite good, you know. Those lobster tarts last time were lovely…'

Clio laughed. 'Father, I vow you begin to think only of your stomach! But we can attend, if you like.'

'Perhaps she would let me participate in the theatricals,' Thalia said, pouring herself more chocolate. 'I would like to try out some of my *Antigone* lines on an audience. I am not sure my delivery is quite correct. It all sounds very well in the amphitheatre, but then anything would be terribly dramatic there! I do want it to be right.'

'Have you yet found anyone for the role of Haemon?' Clio asked.

Thalia shook her head. 'All the Sicilians speak so little English, and all the Englishmen lack passion! I don't know what to do. Perform it all in Greek? Everyone seems to speak it around here.'

'Lady Riverton will be able to help, I'm sure, Thalia dear,' Sir Walter said. 'She does appear to know absolutely everyone.'

'And she's a terrible busybody,' Thalia answered. 'I don't want her taking over my play! But I will certainly call on her to ask about the theatricals. Will you come with me, Clio?'

Clio glanced again out the window, where the sky seemed even darker. She hurriedly gulped the last of her tea and said, 'If you go this afternoon, I can come with you. But I must run an errand this morning. If you will excuse me, Father?'

Sir Walter nodded distractedly as he read another invitation. He was quite accustomed to Clio dashing away at all hours now, which was how she liked it. Even the time she had gone off with the Darbys to see the temple at Agrigento with only a day's notice had not caused him to bat an eye.

As Clio hurried from the breakfast room, she heard her sister Cory say plaintively, 'May I go to Lady Riverton's, too? Please? I have been to no parties at all since we came here, and I am nearly fifteen.'

'That is because until October you are still only

fourteen,' Thalia answered. 'You are not out yet, and you should feel lucky for that. You have no social obligations at all, and can do what you please!'

Clio paused at the front door to change to her sturdy boots. If she ran, surely she could stay ahead of the rain and return in plenty of time to call on Lady Riverton. She dashed out the door and down the narrow lane that skirted past the cathedral and into the main square of Santa Lucia.

The village was just stirring to life for the day, fruit, vegetable and fish sellers setting up their booths, the bakery and patisserie opening their doors in a flood of sweet-sugar smells. Maids were fetching water from the fountain, gossiping and laughing. The great carved doors of the cathedral were still closed for morning mass, but soon they would open, letting out the prosperous matrons and pretty maidens of the town. The darkly dangerous-looking men were lounging in the shadows.

The day was still cool, but later the warm sun would bring out the smells of all this life, the salty fish and pungent herbs, the sweet cakes, the earthiness of the horses and dogs. The cathedral bells would ring out, crowds would flood forth to do their marketing, and the English tourists would dash away to view the ancient temples, and the day of Santa Lucia would begin in earnest. The wider politics of the world, King Ferdinand, the ruler of the Kingdom of Two Sicilies, far away in Naples with his young Sicilian bride, the collapse of the Sicilian feudal system after the withdrawal of the English forces—none of it mattered here. Not yet, not now. There was shopping and cooking to be done.

Marie, the baker's wife, leaned from the window to hand her a fresh roll as she dashed by. 'It will rain, *signorina*! You should stay inside this morning.'

Clio dashed past Lady Riverton's grand palazzo. The windows were still shuttered, but when they were opened Lady Riverton could spy on all that happened in Santa Lucia—which was surely just as the youngish widow wanted it.

Clio never really minded attending gatherings there. They were certainly dull enough, to be sure, especially when she had studies of her own to attend to and was forced instead to make polite conversation or listen to some young, talentless miss play at the pianoforte. But most of Lady Riverton's guests were also interested in antiquities, and the talk was usually lively. And, as her father had said, the food was quite good. If there was something rather *odd* about Lady Riverton, well, that was no different from dozens of other bored society matrons.

At the edge of town, also with a fine view of things and perched dramatically on the hillside, was the palazzo of the Baroness Picini. It had stood empty since the Chases had arrived at Santa Lucia, the baroness having taken herself off to Naples in the court of the new queen. Today, though, the vast old place was swarming with activity, servants hurrying in and out bearing trunks and crates and furniture. The courtyard gates stood wide open.

More guests for Lady Riverton, then, Clio thought. Despite her curiosity about who might dare to live in the mouldy old pile, she still had work to do, and turned down the steep pathway to the valley.

She reached the farmhouse site just as the first rain-drops started to fall. The sunken cellar area where she had begun excavating, digging out clay amphorae and jars once used for oil and wine, smelled of the sweet, earthy rain, the sulphur of lightning and the imagined remnants of the old wine. Clio shook out a tarpaulin, dragging it up and over the cellar opening and tying it down to the limestone walls. She had done it several times before, so it was quick work.

It wasn't much, but at least it would keep the rain from filling up her excavation trenches before she had finished. So far she had found only the storage jars, a terracotta altar set and one battered silver goblet, but she hoped to discover coins, jewelled goblets and crockery, perhaps even some jewellery. Something to show her father and his friends, so they would not think she had wasted her time on an insignificant site!

She secured the tarpaulin as the rain began to fall in earnest, a soft, warm shower that pattered against the oiled canvas. Clio sat down on another square of canvas spread out on the packed dirt of the cellar, hugging her knees to her chest as she listened to the rain above her head.

It was a strangely soothing sound, cosy as she sat in her ancient house, imagining the blessing of the water falling on the crops in the fields, the flowering orchards. Surely the people who once lived here had done the same thing, thanking Demeter, goddess of the earth and all growing things, for her bounty, making offerings in hopes of a good harvest.

Clio had always loved envisioning the lives of the past. She could hardly get away from history, not with her family! There was her grandfather, who had written a famous treatise, *The Archeology of the Ancients*; her father, who had so richly inherited those scholarly sensibilities and had used them to co-found the Antiquities

Society; her mother, the daughter of a French comte renowned for his collection of Hellenistic silver; her sisters, all the Muses. They had been fed on tales of the old gods, old battles and love affairs, glories that would never die, from the time they were in their cradles.

The classical world was as real to Clio as the everyday life of the London streets and squares—no, it was *more* real. More vital and true. She always took those stories far more to heart than even her sisters did, and it led her into trouble time and again—until it had all come to a terrible crescendo with the Lily Thief.

Clio closed her eyes tightly as the rain pounded louder above her, trying to block out the memory of Calliope's shocked eyes as she saw the truth—that Clio was the Lily Thief. *'How could you do this, Clio?'*

Clio never wanted to hurt her sister. She loved Cal so much, loved them all, her entire boisterous, noisy, eccentric family. But so often she felt alone, even when she stood in their midst. Even as the sound and passion broke all around her, just like the rain.

Things had changed since Cal had married and they had come to Sicily, though. Clio loved this island, loved its windswept whispers that seemed to speak only to her. She loved the roughness of the land and the people, the layers of history in the very earth itself. Just like this house, or what was left of it, where families had lived their daily lives, laughed together, made love, quarrelled and died, she felt herself slowly stirring back to warm, vivid life. She poured all her work, her secrets, into this place, and in return it gave her back herself.

Not that everything could be left behind, of course. At night, when she tumbled exhausted into bed, she had such dreams. Such vivid flashes of memory. The Duke of Averton, how his lips felt on hers, the cool brush of his breath on her skin, the heat and *life* of him, before she had driven him so violently away. The way he watched her, as if he could see into her very soul. See everything about her…

Thunder cracked overhead, loud as a cannon shot, and Clio reared back in surprise. She had almost forgotten where she was, lost in the haze of those memories. The dark gold-green of the duke's eyes, drawing her ever closer, so close she could almost drown in him.

She peered up to find her tarpaulin still securely bound, though bowed in the centre by the weight of the rain. Surely it would cease soon; these morning showers always passed, the thirsty land soaking up every drop until there was no sign of rain at all. Even now she could hear the thunder retreating back along the valley.

Clio took out her small spade again and went to work on her newest excavation, near the remains of the old stone staircase that once led to the upper floors of the house. She would probably have more luck if she worked faster, Clio thought as she carefully measured out a trench in the pockmarked earth. Tear up the floor and be done with it, as anyone else would. As those deceptively lazy men in Santa Lucia would. But then she couldn't come here alone, to her quiet sanctuary. Couldn't lose herself in work and dreams.

She had barely started digging when she noticed something odd, something that hadn't been there before. An indentation in the dirt, maybe. An old trench someone else had once dug. She pushed her spectacles atop her head, tangling them in her hair, and leaned in to peer closer…

Just then she heard a rumbling noise overhead, like the thunder except it persisted, growing ever louder. She froze, sitting back on her heels, tense, as she realised what it was.

Hoofbeats.

Her skin turned suddenly cold, the back of her neck prickling. The blood quickened in her veins, as it had not since she had left the Lily Thief behind for good. No one ever came out here; the old farm site was too isolated, too insignificant for tourists. She had been warned about bandits, of course, and thieves—Sicily could be a wild, dangerous place. But she had never seen any.

Was that about to change?

Clio carefully laid down the spade, and reached under her skirt for the sheath strapped to her leg just above the boot. In one smooth, silent movement, she drew out her dagger.

It was no dainty, ornamental little antique, but a well-honed, sturdy knife, forged to razor sharpness in the Santa Lucia smithy. Their Sicilian cook and her husband had given it to her when she kept insisting on wandering off by herself. At first they were utterly scandalised. Upper-class Sicilian girls were even *more* strictly chaperoned and protected than English girls! But when she had persisted, they had given her the dagger, certain that any lady as strangely independent as Clio would know how to use it.

Their kind confidence was not misplaced. Clio had once been the most famous thief in London. She could use a dagger if she had to. But she hoped she would not.

Surely the hoofbeats, which came ever closer, were only those of a traveller who would quickly pass by on the way to more elaborate sites. Still, she had to be careful. Clio silently crept up a few of the crumbling stone steps, poised on her toes, until she could ease back the corner of the tarpaulin and peer out on to the world.

The rain had finally ceased, leaving behind a damp, rich scent, a land that sparkled with waterdrops on flowers and treetops. The sky was still grey, but a few chalky sunbeams broke through. The horse was coming from behind the farmhouse, along the old, overgrown roadway.

Balancing the dagger hilt in one hand, Clio folded back the tarpaulin a bit more, until she could see past the canvas edge. 'Blast it all,' she muttered, wondering if she had fallen asleep on the dirt floor and was dreaming—or having a nightmare.

A glossy black horse, much like the ones that had probably drawn Hades' chariot as he had born down on hapless Persephone, galloped along the road where it skirted around the farm site. And riding it was the very man she believed, or hoped, to be hundreds of miles away. *Averton*. It could be no other. His bright, Viking hair was loose in the breeze, even longer than when she had last seen him in Yorkshire, falling to his shoulders. His black riding clothes and high leather boots stood in stark contrast to its glow, making him seem one with the horse.

A marauding centaur, then, as well as Hades. A dangerously handsome lord who took what he wanted, regardless of the consequences.

He drew up the horse just beyond the rim of the foundation, so near she could see the sheen of his bronzed skin, shining with rain and sweat. His face, all hard, sharp angles, was expressionless as he gazed around the site. She could feel the fire of his eyes, even across the distance.

White-hot anger burned away her icy poise, her calm wariness. How *dare* he come here, after all that had happened in England! How dare he invade her farmhouse, her one special place? All her old feelings—her fright, her fury, her fascination—boiled over, and she could be silent no longer.

She threw back the tarpaulin, rushing up the last of the old steps with her blade in hand, as if charging into battle.

'What are *you* doing here?' she demanded. 'You, Averton, are on private property, and I will thank you to depart immediately!'

He gazed down at her. His expression did not change—it so seldom did, remaining in its cool lines of ducal contempt even when he confronted thieves in his house. Only a very few times had she seen it alter, that veil of handsome privilege falling away to reveal seething passions and needs that were fearsome to behold.

But his eyes widened a bit as he saw her, the green as bright as sea glass, and she noticed the jagged white scar on his forehead.

'Oh, so you are suddenly the protector of private property, are you now, Clio Chase?' he said mockingly. 'That makes a fascinating change.'

'What do you want?' Clio said. She planted her booted feet solidly in the dirt, tightening her fingers on the dagger hilt even as she longed to flee back to her safe, hidden cellar. Back to an hour ago, when she thought him so far away.

'I want to talk to you,' he said, in a soft, steady voice. A coaxing voice. 'That is all, I swear.'

'So talk.'

His horse pawed at the ground, restless at standing

still, and Averton's black-gloved hands tightened on the reins. 'If I dismount, will I be in danger of being disembowelled by that rather efficient-looking blade in your hand?'

Clio studied him carefully, eye to eye for one long, tense moment. She had seldom met anyone in her life quite as determined as she was herself. That stubbornness meant she usually got her own way, even in a big family. But she knew, just by looking at him now, just by remembering their past encounters, that here was someone of determination to match her own. He wouldn't go away easily, and if she tried to run he would just mow her down with his fearsome steed.

She gave a brusque nod. 'Very well. But stay over there. Don't come near my house.'

His brow arched sardonically. '*Your* house, is it?' But he followed her instructions, swinging down from his horse yet staying several feet away, holding loosely to the reins as his horse began to crop at the clover. 'Is this far enough?'

Clio nodded again. 'You said you wanted to talk, Averton. It must be something important indeed to bring you all this way.'

'It is,' he answered. Yet then he fell silent, just watching her as if he had never seen her before in his life. As if she were some strange creature, a unicorn or phoenix, maybe, that he could not understand.

Clio shifted on her feet. 'Did someone snatch away your precious Alabaster Goddess? It was not me, I vow. I have been in Sicily for weeks. Or perhaps it was—'

'Clio,' he said, in a voice that was quiet, soft, but full of steely command. 'I have come here because you are in danger.'

Chapter Four

❦

Clio could scarcely understand what she was hearing. *Could* this just be a dream after all? Every moment she had ever spent with Averton had been bizarre, to be sure, but this…

'Did you just say I am in danger?' she asked, studying his face for signs of—what? Joking? Subterfuge? It was not the Duke's way to make jests, nor hers.

There was no hint of humour or deception in his face, though. No change in those Viking-warrior features at all, except for a tiny tic in the muscle along his jaw as he stared at her.

Clio stared back, hardly daring to move, to breathe. The thunderstorm had left the air heavy and thick, the breeze practically crackling around her. Around *them*. It was as if snapping tendrils snaked out from the grey sky, wrapping ever tighter around her, binding her closer and closer to him.

It was like a myth, a tale of jealous gods and enchanted spells that bound mortals to them against their every sensible inclination. Every shred of sense.

Clio shook her head, trying to clear it of such dark fancies. It was just this place making her feel so, that web of myth and fantasy that had been woven around her ever since she was a child. And being faced with Averton, of all people, when she least expected him! Was least prepared for him, and the effect he always had on her.

As if she ever *could* be prepared for him. Every single time she saw him, it was like a lightning storm all over again. Beautiful, treacherous and so completely disorienting.

She took a step back. 'I know of no dangers here except you. You needn't have gone to all this trouble to warn me of *that*.'

His brow creased, as if in a flash of pain, yet that spasm was gone in an instant, banished under a mocking smile. 'Did I not prove to you in Yorkshire that you are never in danger from me? I sent you and your friend— Marco, was it?—on your merry way, with scarcely a scolding word. Even though you were in the midst of stealing from me. I am the last person you need fear, Clio.'

She swallowed hard, remembering another night, that gallery at Acropolis House. 'Indeed?'

'Indeed. I want to be your friend, if you will let me.'

'My friend, is it?' she said, nearly choking on a humourless laugh. 'So, that is why you are here? To offer friendship, along with cryptic warnings of danger? I think it more likely you are here to see what my father has found in his Greek villa. To see what you can snatch to add to your vaunted collections, hidden away in the darkness so no one else can ever see them.'

'Clio!' he growled, his icy calm cracking at last. He dropped the reins, his hands curling into fists.

And Clio felt a stirring of some strange satisfaction.

'You are the most obstinate woman I have ever met,' he muttered. 'Why can you not just listen to me for once in your life?'

'Just listen to you? Quietly do what you want, just as everyone does with the exalted duke? Well, I'm sorry, your Grace, but I am too busy to stand here arguing with you any longer.' She strode past him, not sure where she was going, only knowing that she had to get away. Had to escape from those crackling bonds before she exploded!

She gave Averton a wide berth, yet not quite wide enough. Before she had even seen him move, he had caught her by the wrists, pulling her close to him. Startled, she dropped her dagger. It landed mere inches from his booted foot, yet he did not glance at it at all. He only watched her.

As she stared up into his face, into the glow of his eyes, those bonds grew tighter and tighter. She could not breathe, could not move at all. She flexed her wrists in his grasp, the fingers of her right hand splayed out until she touched the very edge of his sleeve. The hot, smooth skin of his wrist. She felt the thrum of his pulse there, the tumbling rush of his life's blood, and his heartbeat seemed to meld with her own.

She heard the quick rush of his breath in her ear, smelled the clean, spicy scent of his skin. He was all around her, a part of her she could not escape, for truly he was not something outside, not a separate being she could run from, deny. He was inside her, part of her very breath and blood.

She arched in his grasp, her head thrown back like Persephone's as she tried to escape, tried to leap from the speeding chariot to safety. Escape, even as she longed to stay.

'Then tell me what it is you want here,' she whispered. 'Why you came here to find me.'

'Will you listen, then?' he said hoarsely. 'For once?'

'I...' she answered. 'It depends on what you say, I suppose.'

He gave a bark of laughter, his clasp loosening on her wrists. 'Of course. Always conditions. Always wanting things your own way.'

'Muses are as spoiled as dukes when it comes to that,' she said. She raised her hand, still caught in that dream where she was not herself. She lightly touched the white scar with her fingertips, feeling the uneven ridge of it under her touch.

He tensed, as taut as a bowstring, but he did not move away. Perhaps he was as enchanted as she was. She trailed her touch over his temple, the pulse that thrummed there; over his sharp cheekbone, the crooked nose Cam de Vere had once broken in some unspecified brawl. A loose strand of his hair, bright silk, brushed against her hand, clinging. She traced its wave until she found the curve of his lips.

Her fingers hovered over them as they parted, and she felt his very life's breath. How close, how very close...

'Clio,' he groaned. His arms came around her waist, dragging her against him until there was not even a whisper between them. She was a tall woman, nearly as tall as he, but she felt fragile as his hot strength wrapped around her and she was surrounded by only him. She looped her arms about his neck, making him her captive just as she was his.

Their lips met, and there was nothing tentative or shy about the caress. It was quick, hot, desperate. A fervent need to be as one, to fall down into the dark myth and be lost for ever. That was what it was like when she kissed him—like being lost in the corridors of the underworld among all the shades, the misty illusions. She was a fool, an utter fool, to give in again. To reach for something that could only do her ill in the end.

But neither could she turn away, any more than she could tear her own soul out.

She dug her fingers into the fall of his hair, holding him to her as she felt the smooth leather of his gloved caress slide across her shoulders, skimming along her bare skin until she shivered. She leaned deeper into him, losing herself, losing everything…

'Clio!' he said, tearing his lips from hers. His hands tightened on her shoulders, pressing her back from him. 'Clio, what am I doing? I did not come here to…'

And the spell was broken, like one of those invisible cords that bound her to him. She stumbled away, still intoxicated with the smell and taste of him. With the bizarre alchemy that happened whenever they were close.

She glanced away from him, covering her mouth with her trembling hands. She had to get away from him, now! 'No, you came here to *warn* me. Well, Averton, consider me warned.'

She snatched up her dagger from the dirt, in the process losing the spectacles she had pushed atop her head while she was digging. She scarcely noticed, though. She was too busy running away, dashing for the footpath along the hills that she knew his horse could not follow.

'Fool, fool,' she muttered, scrubbing at her aching eyes with the back of her hand. 'Bloody *fool*! How dare you?'

Yet she did not know if she talked to him—or herself.

'Damn it all!' Edward cursed, kicking violently at the dirt. This was not what he had planned!

He meant to gently alert Clio to his presence in Sicily, to be polite and calm, and make her see he meant her no harm before he revealed his true purpose. Or part of it, anyway. He had not even known she would be here today. The rain would have kept away any other would-be antiquities hunter. He should have known that it would take more than a bit of thunder to keep Clio Chase away! But he had wanted to see the site, do a bit of reconnaissance work while no one else was about. Get to know his opponent.

Then there she was, suddenly appearing before him, fierce as any Fury, her dagger in hand. Her eyes, usually a serene spring-green, sparkled with shock and anger. '*You!*' she had cried, as if a demon had landed in front of her.

And all his careful, measured plans, his resolve to not get close to her, exploded and disappeared like a cloud of smoke. That raw, passionate *need* that drew him to her whenever he saw her, that force that drove him to touch her, be close to her, was there. He could not resist it, any more than he could resist breathing. He forced himself, by sheer steely will, to stay where he was—until she hurried past him, ignoring his warnings with her maddening wilfulness.

Edward pounded his fist against a tree trunk, cursing, oblivious to the slivers that drove themselves through his glove. Oblivious to everything but the way he still smelled her white lily perfume on his skin.

Why, *why*, had he kissed her? Why had she kissed him? He had understood it far better when she had knocked him senseless with the Alabaster Goddess. He deserved no less. But now he wanted her to be safe, to listen to his warnings and stay out of his way.

Well, that was not *all* he wanted. Their little scene here, as well as what had happened at Acropolis House, clearly demonstrated that. He wanted Clio in his bed, in his arms, all her passion his at last. Her long legs wrapped around his hips, her head thrown back in a tangle of auburn hair as she cried out his name.

But their kisses could change nothing.

Edward strode toward his horse. As he caught up the reins, he saw the glint of sunlight on Clio's spectacles. They lay in the dirt, apparently lost when she had stormed away. He picked them up carefully, holding them up to the light. The lenses were strong, but not hugely so; the ground glass magnified the limestone walls only a bit, showing up the old cracks and pits. So, she did need them for the close, painstaking work she did, but she was not blind without them. Perhaps they were a sort of armour, as well. Something to hide behind.

He tucked them carefully inside his coat, and swung up into the saddle. Well, surely she would need them back again. Very soon.

Chapter Five

Earth with its wide roads gaped, and then over the Nysian field the lord and All-receiver, the many-named son of Kronos, sprang out upon her with his immortal horses...

Clio groaned, and slammed the book shut, pushing it away from her. Perhaps that particular one of the *Homeric Hymns*, the tale of Hades and Persephone, was not the best choice of reading material this afternoon.

She rubbed her hand over her aching head. In truth, she doubted she could concentrate on anything at all, even so much as a fashion paper. Her thoughts kept turning, leaping, back to the farmhouse, to Averton and his appearance there. As sudden and shocking as if he had 'sprung out upon her with his immortal horses'.

She had crept back to try to find her spectacles, peering from over the rocky ridge of the hills to be sure he was gone. And so he was, not a trace of him remaining at all. Perhaps she had just imagined him after all? Perhaps he, and his kisses, were the product of sunstroke. Of overwork and exhaustion.

Yet as she tiptoed closer, she saw the marks of horse's hoofs in the dirt. And her spectacles were gone.

She had hurriedly secured the site, putting away the tarpaulin and tools, and had run home for a quiet afternoon of study. Or so she'd hoped.

Clio could not fathom what had come over her. *Kissing* Averton? Touching him! Not wanting it all to end, even as every ounce of her good sense screamed at her to get away from him. The man who was rumoured to be a terrible libertine, who respected no wishes not his own, who took every shameful advantage of his exalted rank. Who was, worst of all, a hoarder of antiquities!

Yet she had kissed him. And wanted so much more.

Clio groaned, dropping her head to the hard, polished surface of the desk. If only she could leave this place, this island she loved with such fervour, which had been her refuge until today. She could go back to England, to see how her younger sisters fared at Chase Lodge. She could—

No. The Chase Muses were no cowards. She might not possess the reckless, headlong courage of Thalia, who swam icy lakes and scaled mountains without a care, or the rare grace of Calliope. But she had to be strong, to stand her ground. Even in the face of Averton. Who would work on the farmhouse if she left? Who would discover its secrets?

The Duke himself, probably. He had seemed rather interested in the site that morning, before he realised she was there. And that she could not allow.

Clio pushed herself up from her chair, walking over to the window as she stretched her aching shoulders. She gazed down at their little patch of garden, at the

road that led around the cathedral and out to the square.
It was quiet in Santa Lucia now, the shops closed for
the afternoon siesta as a warm, sunny somnolence
settled over the place. Her father sat beneath the shade
of their almond tree, reading with Lady Rushworth and
Cory, but they were the only living things to be seen.

Clio thought about going for a rest herself, crawling
under the brocade blanket of the *chaise* in her chamber
and forgetting the Duke in sleep. But she dismissed the
notion. Afternoon sleep was always feverish for her,
bringing strange dreams. He would surely appear *there*,
and she didn't want to see what would happen.

Yet neither could she read and study. She was too
restless, too scattered.

There was a knock at the library door, and Clio
turned toward it, eager for fresh distraction. 'Come in!'

It was Thalia who peeped around the threshold. She
had changed her classical Antigone robes and veil for
a stylish blue-dotted white muslin dress and blue
spencer, a chip-straw bonnet with pink ribbons tucked
under her arm. With her golden curls swept up and
bound with more pink ribbons, her wide blue eyes and
creamy skin, she looked the perfect porcelain shepherdess. The angelic beauty.

Many men had been fooled by her pretty, innocent
façade—and had been sorry when they discovered the
warrior-woman beneath. She often declared she was
far too busy to marry, and Clio was inclined to believe
her. Where could she find her match, a man with the
power *and* the trickery of Zeus, the golden looks of
Apollo, the strength of Hercules?

Thalia, with all her adventurous 'projects', was endlessly diverting, always entertaining, and sometimes

exhausting. Today, though, Clio was entirely glad of her company.

'Are you working?' Thalia asked. She hurried over to the desk, rifling curiously through the books and papers.

'I was,' Clio answered. She leaned back against the windowsill, her arms crossed at her waist, watching as Thalia examined first one title, then another. 'But I can't seem to concentrate for some reason.'

'Me, neither. I think it's the heat. Rosa says summer is coming on, and soon the sun will burn everything brown.'

'I hope not yet! I need to finish the farmhouse cellar first.'

'And I'll have to perform my play. If it is too hot, no one will want to sit on those stone seats and watch.'

'Except for every young swain in town! They would happily sit and watch you for hours. They're all achingly in love with you, you know.'

Thalia made a dismissive wave of her hand, tossing the book she held back to the desk. 'A whole village full of men, English and Italian both, and not one with a jot of interesting conversation in him! They just want to sit and stare like a pack of half-wits.'

Clio laughed. 'And send flowers, and serenade outside your window.'

'I haven't time for such things.'

'One day you will have to make time. So shall we all, I expect.'

'What do you mean?'

'Now that Calliope is married, everyone will expect you and me to be next.'

Thalia shook her head. 'Father doesn't care if we marry or not! He's too busy with his villa and mosaics to worry about such trifles.'

Clio glanced back to the garden below, to their father and Lady Rushworth reading together so companionably. He smiled as Lady Rushworth pointed to something in their book, catching her hand to press a quick kiss to her gloved fingers. Lady Rushworth, a widow herself with two grown sons and grandchildren, blushed. Clio had not seen her father so happy since her mother had died.

'Then again, perhaps the next Chase to wed won't be a Muse at all,' she said.

Thalia hurried to her side, gazing down at the scene. 'You don't mean—Father will marry Lady Rushworth?'

'Perhaps.'

'But they are just friends!'

'Maybe. But if they *do* wed, Father won't want so many Muses underfoot for a while. And, since you are the most beautiful of all of us, you will probably be next.'

Thalia frowned, turning away from the window. 'Me? I look like a bonbon, whereas *you* look like a goddess. You are sure to attract someone interesting, someone strong and clever and...' Her voice trailed away, and Clio saw her golden head bow.

Clio was suddenly worried. Thalia was seldom anything less than running at top speed, charging ahead with her glorious confidence. She reached out and caught Thalia's hand, drawing her sister back to her side. 'What's wrong, Thalia dear? Has something happened?'

Thalia tilted her chin up, smiling, but her china-blue eyes still held a strange glitter. 'Of course not, Clio. What could possibly have happened? I just don't care for all this marriage talk, that's all! Not when I am in danger of being stuck with one of my horrid suitors.'

'Thalia, there is no danger of being "stuck"! If you really don't want to marry…'

'I will marry—when I meet someone who suits me as Cameron does Calliope.' Thalia gave Clio's hand a reassuring squeeze before letting go to stroll back to the desk. She reached for a fat letter, holding it up. 'And I see you've heard from Calliope, the new Lady Westwood, today!'

'Yes, I thought we could all read Calliope's news together after dinner,' Clio answered.

Thalia turned the missive over in her hand. 'Where are they now, do you think? Capri? Tuscany? Venice?'

'On their way back to England, I expect. Hopefully, they'll be waiting for us when we return ourselves.'

'With a new little Chase-de Vere infant on the way.' Thalia put down the letter. 'Do you miss her terribly?'

'Calliope?' Clio remembered sitting by a Yorkshire stream with Cal. *"You can tell me anything from now on, Clio."* Clio had promised she would keep no more secrets, that she was done with the Lily Thief. And she had truly tried to keep that promise. Tried to live up to her older sister's confidence. It had gone well, until that very morning, when Averton had appeared. 'Of course. None of us have ever been parted for long before. Don't you miss her?'

'Very much. I just thought it must be worse for you. You and Cal were always so close.'

'Yes. But I still have you! And I always will, if we're going to be spinster Muses together.'

Thalia laughed, and the merry sound seemed to help her shrug off whatever hint of melancholy she was suffering. She twirled around and caught Clio's hand in hers. 'Cal's children will be sorry to have such formidable old aunts! I will teach them music and drama, and how to shoot a bow and arrow. You will teach them how to swim for miles, just like you, and how to read history from just a shard of pottery.'

Clio laughed, too, going along with her. 'How to sew very, very badly?'

'That, too. But as the child is not here yet we shall have to—oh!'

'What?'

'I forgot why I came in here in the first place. I am going to call on Lady Riverton, and you promised to come with me.'

Clio felt a sinking in the pit of her stomach at the mention of Lady Riverton. The widow was the self-styled 'social leader' of the small band of English travellers in Santa Lucia. People who, like the Chases, were deeply interested in history and antiquities. Everyone else was sensible, and stayed near the cool delights of the shore, the relative culture of Palermo.

Viscount Riverton had possessed a considerable collection himself, especially of Greek coins. His widow, while she claimed to be carrying on his work, seemed to be only really interested in parties, gossip and hats. She had lots and lots of hats. Clio often thought it was a pity she didn't also have a many-headed Cerberus to guard her door; then it could wear all of them at once.

But Clio *had* promised Thalia. 'I'll have to change my clothes,' Clio said, gesturing to her garb. She had left off her heavy boots, but still wore her old brown muslin with its dusty hem. Her hair fell down her back in an untidy auburn plait.

'Just plop on a fancy bonnet!' Thalia said. 'She'll never notice the rest.' She 'plopped' her own hat on to

Clio's head, tugging at the pink ribbons and singing, 'Oh la la, aren't the Chase sisters so terribly *à la mode*!'

Clio laughed helplessly, trying to spin away from her sister. Thalia wouldn't let go. 'Brown and pink, Clio, all the rage from Paris! You must be—oh, I say. Where are your spectacles?'

Chapter Six

Lady Riverton's palazzo was the grandest in town, if not as dramatically situated as the Baroness Picini's rambling manse. Lady Riverton's abode had been refurbished before she took possession, freshly stuccoed and painted so that it gleamed a bright, artificial white in the sun. There were no gaps in the tiles of the roof, no overgrown ivy, no slats missing from the shutters, no chips in her garden fountain, which splashed and gurgled as Clio and Thalia turned in through her polished black gates.

'We won't stay long,' Clio said, waiting for their knock to be answered.

'Of course not,' Thalia answered, smoothing her pink kid gloves. 'I don't think we could take more than an hour without screaming, do you?'

The butler opened the doors, and Clio thought, as she always did when coming to visit Lady Riverton, that it was like stepping back into England. Unlike the Chases' own rented house, furnished with comfortable, slightly shabby pieces, Lady Riverton had filled her space with dark, gleaming tables and cabinets. Chairs, couches and hassocks upholstered in blue-striped satin, interspersed with displays of her collections: vases, coffers, fragments of statues, cases showing off her husband's ancient coins.

Lady Riverton herself sat on a throne-like chair and presided over an elaborate tea table, set with silver, porcelain, platters of tiny sandwiches and pink-iced cakes. Her light brown hair, untouched by any hint of grey, was crowned with a dainty lace cap matching the filmy fichu tucked into her pale green muslin gown. A pair of antique cameos dangled from her ears.

Once, in a different life, those earrings had been just the sort of thing to tempt Clio to 'liberate' them. But she had made promises, so all she said as she greeted Lady Riverton was, 'Such charming earrings.'

Lady Riverton trilled a light laugh, reaching up to toy with one of the fragile cameos. 'A gift from my dear late husband. He had such excellent taste! I am honoured you have decided to grace my tea table this afternoon, Miss Chase, Miss Thalia. We see so little of you lately, you always seem to be trailing around the fields with your father.'

Clio nodded at the other guests, Lady Elliott—whose husband helped her father at the villa site—and her daughters, Mrs Darby and *her* daughter—who had taken Clio on their impromptu Agrigento tour—as she and Thalia took their seats. Lady Riverton's friend, her 'cicisbeo' as Thalia called him, Ronald Frobisher, was not present, which was most unusual. 'There is certainly a great deal to see in Sicily,' Clio said, accepting a cup of tea. 'Much work to be done.'

Lady Riverton laughed again. 'Oh, certainly I know

all about that! Viscount Riverton was one of the first to see the vast potential of this site. It was just a dusty valley when he came here with Nelson! I'm most gratified to see his work being carried on so admirably. But I also know that young ladies must have their share of amusement. Before I married, I had far too much energy and natural merriment to live by digging alone!'

'That is so true!' cried Miss Darby. 'I am always telling Mama—'

Mrs Darby laid a gentle hand on her daughter's arm, stilling the excited flow of words. 'And we are very gratified you provide such—amusements, Lady Riverton.'

'Not at all. I so vastly enjoy entertaining, and my dear husband always said my parties were so very elegant.' She gave another little laugh. 'He was so indulgent. But I do hope you will all be at my next gathering! An evening of amateur theatricals, very diverting. You all received your invitations?'

Clio calmly sipped at her tea, silently willing Thalia not to have an excited outburst *à la* Miss Darby. Lady Riverton hardly needed any fodder for her 'Gracious Hostess' act. 'Indeed we did, Lady Riverton. We will be most happy to attend.'

'So kind of you to ask us,' Thalia said coolly. Clio was proud of her. 'That is one thing I miss so much about London, the theatre.'

'As do I, Miss Thalia,' Lady Riverton answered. 'We are both cultured souls, I see! While I cannot procure the likes of Mrs Siddons, I fear, I do hope to show off some of our local talent, which I suspect is quite great. The Manning-Smythes have agreed to stage a scene from *Romeo and Juliet*. So appropriate, is it not, since they are on their honeymoon? And Miss Darby here will do Ophelia's mad scene. It is so important to include Shakespeare! His more *appropriate* bits, at least.'

'Oh, yes,' Clio said. 'The Bard is always welcome. But, as this is Sicily, would it not be a fine thing to include some classical playwrights? For is this not where Ovid and Aeschylus worked?'

'But the Greeks and Romans are so very violent, aren't they?' Lady Riverton murmured, her lace cap quivering. 'So much blood and vengeance!'

Unlike Shakespeare, of course, Clio thought wryly. No blood or vengeance there.

'But always so vastly exciting,' Lady Elliott said over her sandwiches. 'You have been working yourself on some Sophocles, have you not, Miss Thalia?'

'Indeed,' Thalia answered. '*Antigone*. The amphitheatre here is so wondrous, with superb acoustics, it just seemed to call out to be brought to life again! To be used for its true purpose. Yet I fear *Antigone* features no blood at all.'

'Yes. All the death is offstage, is it not?' Mrs Darby said. 'Still, very dramatic.'

'No blood, you say?' Lady Riverton said. 'How interesting. Perhaps, Miss Thalia, you might grace us with a monologue at my little theatricals? Add some *appropriate* classicism to the proceedings.'

Thalia gave her a gracious smile. 'If you think your guests would enjoy it, Lady Riverton.'

The purpose of their visit now so neatly achieved, Thalia went on to chat with their hostess about the newest fashions in bonnets—feathers or fruit?—while Clio turned to Mrs Darby. They had become friends on that tour of the 'valley of the temples' at Agrigento, but did not see each other as often now that Mr Darby had turned his activities from excavating to writing. A novel, everyone heard, about the original destruction of the old Greek town during the Punic Wars.

'And how is Mr Darby's book progressing?' Clio asked.

Mrs Darby laughed. 'Well enough, I suppose. He hides himself away in his library after breakfast and does not emerge all day, so *something* is being worked on.'

'What do you do yourself, then, while he is scribbling away?'

'Pay calls, as you see. Go on excursions. I fear it's becoming rather dull for poor Susan.' Mrs Darby glanced at her daughter, who was nibbling at a cake with a very dreamy look in her eyes. 'We have been thinking of hiring a yacht to take us out to some of the other islands. Motya, for the Phoenician sites, perhaps. Maybe you would care to join us?'

Clio thought again of the Duke, of their kiss. Now that he was here, he was not likely to go away again any time soon. It was terribly tempting to run away, to sail off and put the endless blue sea between them! But she could not leave her work. Not just yet. 'That is very kind of you, Mrs Darby. I have heard such enticing things about the necropolis there. But I am not sure I can leave my family just now.'

'Yes. We have heard you are hard at work on a more remote site while your father explores that villa of his. It is very brave of you, I must say!'

'Brave? Not at all. *Dull* is what most people would call it. The site is just an old ruined farmhouse, but I am enjoying finding clues to everyday life here.'

'Yet it is so remote! I would fear for Susan out there. And, of course, there is the curse.'

Clio felt a tiny cold shiver along her spine. 'Curse, Mrs Darby? Is your husband by some chance writing a horrid novel?'

Mrs Darby smiled and shook her head. 'Oh, Miss Clio. I myself do not believe in such nonsense. I simply happened to overhear your cook gossiping with our housemaid, who I think is her daughter. They didn't seem to know I speak Italian. They were saying how courageous you are to brave the curse.'

Clio laughed, though she still felt inexplicably cold. As if a goose had walked over her grave. 'How very amusing. I wonder who placed this curse?'

Mrs Darby shrugged. 'It seems something terribly violent happened at your farmhouse before it was destroyed. Something that deeply angered the gods. Now it is said that anyone unworthy who dares disturb the ground will be terribly punished. That's why the site has been so undisturbed all these years.'

'Perhaps the curse has a time limit,' Clio suggested, 'for I am still here.'

'Or maybe you are considered worthy. Oh, Miss Clio, Sicily is ever fascinating, is it not?'

'Indeed it is,' Clio murmured. Well, at least this little tale explained why she had trouble hiring assistants. If only ancient curses could keep Averton away, too.

The drawing room opened amid the quiet buzz of conversation, and the butler announced, 'The Count di Fabrizzi, my lady.'

Clio's teacup clattered in its saucer at the sudden announcement. *No!* Perhaps there were two Fabrizzis in Italy? There simply had to be. She couldn't take another sudden reappearance, not in one day.

She carefully put the cup and saucer down, school-

ing her expression into cool lines of casual interest
before she looked toward the door.

There were not, after all, two Count Fabrizzis. Only
the one she already knew—Marco, who had been one
of the Lily Thief's cohorts, a man deeply concerned
with the lost heritage of his homeland. And there he
stood, raising Lady Riverton's lace-mittened hand to his
lips for a polite salute as she giggled and blushed.

When she had known him in England, she had been
quite aware that he was a titled nobleman from an old
Florentine family. Yet he had been disguised as a gypsy,
his long black hair tied back with a red bandanna,
dressed in plain white shirts and scuffed boots. Now his
hair was expertly trimmed into a glossy dark cap that
emphasised his chocolate-brown eyes and high Italian
cheekbones. He was dressed simply but expensively in
a well-cut bottle-green coat, buckskin breeches and a
gold-striped silk waistcoat.

Clio folded her hands in her lap, watching the scene
warily. She did not feel that lightning shock that went
all through her when Averton appeared, that hot fear
and excitement. She knew very well Marco would
never give away her secrets. But his arrival in Lady
Riverton's drawing room *was* an unexpected wrinkle
in her plans. What was he doing here? What did he
hope to gain in Sicily?

If he looked to reincarnate the Lily Thief…

'Good heavens,' Mrs Darby murmured. 'What a
beauty.'

Her daughter just giggled, hiding the giddy sound
behind her fan.

'Indeed,' Clio said, glancing at her sister. Thalia had
a frighteningly speculative gleam in her eye. She

couldn't be thinking of recruiting Marco for her play! Could she?

Lady Riverton stood and took Marco's arm, turning him toward their eager little group. 'This is the Count di Fabrizzi, who has come all the way from Florence to grace our little society here! He and my dear Lord Riverton were such good friends, you see.'

'He would never forgive me if I did not pay my deepest respects to his lovely widow,' Marco said in his liquid accent, giving her a charming smile that made her plump, pretty cheeks turn bright pink. 'But I fear I will only be in Santa Lucia for a very few days. I have business in Palermo.'

'Oh, no!' Lady Riverton cried. 'Surely your business *here* cannot be concluded so quickly. And Santa Lucia is so diverting this spring, as I'm sure my friends can tell you. Let me introduce you. Lady Elliott and the Misses Elliott, Mrs Darby and Miss Darby. And the Misses Chase, Clio and Thalia, whom you must have heard of. They are the famous Chase Muses. Ladies, you must join me in urging the Count to stay a little longer.'

'Oh, yes!' Lady Elliott declared. 'If you were a friend of Lord Riverton, you must enjoy antiquities. There are so many around here.'

Lady Riverton urged Marco to sit down in the chair next to hers, pressing a cup of tea and some sandwiches on him. 'Yes, quite,' he answered. 'Ancient history is one of the great passions of my life.'

Miss Darby giggled again behind that fan, until her mother shot her a stern glance.

'Then you should stay and meet our husbands,' Lady Elliott went on. 'As well as Mr Frobisher and the

Manning-Smythes. Most of them are working on the site of an ancient Greek town, and have already found many exquisite objects. We expect more great things. I'm sure they would welcome your expertise.'

'Welcome the free labour,' Thalia muttered to Clio.

'You must at least stay for my theatrical evening,' Lady Riverton said.

'It sounds most—diverting,' Marco answered. He gave their hostess another smile, displaying a deep-set dimple in his olive-complected cheek that made even Mrs Darby sigh.

'You enjoy the theatre, Count?' Thalia said.

'When I have the chance to attend,' Marco answered. He turned his smile on to Thalia, but it turned to a frown of puzzlement when he met her frank, speculative blue eyes.

Well, Clio thought, she could not save Marco if Thalia had decided he would act in her play. Anyone caught in Thalia's crosshairs was doomed. But she still could not decipher what he was doing here. Marco and the Duke in one place? So strange.

The conversation went along most politely, turning to the social events of Santa Lucia, the *objets* that had been found thus far in the Greek town. Clio sipped at a fresh cup of tea, studying Marco over the painted china rim. They exchanged only one meaningful glance, a long look that promised much conversation later, but other than that he gave no sign at all that he had ever seen her before. Perhaps Thalia was right about his potential acting skills.

And Clio had to keep up her own, too. Luckily, deception had become second nature to her in her Lily Thief days. But this afternoon, smiling and chatting as if she hadn't a care, she felt as if a bar of cold iron was pressing down on her. Making her want to scream.

Her cheeks hurt from all that smiling, too.

At last, the half-hour deemed polite for a social call passed, giving Clio and Thalia the excuse they needed to escape. As they collected their shawls and gloves and thanked Lady Riverton, the footman appeared again with a note on a silver tray. Lady Riverton scanned it quickly, and suddenly broke into a triumphant laugh.

Curious, Clio paused in drawing on her gloves. Surely there was little in Santa Lucia correspondence that could be *that* exciting. Not very much changed here from day to day. Until now.

'Oh, Count di Fabrizzi, now you really must come to my theatricals!' Lady Riverton said, carefully refolding the note. 'It would be quite the triumph to have in attendance both an Italian count *and* an English duke. Two handsome young noblemen to grace my drawing room!'

'A *duke*?' exclaimed Lady Elliott. 'I was not aware there were any such personages in the neighborhood.'

'There is now. He has just accepted my invitation, which I sent round as soon as I heard who had taken the Picini palazzo.' Lady Riverton gave them a supremely satisfied smile. 'And you will never guess who it is.'

'Devonshire!' guessed Miss Darby.

'Clarence,' suggested Thalia. 'Oh, no. He would be too fat to get up the hill.'

'Better,' Lady Riverton said. 'It is *the* Duke of Averton. So handsome and delightful! And he will actually be here for my theatrical evening. Won't it be glorious?'

Thalia glanced at Clio, her eyes wide. 'But how could…?'

Clio grabbed her hand, holding it tightly. 'Glorious, indeed. We do look forward to it, Lady Riverton, but now we really must go before our father misses us. It was lovely to make your acquaintance, Count di Fabrizzi.'

'Oh, no, Miss Chase,' Marco said, giving her an elaborate bow. Only the merest shadow in his dark eyes reflected a certain dismay at the mention of the name 'Averton'. He, too, remembered the Yorkshire dungeon. 'The pleasure was entirely mine.'

Clio left Lady Riverton's house, still holding on to Thalia's hand until they were at a safe distance on the street. When she let go, it was like releasing a tidal wave.

'Averton!' Thalia exploded. 'What is *he* doing here? How dare he show his face where we are, how dare he come as near us as—as Rome! Handsome he may be, but he is naught but a freebooter, a—'

'A freebooter?' Clio said, laughing despite herself. 'Thalia, he is hardly Drake on the *Golden Hind*.'

'No, he is worse. I would wager he only comes here to steal whatever Father finds in his villa. And to harass *you* some more.'

'And don't forget, to attend Lady Riverton's party. He has definitely come for that.' Clio spoke with a lightness she was far from feeling, hurrying her steps towards home. She longed for the quiet of her own room. The safe haven she had always found in Santa Lucia felt torn now, reshaped with the arrivals of Averton and Marco. Something was definitely afoot, something she could not see or understand. Not yet, anyway. 'Danger,' the Duke had said. How right he was.

Thalia hurried after her. 'Well, then, I *won't* go to that party. I have no wish to see that spoiled, arrogant—'

'Freebooter? Oh, Thalia, we have to go. We told Lady Riverton we would, and you were looking forward to it. Everyone will need your wonderful Antigone to save them from drowning in sugary faux-Shakespeare-ness. There will be lots of people there, we won't even notice Averton. Handsome or not.'

'Perhaps not,' Thalia said reluctantly. She was silent for a moment, then added, 'But we will be sure to notice Count Adonis! And *he* will notice *you*.'

Clio was careful not to look at her sister, just walking a bit faster on their way home. 'Don't be silly. Why would a gorgeous Italian count notice me, when your golden beauty or Miss Darby's conspicuous giggles will be near?'

'He kept looking at you just now,' Thalia said. Not for the first time, Clio cursed Thalia's powers of observation. 'If I was a reader of horrid novels, like our friend Lotty, I would call them "speaking glances".'

'You are just imagining things. I think all the theatricality is getting to you.'

'I think not.' Thalia opened their own garden gate, and went prancing up to the front door, chanting, 'Clio has a new admirer!'

'What?' cried Cory, who came into the foyer just in time to hear this bit of news. 'Clio has an admirer? Who is it? Oh! Not that silly Peter Elliott? I thought he was in love with *you*, Thalia.'

'Far better,' Thalia said. 'A dark Italian count! He kept staring at her over Lady Riverton's tea table. And he is *beautiful*.'

'Perhaps Clio will soon be a contessa!' Cory said, pretending to swoon. 'And we will all live with her in

Italy for ever. In her grand palazzo, with her hundreds of servants and vast marble halls.'

Clio fled their merry laughter, taking the stairs two at a time until she could slam her chamber door behind her and be alone, in silence, at last. Heaven deliver her from *sisters*!

And from English Viking dukes and 'dark Italian counts'. They all knew far too many of her secrets already.

Chapter Seven

Edward watched the sun set from his overgrown back garden, seated on the edge of the old fountain, a Turkish cigarillo in hand. The vast sky was a swirling blend of orange and blood-red, streaked with shimmering gold dust, smoky lavender at the edges. Etna dominated the horizon like a silent queen, swathed in silver mists like a torn bridal veil. The breeze that swept up from the valley was cool, carrying away the heat of the afternoon.

It was unlike anything he had ever seen in all his travels—silent, eternal, dramatic. Every instant the sky shifted and changed. The vestiges of modern Sicily, the bustle of the village streets, the vast tides of tourists, receded and there was only the land itself.

It was like Clio. Changeable, mysterious, remote. Beautiful.

Not that she had been so very *remote* when they had met that morning. He exhaled a grey plume of smoke, remembering the feel of her in his arms, the taste of her mouth. She was intoxicating, worse than the brandy he

had given up years ago. Every time he was near her, he
wanted more and more of her! He wanted everything.

Her kisses took him out of himself, until there was
only her. Only the two of them, floating high above the
dark world, lost in a passion that promised everything.
But the problem with soaring above the earth, touching
the glory of the sun, was that he always fell, Icarus-like,
to the rocks below. He had no heart left to offer her.

Edward took another long drag of the cigarillo,
drawing the sour smoke deep inside, feeling it burn its
way down his throat as he looked down to the marble
ledge beside him. Clio's spectacles lay there, the vivid
sunset glowing on the lenses, reflecting the light back
to him. 'Remember why you're here,' he muttered. To
finish his task. To make sure no one else got hurt. Not
to kiss Clio Chase.

He ground the last of the cigarillo out beneath his
boot. Maybe one day she might understand. Clio saw
things even *he* could not fathom; so much was hidden
in her eyes. Even if she never understood, never saw,
he would take care of her. He thought about his first invitation here in Santa Lucia, to Lady Riverton's 'theatrical evening'. It was just the first step in his plan.

Edward turned and strode into the palazzo, wrapping
the spectacles up in his silk handkerchief. He shoved the
makeshift package at one of the footmen, and said,
'Deliver this to Miss Chase immediately.'

After dinner, when her father, Thalia and Cory were
settled to reading in the drawing room, Clio crept down
the back staircase to the kitchens. Lady Riverton
thought she knew everything that happened in Santa
Lucia, but Clio was sure her ladyship saw only the

merest surface. Only the polite *English* side of things. Clio knew that if she wanted the whole truth, she needed to go to Rosa, their cook.

Rosa had a vast family, sons and daughters, nieces and nephews, who worked in every corner of Santa Lucia, the hills and the valleys, both in legitimate venues and those that were less so. Especially her strange younger son, Giacomo, who appeared to have no profession at all, one of the seemingly indolent men in the piazza. If anyone had heard anything of the English duke, it would be Rosa.

The cook was sitting by the kitchen fire, shelling fresh peas and chatting with her husband, Paolo, who ran the stables. A lamb lay on the table, ready to be dressed for tomorrow's dinner, which meant her butcher son must have been by. Or perhaps the shepherd son.

Clio sat down with them, enjoying the cosy crackle of the flames against the cool evening. Rosa and Paolo just smiled at her, used to her strange ways by now. Paolo held up a bottle of clear liquid.

'Grappa, *signorina*?' he asked.

'Yes, *grazie*,' Clio answered, watching as he poured out a generous glassful and passed it to her. One of their other sons distilled it himself, and it was rough and strong as she sipped at it. She laughed, wiping at her stinging eyes. 'It's, er, very good.'

Rosa laughed. 'Oh, Signorina Clio! You are an odd one.'

'Yes, I know. I've often been told that.' If they only knew just *how* odd. But no one knew, really. No one but Averton. And he was an odd one himself. 'Rosa, what do you know about the farmhouse site being cursed?'

Rosa made a quick gesture to deflect evil before going on with her pea-shelling, not looking at Clio. 'Cursed?'

'Yes. I heard something about it today, and I was surprised you hadn't warned me.'

'Pah! You are *Inglese*, it can't hurt you.'

Clio took another drink of the grappa. It was really quite nice once she got used to it. So, she took yet another. 'A strange curse, to respect national boundaries like that.'

'What Rosa means,' Paolo said, 'is that you have to believe in a curse for it to work.'

'How do you know I don't?'

Rosa gave a sharp laugh. 'You're still here, aren't you, *signorina*?'

'Are you saying there are some who are not still here? Victims of this curse?'

Paolo shrugged. 'That house was destroyed in a time of great violence. Bloodshed, battles, much fear. The last family who lived there, a Greek family, fled as the Romans drew near. But they were acolytes of Demeter, they called on their goddess to avenge them for the loss of their home as they left. Since that long-ago day, anyone who tries to live there, grow crops there, they fail. They die horrible deaths.'

'They see the ghosts,' Rosa added. 'It drives them mad.'

'Hmm,' Clio said thoughtfully. 'Maybe the ghosts leave me alone because I don't try to live there. Because my work is meant to help those people who fled, to tell their story.'

'Perhaps,' Rosa said. 'But if anyone comes there with evil intentions…'

Like Averton? Were his intentions 'evil'? 'What have you heard about the Englishman who has taken the Picini palazzo?'

Rosa and Paolo exchanged a long glance. 'Not a

great deal yet,' Rosa said. 'Our youngest son got a place as footman there. He says this man is very great in your country. A prince of some sort.'

Clio laughed to envision Averton with a crown perched crookedly on his golden head. That grappa was certainly doing its work! She felt all warm and content. Even curses and dukes couldn't affect her, not now. 'Not a prince exactly. But very important, yes. I'm surprised to see him here.'

'You knew him before, *signorina*?'

'Yes, in England.'

'Ah. Our son says this prince seems to have come here for the antiquities, as so many do. He has many objects he moved into the palazzo. He keeps them in his very bedchamber!'

'Really?' Clio leaned forward, her interest sharpening. 'What sort of objects?'

'Vases, statues.'

'A statue of Artemis, perhaps? About as tall as me? Alabaster?'

'I don't know,' Rosa said. 'I will ask Lorenzo. Is this statue important?'

'It could be.' Clio sat back, sipping the last of her grappa. 'If you hear anything else interesting from Lorenzo, will you tell me? I'd like to know what he's doing here.'

'Of course, *signorina*. Is he a bad man, this prince of yours?'

Clio considered this, thought about their kiss, his touch. The madness that came over her every time she saw him. 'I don't know yet.'

She thanked Rosa and Paolo for the drink and the information, and left them to their own gossip. At the top of the stairs, she could hear the low murmur of voices from the drawing room, the sound of Thalia playing old English madrigals at the pianoforte. She should rejoin them, but her head was spinning with the grappa, curses, ghosts and thoroughly baffling princes. Instead, she turned toward the second flight of stairs leading to the bedchambers.

Her own room was silent and dark. No one had come yet to light the candles or turn back the bed. Clio walked unsteadily to the window, opening it to lean out and take a deep breath. The vast sky was indigo blue, with only one tiny star and a crescent of moon to light the inky expanse. It was still early; soon, the pearly stars would blink on one by one. Distant Etna was just a blur without her spectacles.

It would be a good night for the Lily Thief, Clio thought idly. Dark enough to avoid detection. But Santa Lucia was quiet, with nothing to distract people from their purloined ancient treasures. Maybe later, when everyone was cosy in bed…

She perched on the wide windowsill, tucking the Turkey-red muslin skirts of her evening gown around her. Those thieving days were behind her now, which was a pity considering the Alabaster Goddess might be so near. Clio peered out over the roofs, past the bulk of the cathedral, to the edge of the Duke's palazzo. It, too, was a bit blurry, but some of the windows were lit up, glowing bright squares. Someone was home.

What was he doing in there right now? she wondered. Did he gloat over his treasures? Plan how best to drive her even more insane? Did he consider whatever it was that had brought him to Santa Lucia in the first place?

Rosa said it was the hunt for antiquities, like almost everyone else here. But Clio had learned the hard way that Averton never did things as 'everyone else' did, and never for the expected reasons. He was a world unto himself, completely indecipherable.

Clio doubted his appearance here in sleepy Santa Lucia, so far from his ducal empire, could be a mere co-incidence. So, what was it?

'I will just have to find out,' she murmured. She had gained many skills in her Lily Thief days. Maybe it was time to put them to use again. And, with Marco in town, she had a potential accomplice.

If *he* wasn't up to mischief himself. Marco was always up to mischief. The question was, what sort was it? What was happening behind the sleepy façades of Santa Lucia?

A knock sounded at her chamber door, and Clio stood up, shaking out her skirts. 'Yes?'

'A delivery for you, Miss Chase,' a maid said.

'Come in.' It was a strange package, a lump of white silk tied with a bit of string. Clio quickly unrolled it, catching her spectacles in her hand. There was no note, no message. Just the scarlet letters embroidered on a corner of the silk.

ER.

'Edward Radcliffe,' she whispered.

It seemed so strange that he even possessed a given name.

'Edward,' she whispered again, crumpling the hand-kerchief in her palm. 'I promise I will find out what you're doing. You can't escape from me. Prince or not.'

It was definitely not one of the finer streets of Santa Lucia.

Edward nudged aside a pile of rubbish with the toe

of his boot. The cobblestones were old and cracked, streaked with refuse; the lane itself was narrow and dark, close-packed with ancient buildings that faced the world with barred doors and broken, shuttered windows, with walls of peeling, grimy stucco. From behind those walls he could hear the shriek of drunken laughter, the crash of quarrels, the two barely distinguishable from each other. The smell of rotting vegetables, sour grappa and old chamber pots hung heavy in the still night air. It was after midnight, but he knew it would be little different at midday.

This street was far from the Picini palazzo, or even from the smaller, respectable abodes of shopkeepers and servants. This was another world entirely, one kept far from the tourists, the wealthy. Yet this was the only place where he could find what he sought.

There were surely answers behind those barred doors, answers that would never be easily given up. So, he would have to take them.

He paused, his black clothes and dark cap blending with the shadows as he studied the dwelling opposite. It appeared to be deserted, a dilapidated structure, yet it had to be the one he sought. He settled in to wait, his arms crossed over his chest. In his work, cool, predatory patience was a necessity, and he had learned it at long last after all his wildly impulsive years.

Like the impulse that led him to kiss Clio Chase at her farmhouse—despite what had happened in London.

He reached up to rub at the scar on his brow, that rough reminder of where 'impulse' had got him. He had a task here, one that included keeping Clio far away from it all. Far from places like this, and from him.

He was not doing a very good job of it so far.

Kissing her; agreeing to meet her father. But that would change.

Right now, it seemed. A small, flickering light appeared in one of the broken upper windows. Someone was home.

Edward crept across the lane, drawing a dagger from its sheath beneath his sleeve. Holding it balanced on his leather-gloved palm, he made his way around the house to its back door. It faced on to an alleyway even narrower than the front street, barely wide enough for one man to walk down. More refuse was piled in the doorway, but, as he had suspected, it was not barred. The tip of his knife made quick work of the flimsy lock.

The corridor inside was dark and dank, smelling of dusty disuse. Surely no one lived here but the mice; it was perfect for nefarious plots. Everyone in Santa Lucia surely knew what went on here, but no one would ever speak of it. Tomb-raiding was the pastime of centuries here, the key to ill-gotten prosperity.

But that was also about to change.

Moving silently on the balls of his booted feet, Edward made his way up a narrow staircase. He did not stop at the lighted room, but kept going ever upwards until he found a narrow space under the eaves, just as his informant had said. There was a gap in the floorboards there, where he could hear and see everything that went on in that room below. But *they* could not see *him*, and would thus blithely go on with their plans.

Oh, yes. Things were about to change indeed.

Chapter Eight

The next day Clio did not go to her farmhouse, but to the villa with her father and sisters. She was tired from the sleepless night, the grappa, and was not sure if she should be alone in the secluded meadow until she knew more about the enemy's plans. She might have been a thief, but never an impulsive one. It didn't pay to act rashly, if a person wanted to achieve their goals and come out of the fray unscathed.

She had made the mistake of jumping in without the proper preparation in Yorkshire. She would not do that again.

She sat at the edge of the partially uncovered banquet hall of the villa, sketching the elaborate mosaic floor, carefully noting measurements. The people who once lived here were rather different from her prosperous but hard-working farmers. These had been the rulers of this distant outpost, this luxurious little colony built up from nothing to be the breadbasket of a kingdom. And their villa reflected that status, full of sumptuous touches like a thermal bath and elaborate courtyard gardens.

Here, in the banquet hall, the borders of the floor were inlaid with grapes, figs and pomegranates, common Greek fertility symbols, the purple and red colours still lush and glistening after all these years. They framed scenes of parties such as the ones that must have gone on long into the night here. Diners clad in purple, blue and white robes, lounging on low couches as they gorged themselves on delicacies such as fishcakes, white breads, honeyed sweets and copious vats of wine.

Clio smiled as she drew their laughing, satisfied faces, imagining their drunken conversations. The gossip about the sexual orgies of powerful officials, the talents of actors seen recently at the amphitheatre, favourite poets, onerous new taxes. The peccadilloes of their neighbors. Surely not much had changed over the centuries. Very similar talk could be heard at Lady Riverton's house, too.

Except for the orgies, of course. No one would even *say* such a word in the presence of an unmarried English lady! Clio laughed aloud. If only they knew how she had augmented her already surprisingly frank classical education with information from Rosa and the other Sicilians. If she had to, she now knew the best ways to breed strong goats. The best sexual positions for a human woman, too, if she wanted to conceive a boy child. The best herbal potions to use if she didn't want to conceive a child at all. That would surely some day be useful.

'Shocking,' she murmured. Yes, if they all knew, Lady Riverton, the Darbys and Elliotts, the Manning-Smythes, she would be cast out of 'good' society.

Would that be a terrible thing? Not for herself, maybe, but for her father and sisters. They were what kept her tethered to reality.

'What is shocking, Clio dear?' her father asked, coming up beside her to sit down at the edge of the floor.

'The colours of the tiles,' Clio answered, gesturing to a pomegranate bursting with ruby-coloured seeds. 'They could have been laid yesterday.'

'It's the soil, of course,' Sir Walter said. 'Perfect conditions for preservation, just the right level of acidity. We are quite fortunate.'

'Indeed we are. Travelling here was a very good idea.' Clio examined her father over the edge of her sketchbook. He seemed rather tired today, his face reddened from the southern sun, his eyes lined with purplish shadows. He appeared thinner, too, despite Rosa's excellent cooking.

This kind of work had been his life for so long, but he was not as young as he used to be. Perhaps if he *did* marry Lady Rushworth, it would be a good thing. She would take care of him, as Clio's mother once had.

He took the book from her hands, examining the drawings. 'Such careful measurements and proportions, Clio. You were always good at such things.'

'But not nearly as artistic as Cory! Her sketches grow more accomplished every day.' Clio gestured toward her sister, working with her watercolour box under the canvas pavilion.

'So she does. Her works bring this place back to life.' Sir Walter laughed. 'She talks of joining an expedition to Egypt when she is older! Painting the pyramids and hieroglyphs.'

'She would be excellent at that, I'm sure.'

'My dearest girls. You all were always so fanciful.'

Were? 'That is because of you and Mother. You always gave us much to be fanciful about.'

'Indeed we did. Yet I sometimes wonder…' His voice trailed away, and he stared out into the distance, to the ever-vigilant, ever-patient hulk of Etna.

'Wonder what, Father?'

'If we raised all of you the wrong way. We wanted you to love what we loved, to see the great importance of history and art. To think for yourselves.'

Clio laughed. 'We most assuredly do *that*!'

'Perhaps we should have been more realistic, though. Should have taught you more of the things young ladies of your position ought to know, and lived less in our own world with our own friends. I begin to fear we did not prepare you well for life.'

'Oh, no!' Clio cried. 'We all love you and Mother so very much. We love the life you've given us. None of us could bear the usual missish sort of existence, needlework and idle gossip…'

'Husband hunting?' he said teasingly, a glint in his eye.

'Especially that.'

'Oh, well, that is another way I have failed you. If your mother were here, she would know how to find suitable matches. I have been shockingly remiss, just drifting along, year after year, selfishly keeping you with me.'

'Not at all! Isn't Calliope well married? She's a countess now. And Cameron is a good man. He loves her very much.'

'Yes. Love. We never thought of that sort of thing when I was young. But I suppose you modern young Muses won't do without it.'

'You suppose correctly! But weren't you and Mother in love? Despite—' Clio snapped her mouth shut before she could let out those dreadful words. The secret knowledge she had held all these years, would hold for ever. 'Despite being so young when you married.'

He smiled sadly. 'Of course I loved your mother. Who could not? She was so beautiful, so—temperamental. Full of fire. Just like you, Clio.'

'Like me?'

'Of all my girls, you are the most like my Celeste. You have her hair, her eyes. Her passion.'

Clio reached out and gently touched his hand. 'Then I must wait for my perfect match, as she did.'

He laughed. 'I could never *match* Celeste! No one could. You must simply find someone who can keep up with you, a Herculean task in itself.' He stood up, prodding at a mosaic flute girl with his walking stick. 'Oh, I almost forgot! I have invited someone to take a look at the villa this morning. He'll probably stay and share our picnic luncheon, too.'

Clio slowly closed her sketchbook. Guests at the villa were certainly nothing new. All the English tourists who visited Santa Lucia were avid to see ruins. And they often stayed to eat, too, discussing antiquities far into the siesta hours. But something in her father's tone, in the way he refused to meet her gaze, aroused her suspicions.

'What sort of visitors?' she asked. 'Not one of those odd men from Palermo who are always offering to be a "security guard"? I don't trust them!'

'Certainly not. They only want to steal what they can dig up and sell, destroying everything else in the process. We have our own "security". No, my dear, it is—well, it is the Duke of Averton.'

'Averton?' Clio muttered. She knew she should not be surprised. The man had such a knack for insinuating himself into her life. A duke was always welcome everywhere. But now her own *father*? She had thought he did not much like Averton, or indeed any of the Radcliffes.

But then, Sir Walter knew nothing of what had happened between her and Averton last year. If Clio had her way, he never would.

'Yes,' he said, his voice far too cheerful. 'Thalia told me Lady Riverton said he was in Santa Lucia, and I thought he might be interested to see what we're doing here.'

'But, Father! He is so…'

He held up his hand. 'I know he is a bit more *avid* in his collecting habits than you would like. Yet he is not so bad as you seem to think, Clio. He is a great scholar, particularly knowledgeable about the Punic Wars, which would be very helpful to us at this site.'

He leaned down, laying a gentle touch on her arm, much as one would with a skittish horse. 'He did make many mistakes when he was a young man, that is true. But, my dear, I have heard that he is trying to make a new start. To live up to his title, his family and responsibilities. Look at the work he has done for the Antiquities Society! I feel we should give him a chance.'

'Then of course I will welcome him politely, Father. You and Mother *did* raise me to have proper manners, no matter what your doubts on that score.' And they were surrounded by people here. That would definitely limit the trouble she and Averton could get into. 'Do we have enough food and wine?'

Her father gave her a relieved smile. Apparently, being so much like her French mother made her unpredictable, too. 'Lady Rushworth has gone back to Santa Lucia to fetch more provisions, plus some footmen to set up more tables under the pavilion. Silver and china, linens and such.'

Clio laughed. 'What, is he bringing an army with him? An entourage of retainers?'

'One never knows with dukes, my dear. Lady Rushworth just thought we should be prepared.' He paused. 'But then, Averton has never been like most dukes, has he?'

No, indeed, Clio thought wryly. Averton had never been like anyone else at all. 'I will go and help Cory to clear up her paints, then. If I had known we were to have such exalted company, I would have worn my silks and feathers!'

Her father kissed her cheek. 'You look beautiful no matter what you wear, Clio. I have the suspicion that his Grace thinks so, as well.'

Before Clio could even begin to argue with him, Sir Walter strolled quickly away, whistling as he swung his walking stick. Exactly how much did her father know? And how much did he know that *she* knew?

Along with her worries about Marco's appearance, and about what Averton knew that she did not, it made her head spin more than any amount of grappa.

Clio helped Cory pack her paintboxes away in her baskets, hanging up finished watercolours to dry along a line specially hung for that purpose. They were really wonderful, Clio thought, examining a scene that was a reconstruction of the villa as it would have been in its prime. The frescoes on the walls were perfectly detailed, the water in the fountain sparkling. Far better than anything Denon had done in Egypt.

'These are truly wonderful, Cory,' Clio said.

'They're all right,' Cory answered. 'I'm having some trouble with the perspective in the thermal baths. If I could just work on it some more today, instead of having to pack it all up! Just to give luncheon to a stupid old duke.'

Clio smothered a laugh at her sister's petulant irreverence. It would never do to encourage her! Yet it was still quite funny. *Stupid duke*, indeed.

Cory was quite serious, though. 'I wouldn't think *you* would care to see him, Clio,' she said, taking off her paint-splattered apron and smoothing her pink muslin dress. Like Calliope, she had black hair and fair skin that glowed in pink. The colour just made Clio look like a demented strawberry. Not that her grey work frock was any better.

'Why is that?' Clio asked. 'I don't mind Father's guests.'

Cory glanced at her from the corner of her eye. 'Well, after that quarrel you had with the Duke at the British Museum last year…'

Clio froze. *Oh, blast.* How could she have forgotten that? Cory had been right there in the Elgin room when Averton had cornered Clio and tried to talk to her about the Lily Thief. When she had nearly stabbed him with her hatpin before Cameron de Vere had separated them. She had foolishly thought Cory had not noticed, being so preoccupied with her sketching, but she should have known better. Cory was a Chase, after all. Observation—some might unkindly call it snooping—was their *raison d'être*.

'That was just a misunderstanding,' Clio said.

'Was it?' Cory answered. 'You and the Duke seem to *misunderstand* each other a lot. Like that time at Herr Mueller's lecture at the Antiquities Society…'

'Well, we're not going to have any such misunder-standings today,' Clio said firmly. 'We're all going to be perfectly polite and have a pleasant luncheon. Correct?'

Cory gave a most impolite snort. 'I wouldn't count on that if Thalia comes back from the theatre. She doesn't like him, either, and you know Thalia is likely to say anything.'

Clio sighed. She *did* know that. Calliope, the most sensible and organised of them, had once likened managing her sisters to herding a pack of feral cats. Not flattering, but probably true. Maybe her father was right about their upbringing.

'Thalia will be polite, too,' Clio said sternly, trying to sound like Calliope. 'We are *all* going to be polite. Yes, Terpsichore?'

'I will if you won't call me that.' Cory hated her full name.

There was no time to remonstrate further. The Duke himself came into the valley on his gleaming black horse, gazing around him with an air of wary interest. He had no entourage at all, no army of hangers-on. Not even a groom. Just himself, yet he alone seemed to fill up every corner with his vast presence.

He had left off his black garb in the afternoon heat, wearing instead a wheat-coloured linen coat over his buckskin breeches and high boots. His bright hair fell to his shoulders, under the shadowing brim of his hat.

Sir Walter hurried forward to greet him, and even Cory followed, dragging her feet only a bit before making a proper, pretty curtsy. But Clio found she was quite frozen to the spot, unable to move even one step on seeing him again. Seeing, feeling, the reality of his presence.

It was one thing to think about him, to ponder his mysterious motives and try to push away her own tangled feelings for him. But it was always something else entirely to be face to face with him in the stark light of day.

He swung down from his horse, shaking hands with Sir Walter, bowing to Cory. He slowly drew off his riding gloves, watching thoughtfully as her father gestured to the villa, the cracked steps leading to the agora. She saw that he did not wear his rings today. There was no gaudy sparkle of emeralds or rubies, no antique stickpin in his simply tied neckcloth. No satin waistcoat, either. Nothing to distract from his austere beauty. His simple clothes, his solemn mien, it all spoke of a seriousness of purpose here.

A purpose she still could not get to the bottom of.

Her father and Averton turned toward the pavilion where Clio stood, making their way slowly as Sir Walter talked and gestured avidly. Averton nodded, listening intently.

Edward, she thought suddenly. He was not the Duke today. He was Edward.

And she was shocked to realise she wanted to run forwards and throw her arms around *Edward*'s neck. To feel the press of his lips on hers as he lifted her from her feet, twirling her around and around as the world blurred and crumbled around them. No Duke, no Lily Thief, just Clio and Edward, free to feel and do whatever they chose. To forget the past.

As if such a thing was even possible. Clio was too much a realist to believe *that*.

She smoothed her skirt as they drew closer, folding her hands tightly to still their trembling. To keep them from reaching out for him.

'…should be here soon with our meal,' Sir Walter was saying. 'In the meantime, perhaps you'd care to see the mosaics of the villa. They are extraordinarily well-preserved.'

'I would like that very much, Sir Walter,' Averton answered. 'Everyone speaks of their beauty. Good day, Miss Clio. It is most pleasant to see you again.'

Clio swallowed past the dry knot in her throat. Where was that grappa when she really needed it? 'And you, your Grace. Father is always so happy to have someone new to Santa Lucia to show off his villa.'

'I'm honoured to be allowed to see it. I haven't yet had time to see any of the sites of Enna properly.'

'I think there are too many to see "properly" in a decade,' Clio said, surprised to find that she *could* chat politely with him. 'We have been here many weeks now, and my family have not even been to the castle. We've just seen it from a distance.'

'It isn't *Greek*, of course,' her father said dismissively. 'Just thirteenth century. Far too new for me.'

'But lovely, or so Rosa says,' Clio answered. Rosa also said it was haunted, just like Clio's 'cursed' farmhouse, but she didn't mention that.

'Rosa?' Averton asked.

'Our cook,' said Clio. 'Her family has lived in Santa Lucia for generations. She seems to know every inch of the land.'

'Then if she says the castle is worth seeing, she must be right.' Averton glanced at Clio, his expression unreadable under the shadow of his hat. 'Perhaps you would care to accompany me there after luncheon, Miss Clio? We could discover it together. And you, too, of course, Sir Walter.'

Her father laughed. 'Oh, no, not me! I have work to do on things that are truly old. But you two must go. Clio has been wanting to see it, have you not, my dear?'

'Well, yes, but…' she began.

'Then it is settled. Now, you really must let me show you the mosaics, Averton. Especially the mermaid in the baths. So extraordinarily well preserved.'

Clio watched helplessly as her father led Averton away. It seemed she was now committed to an outing with the Duke. Or was it with Edward?

Either way, she would have to watch her step very carefully. Any unwary move in this slippery game they played would send her tumbling right down into a new abyss.

'Just don't push him off the battlements, Clio,' Cory whispered. 'That would surely not be polite.'

Edward nodded as Sir Walter pointed out the sections of his villa, the old peristyle hall, the long space where the women had their weaving looms, the walled gardens. He listened closely, yet his attention was not on the ancient past. It was on the all-too-near present.

Clio sat with her younger sister in a pavilion, her dark red hair cast in shadow, her face unreadable. Servants scurried around them, setting up their luncheon, yet she was an island of stillness.

She had agreed to show him the medieval castle, but how did she feel about that? About spending yet more time with him? How did *he* feel about that?

Edward frowned, nudging at a bright mosaic tile with his boot. Self-examination was not what was needed now; action was. He thought of the dark house on its poor street, of what he had learned in his secret space there. Santa Lucia was not safe for Clio, not if she kept wandering off on her own in the hills. He could warn her again, but would she ever listen?

Truly, Clio Chase was maddening! Every time he determined to stay away from her, from the complications of her fierce intelligence and lithe body, of her tangled past, something pulled him back to her. Pulled them together.

Just like this castle outing. Perhaps it was one last chance, a chance for him to persuade her at last to leave things alone. Persuade *himself* to leave *her* alone! If talking did not work…

Then more drastic measures were called for.

Chapter Nine

Clio led the way up the steep stairs carved in the rocky hillside, the only access to the castle, conscious at every moment of the Duke's footsteps close behind her. Despite the fact that he was a tall man, he walked softly, gracefully, an ever-present ghost. His movements were light, stealthy, as unpredictable as the clouds overhead, and as always when he was near her senses were poised and alert. He had taken her by surprise more than once in the past—he would not do so again.

She glanced back at him as they climbed ever higher, to find him watching her with solemn wariness, his face half-shadowed by the brim of his hat. When she had come to Sicily, she had been so sure she had left him and his all-seeing gaze far behind. Perhaps she had thought she would never even have to face him again! Face the truth of her own feelings. What folly that had been. Even when he was not in the same country, he was always with her.

In her distraction, her boot sole slipped on a loose pebble, and she slid backwards. Caught off guard, her stomach lurching in a sudden jolt of panic, she reached out to steady herself, but clutched only insubstantial air. Before she could tumble off the narrow walkway to the valley far below, a strong arm came around her waist, stopping her in mid-fall.

Breathless, Clio found herself caught against the Duke's warm, muscled chest, his embrace surrounding her, holding her safe above the chasm.

'You should watch your step, Clio,' he whispered. 'These paths are treacherous.'

'The entire world is treacherous, to those who are unwary,' she said hoarsely. She disentangled herself from his arms, pressing close to the rock-cut hillside. She could not leave him entirely, though. He held on to her hand, their bare fingers a lonely connection in that treacherous world. 'Thank you for catching me.'

'Oh, Clio,' he answered, an undertone of sadness in his voice, 'don't you know that I will always catch you?'

Before she could reply, he slipped past her on the narrow path, holding her hand as they finished the climb to the castle. They didn't speak as they walked through the broken archway into the old keep itself. It was not much of a castle any longer; a year-long siege in the twelve hundreds had broken down the sturdy grey stone walls, reducing the twenty towers to ten, then three, and now only one.

But Clio loved the tumbling piles of stones, overgrown with vines and twisted almond trees, the cracked floors and ruined arches, more than she could have loved any intact fortress. There were stories here, thousands of them, tales of heroism and death and passion that whole walls could never hold. The wind whipped through the fissures, bending the overgrown tree limbs, and bright green lizards skittered over the chipped rocks.

The rest of the island seemed so far away, insignificant. And even the Duke seemed to belong here. In London, he was bigger than life, an awe-inspiring figure of brilliant light among the drabness of the grey city. A person of gossip and speculation, of envy for his title, his money, his fine looks. Here, among old scenes of battles and tragedy, of power won and lost, he was no less impressive or unique. But he *belonged*. Belonged in a way he never really did in England.

Which was exactly how Clio herself often felt. Calliope was so good at playing the lady, at being respectable and admirable. Whereas Clio always seemed to find herself floundering, fighting. Endlessly seeking for something, some beacon of meaning that would never be found.

Here, in the silence and the ancient memories, she only had to *be*. Even the Duke—Edward—could not mar that. Indeed, he, too, seemed to find a rare stillness. He played no role of extravagant overlord. He merely stood there, holding her hand, and just *was* in this moment.

If only all time could be like this! But Clio knew well it never could. He would always be a duke. She would always be a thief. And the world would always be waiting, besieging these walls as surely as it had hundreds of years ago.

She gently disentangled her fingers from his, hurrying through the three interconnected courtyards that had once held together the castle towers. She raised the hem of her skirt, stepping carefully over rocks and birds' nests. 'It was built in 1082,' she said, her voice echoing off the walls. 'The Bourbons once used it as a prison, since those stairs on the hillside were the only access and were easily blocked. There used to be twenty towers; now there is only this one still intact.'

'And is it always so deserted?' he asked. 'So— haunted.'

'Not at all. My family haven't been here yet because it always seems so crowded with English tourists. And too many Sicilian guides trying to part them from their coins. They are very good at that!' She threw him a wry smile over her shoulder. 'Everyone must have heard you were coming and obligingly cleared the way.'

'You see, there *are* advantages to a lofty title,' he said. 'Even an unwanted one.'

'I have never heard of a ducal title being unwanted.'

'Well, my dear, there is much about me—and about being a duke—you don't know. Fortunately for us both.' With those puzzling words, he strolled past her to the base of the tower, entering its tall, empty doorway.

The tower, constructed of weathered local grey stone like all the castle and most of the village, rose up three stories in clean, flat straight lines, covered in ropes of emerald-green ivy. A narrow, winding staircase gave the only access to the top, lit by old arrow slits.

Edward waited for her at the foot of the stairs. Without a word, without even looking at her, he held out his hand. *I will always catch you.* Clio slid her fingers into his, and they climbed upwards into the sky itself.

The steep stairs were covered not just with loose pebbles and windblown dirt, but by the detritus of the tourists: torn, trodden handkerchiefs; empty wine bottles; an abandoned phrasebook. Edward nudged all those out of her path with his boot, holding her steady as they moved through the pale, chalky light. She could hear only the scuff of their boots, the distant cooing of birds hidden high in the old beams. The rush of breath, the pounding of her own heart in her ears.

Even during her Lily Thief exploits, she had never been as anxious as she was in his presence. To be alone with him was a dangerous, unpredictable thing. She never knew what he would do; what *she* would do! Kiss him, hit him. Their meetings always ended in one disaster or another.

They emerged into the daylight at the very top of the old battlements. The wind was quick and chilly there, whistling past in swift currents that pulled at her hair and skirts. But the view between the crenellations was glorious. Rolling waves of Sicilian hills, glowing gold and purple all the way to Etna. And, in the other direction, the silvery expanse of Lake Pergusa, where Hades had snatched away Persephone as she gathered flowers.

Yet another unwary female, Clio thought. She herself should learn from Persephone's example. Never take your gaze from the horizon.

Edward leaned his elbows on the wall, his gaze narrowed on the lake. He had taken off his hat, and the wind tangled his hair, tossing it over his shoulders as the sun caught on those beautiful red-gold strands. He looked so alone.

Clio knew what it was to be alone. But even as she felt drawn to his side, she could not give in to sympathy or understanding. When she was weak, that was when she fell. She leaned against the wall beside him, staring out over the rugged landscape.

'I have never seen anything so beautiful,' he said.

'Nor have I,' Clio answered. 'But surely you have seen far more of the world than I have! Are you not a member of the Travellers' Club?'

He gave a half-smile, not looking at her but at the lake, as if he thought to see Persephone herself strolling its banks, flowers falling around her. 'I am.'

'Which means you have travelled to at least four countries. Seen all the loveliest, most exotic parts of the world. Places far more sophisticated and elegant than this rustic place.'

'For sophistication and elegance, Clio, one need not leave London. For real truth and beauty, though, I think a person must come *here*. Why would so many—the Greeks, the Romans, the Byzantines, the Saracens—fight to possess it?'

'And why do *we* come here, struggling to find our own corner of it?'

'Because we, too, belong here, of course.' He turned to her suddenly, his gaze so steady and piercing. As if he could see right to her heart, her most secret desires.

Clio slowly nodded. 'Edward,' she said. The sound of his name was so strange, so delicious, on her tongue. His eyes widened at her word—Edward. 'Why do you and my brother-in-law hate each other?'

His half-smile faded, until it was only a bitter little quirk at the corner of his lips. 'Ah, yes, the esteemed Lord Westwood. I dare say you *have* noticed something of our old—mistrust.'

'I dare say I have. Especially when it came to fisticuffs in Yorkshire.' Clio remembered all too well Cameron's anger that night.

Edward rubbed at his crooked nose, the only flaw in

his handsome, Celtic-god face. 'When I first knew your brother-in-law, we were both young and foolish. Though I admit I was far more foolish than he ever was. He cannot forget what I was in those days.'

Clio studied him carefully in silence. His expression, that mocking smile, did not alter. But it was as if an opaque veil had fallen over his eyes, shielding his deepest thoughts and feelings from her. It was always thus with him, a dark core of truth hidden away. Obscured by the glitter of his position, the sheer strangeness and charisma of his personality.

'How very quizzical you look,' he said.

'I merely try to make out your character,' she answered.

He laughed. 'Such a useless occupation for such an intelligent mind as yours. And how do you make out in such an endeavour?'

'Not well at all. I have never been able to understand you. Even when I think I am close, you change on me.'

'How ironic that *I* puzzle *you*. For you, my dear Miss Chase, are as ungraspable as the sea itself.'

Clio smiled to think of the Mediterranean waves breaking endlessly on the rugged Sicilian shore, blue, green, grey, white, never tamed. There were storms and tides that could kill, hidden glories under the surface, a dangerously beautiful place. One that most people feared, but for a few hardy mariners it was home.

She was not like the sea. She was shore-bound by her family, by expectations. Yet he—he was like the waves. Unpredictable, irresistible. She could not resist moving nearer and nearer, that dangerous undertow catching her skirts and drawing her down for ever.

'What foolish things did you get up to when you were young, then?' she asked.

He shook his head, turning away from her to stare out over the landscape again. The wind tossed his hair over his brow, hiding his face from her. 'You don't really want to know. Young noblemen are a terrible breed.'

'Hmm. It is true that I have no brothers, but I am not entirely a sheltered, delicate miss. I know the sort of japes young men get into at university, or on their Grand Tours. You were probably no worse than dozens of others.'

'I was more spoiled than most,' he said. 'And more angry, too.'

'Angry?' Clio well knew *that* emotion. The burning helplessness of it. She stepped closer to him, then closer still. They did not touch, not even the brush of his sleeve on her hand, but she felt the heat of his skin, the clean, spicy scent of him, reach out to wrap all around her. Binding them together.

'What were you angry about?' she whispered, longing to know, to understand.

'You are thinking that I, a rich duke's son, had nothing to be angry about?' he said lightly. He gazed down at her with those veiled, jewel-like eyes. 'And you would be right.'

'Everyone has something to be angry about. Something to fight against.'

'Well, I fought against myself. Or, I suppose, against expectations of myself. Until my older brother died, of course.'

Clio stared at him, startled by his words, by the hint of pain that lay under them. Like sharks circling under the blue sea surface. Before she could answer, a party of tourists appeared in the courtyard far below them, their laughter echoing off the old walls. Their prosaic reality seemed to pierce the quiet, tense web around her and the Duke, tearing their isolation.

She moved away from him, pressing her back to the wall.

'I beg you, Clio, do not try to make out my character,' he muttered. 'I could not bear for you, of all people, to discover the truth of what I hide there.'

'Discover what?' Clio asked, her throat dry. She felt as if she were teetering on a crumbling precipice, staring down at the rocky shoals of truth. One sharp push would send her tumbling down and down, falling into that whirlpool that was *him*. She was surely closer to discovering the essence of him than ever. Yet did she really, truly want that?

Maybe she *was* one of those eccentric souls who were drawn to the mysteries of the dangerous sea.

'I am many things, Edward, but coward is not one of them,' she said. 'I am not afraid of you, even if your soul is as fearsomely black as this castle's dungeon. There must be a reason we keep meeting. Why our lives keep colliding. Perhaps I am meant to discover it now.'

He studied her for a moment, the air tense between them as the visitors' voices grew closer, louder. Finally, he nodded. 'I know very well you are no coward, Clio. But consider that you are warned. I am no fit company for a young lady.'

'Perhaps you are not. But Muses are contrary beings, are they not? Seldom sensible, and never wanting what is good for them. And I have told you before, I can't bear a mystery.'

'So, I am like one of your antiquary sites, am I?' he said, a thread of shimmering amusement in his voice. 'Just like your farmhouse.'

'Oh, no. You are beyond my poor excavation skills.'

He did not answer, but he held out his hand to her as they turned back towards the stairs. She took it, letting him lead her down the steep, dim tower as if he led her into the puzzles and perils of Hades itself.

Something had changed between them there on that windswept tower; she felt the crack and shift of it deep in her heart. What that change could be—if it would destroy her in the end, keep her as captive as poor Persephone—she did not know. But she realised there was no turning back now.

Edward followed Clio as she led him back down the winding path to the valley where her family waited. Here, in the shadow cast by the castle, the wind ceased its cold moan, sunlight lay in warm, golden ribbons on the dusty earth. Here the world was solid again, they were firmly linked to the elements of growing, living things, of the present and future. Yet the silence was just as profound, just as rich, as it was high up in their fairy-tale tower.

Clio's tall figure moved lightly through the glow of the sun, her skirts catching on the scrubby clusters of lavender and goldenrod. The wind had loosened her hair, long auburn tendrils that escaped their pins and lay against her long neck like silk. She carelessly brushed them back, leaving one dusty smudge on her cheekbone. She did not even seem to notice; her gaze, shielded behind her restored spectacles, was far away, full of inward thought. She didn't even seem to notice his close regard.

But that yearning, that burning desire he felt for her, became ever larger, a palpable, pulsating thing that overcame all else when she was near, when they were together. The touch and taste of her were intoxicating, all-drowning, far more than the alcohol he had craved when he had been young and wild. Clio wrapped around all his senses until she was all he knew, all he wanted. He forgot everything else, and that was dangerous. He needed to be alert here in Sicily, at all times.

She glanced back at him as they made their slow progress down the narrow hillside, her expression serious. 'I have heard many tales of this island since we came here,' she said.

'Magical tales, I'm sure,' he said. 'For Sicily is surely a land of rare enchantment.'

'Indeed it is. I've never been anywhere I loved more.' She paused in her steps, gesturing to the distant mountains, the sea beyond. 'Do you know the story of Erice?'

'Tell me,' he answered, captured by the soft intensity of her voice. The wild timelessness of the land that matched the woman.

'Mount Erice, which guards the port of Trapani, belonged to the Elymians, and is one of the most sacred spots in all the Mediterranean,' she said. 'Its founding stretches back to the very beginning of creation, when the Titans revolted against their father, Uranus. Kronos castrated his father with a great sickle, and threw his, er, organs into the sea off Trapani. And then, to mark the spot where her ancestor had died, Aphrodite, the goddess of love, rose from the sea on her shell and created Erice, making it her home.'

'And it was there she lured Butes, the Argonaut, with the sirens' song. She gave him a son, Eryx…'

'Who gave the mountain its name.' Clio smiled at him. 'You do know the tale.'

'I'm always keenly interested in the doings of Aphrodite.'

'So I've heard. You should know, then, that her feast day is coming soon, according to our cook, Rosa. She says they used to release a flock of white doves from the slopes of Erice, but she doesn't think they do it any longer.'

'And can one steal Daedalus's golden honeycomb there?'

Clio laughed. 'I don't know. It's one of the many mysteries of the island I have yet to discover.'

'Ah, yes. So many mysteries…' And surely the greatest of all was standing before him.

Her laughter faded. 'Indeed. But Demeter's feast day comes before Aphrodite's, far more useful, I think. We should get back to the villa now. My father will be looking for us.'

'Of course.' They continued on their way, the path still too narrow for them to walk side by side. Edward followed her, not holding hands as they had at the castle, yet still bound in some unseen way.

'You are to attend Lady Riverton's theatrical evening?' she asked.

'Yes,' he answered. 'She was the first to send me an invitation here. I must go where I'm invited, or I would be too desolate.'

She laughed. 'I can't imagine *you*, a rich, handsome duke, would ever be left desolate. I would think rather you would have an excess of invitations, and would have to turn most of them down. Not that there is much grand society in Santa Lucia.'

'You think me handsome, then?' he asked lightly.

She looked back at him, one brow raised. 'You know you are.'

'I know no such thing,' he said. 'My mother used to call me her "barbarian", her marauding Viking.'

'Truly? My own mother sometimes said I was an Amazon, taller and wilder than my sisters, and I should have been named Hippolyta. But, of course, after Calliope my father was set on his Muses theme. And my mother obliged by giving him so many daughters.'

'Then perhaps we should forsake Sicily for a colder shore, where our warrior tendencies will be properly appreciated.'

'Is there such a place?' They came around a bend in the path, into sight of the valley. Sir Walter and his younger daughter were seated under the canvas pavilion where they had lunched earlier, their heads bent over a pile of books. Lady Rushworth supervised the servants in packing the used plates and platters.

Clio paused, her head tilted to one side as she watched them. 'I sometimes think I would love to travel for the rest of my life, finding what is beyond each new horizon. Discovering different lives, new stories. Yet even when I do sail seas and climb mountains, it is always the same.' She gave him a sad smile. 'I always just find myself there, going to parties and sipping tea.'

Edward knew how she felt. He found he could never run away from himself, either, no matter where he went. His ducal life was always there, along with the piles of invitations, the clamouring obligations. When all he really wanted right now was to stand for ever on a windswept tower with Clio Chase. How very strange was *that*?

Chapter Ten

Lady Riverton's palazzo was lit up like a Chinese lantern, glowing a hot orange in the dusty-black Sicilian night. Clio gazed up at the windows as she stepped from the carriage, watching as figures already inside strolled past the glass like puppets in a pantomime. They talked and laughed, silent behind the panes, raising glasses of wine, examining proffered trays of delicacies. A liveried footman held the door open for the Chases as they made their way through the manicured courtyard.

How terribly civilised it all was, Clio thought, stepping into that light and noise. As if it were a million miles from the windswept medieval tower, the grey stones that whispered of battles and death and old, old gods.

She remembered what Edward had told her when he had first appeared at her farmhouse, that there was danger here. Well, at *this* house danger surely dared not show its face. The only real peril was in possibly finding oneself cornered and talked at by Lady Riverton's voluble friend, Ronald Frobisher. All in all, Clio preferred curses and spirits.

She surrendered her cloak to another footman, examining herself in one of the gilt-framed mirrors hung on the marble foyer walls. She had left off her brown-and-grey work dresses for a gown in jade-green silk, trimmed on the bodice and cap sleeves with finely spun gold lace. Her hair was smoothed and pinned up, bound by a scarf of more gold lace. She wore a pair of antique Mycenaean gold bracelets over her gloves, pieces that had once been part of her mother's vast jewellery collection. The silk and lace, the gold, it was all an armour of sorts, a disguise carefully constructed to make her appear a fashionable lady, a part of this glittering throng, while her true thoughts were always hidden.

Thalia hurried into the drawing room, her blue eyes glowing with purpose, her pink-and-white muslin skirts whispering softly around her. In her gloved hands she held her rolled *Antigone* script. Clio followed slowly, staying to the back of the room until she had gauged the lay of the land.

Lady Riverton held court by the ornate plaster fireplace, clad in eye-catching red-and-bronze brocade, an elaborate plumed turban atop her curls. Next to her stood Ronald Frobisher, her 'special friend'—or lapdog, as Clio sometimes thought him—a man of delicately slender stature, lovely brown eyes and soft, dark curls. He claimed to be descended from the great Elizabethan mariner, but his life seemed to consist of naught but fetching and fawning. The two of them chatted happily away as they greeted guests, but Lady Riverton kept a sharp eye on the trays of wineglasses and lobster tarts, the new arrivals at the door.

And a great many arrivals there were. Clio slid into a corner near the stage, behind a pair of large comedy/tragedy statues. All the English families were there, the Darbys and Elliotts, the young Manning-Smythes, and also the noble Sicilian families who had not yet decamped to Naples. They stayed mostly in their own tribal clusters at the other end of the room, deigning to grace the foreign proceedings with their dignified presence.

Did they come for the food, then, as her father did? Clio watched as one black-silk-clad matron slid a tart into her reticule. Or perhaps they came to keep an eye on their local antiquities.

Well, whatever their reasons, they certainly added an *ancien régime* dignity to Lady Riverton's proceedings, and filled out her vast rooms quite nicely.

Thalia was making her own progress around the drawing room, trailed by the puppyishly devoted Peter Elliott. She seemed not to notice him, but he now carried her script for her. No doubt he would bear her shawl and reticule, too, if she would let him. Clio's father had found Lady Rushworth, and they were examining one of the cases of the late viscount's coins.

So, Clio thought, everyone was accounted for. Except for the most important piece of all, the Duke. He was nowhere to be seen, and surely if he was there she would sense it. He filled every room he entered; everyone always watched him.

As the moments ticked by, Lady Riverton's smiles became just a tad more brittle, her glances at the door more frequent. She, too, missed her most prominent guest. She took Mr Frobisher's arm, whispering fiercely in his ear until he scurried away on a new errand.

Someone slid up next to Clio in her corner, but she knew it was not Edward. She could sense it.

'Ah, *cara*,' Marco whispered. 'Such an amusing little fête! You English are always so endlessly diverting. I have missed it since I left your shores.'

Clio turned to smile at her old friend, her old partner in crime. He *was* handsome, she had to admit. Probably the most handsome man she had ever seen, a young Roman god with his dark eyes and broad shoulders, with those cut-glass cheekbones and smooth olive skin. He had surely broken hearts in a sad trail from Florence to London and back, hearts he scarcely noticed for he was devoted only to his studies. His burning Florentine patriotism.

But when Clio was near him, she never felt that still, hot *awareness* that came over her when she saw Edward. Marco never made her breath catch, her heart pound. They were friends, that was all; they understood each other, helped each other. It was a great pity, really. Forming an attachment to Marco would be less complicated than carrying a torch for Edward! A lot safer, too.

'So, you did not go on to Palermo after all,' she said.

'And miss this fine party? Never! Especially once I found you were here. It has been far too long, *cara*.' He gave her a melting glance from his chocolate-brown eyes, a woeful, lovelorn gaze that had made many a maiden melt into a puddle on the floor.

It made Clio laugh. 'Shameless, Marco!'

He laughed, too, a rueful sound as he reached for two fresh glasses of wine from a passing footman. He handed her one. 'Ah, Clio, my charms never did work on you. Am I getting old? Losing my romantic touch?'

'Never fear. I just know you far too well. But you are still the loveliest man I have ever met, and you are sure to garner many new hearts here in Santa Lucia. Susan Darby is already in love with you, I think.'

Marco gazed over the gilded rim of his glass toward Thalia, who was laughing with the Elliotts, her blonde hair a luminous halo in the candlelight. 'What of your pretty sister? Is she in love with me?'

Clio snorted. 'Thalia? I wouldn't count on *that*, my friend. She might look like an angel, but she has the soul of a demon. Be careful, or you'll find yourself galloping around the amphitheatre doing her every bidding. She has that effect on men, you see.'

Marco frowned. 'I never do a lady's bidding. Except yours, of course.'

'Only because *my* bidding helped you achieve *your* goals—bringing antiquities back to Italy.'

'Very true. You do know me too well.'

'So, what are your goals here in little Santa Lucia?'

He glanced quickly around the bright, crowded room, and shook his head. 'We shouldn't talk about it here.'

'Of course not.' Despite herself, despite her promises of reform, Clio felt the old excitement flutter deep inside, wakening from its long, respectable sleep. The excitement of secrecy and mischief, of righting old wrongs.

She tightened her clasp on the stem of her glass, until the heavy crystal bit through her glove. *No.* No matter what Marco was up to, she could not be a part of it. She had promised Calliope.

But surely it would not hurt just to *hear* what was afoot...

'Send me a message later,' she whispered.

Marco gave her a solemn glance, quite unlike his usual teasing flirtation. 'Be careful, Clio. There are things going on here, things that could be very dangerous.'

You are in danger—she remembered the Duke's words. Remembered Rosa's ghosts and curses, the deceptively lazy men in the piazza. 'Dangerous? Here in this sleepy town?'

'Surely you know, better than most people, how appearances can be ever so deceiving.' He placed his empty glass on Comedy's pedestal and folded his hands behind his back. 'Just be cautious in your work. Promise me, my friend?'

'I am always cautious.' Almost always, anyway. Just not when she found herself kissing Edward, unable to stop. She gulped down the last of her wine, even though the alcoholic bite of it could not erase the remembered taste of *him*.

Almost as if her thoughts had conjuring powers, the drawing room doors opened and the Duke himself stepped inside. And he *was* the Duke tonight, not Edward, not the man who had stood with her atop the tower and stared down into the whirling maelstrom of something they could not understand. Could not control.

His evening coat was of a glistening sapphire-coloured velvet, with diamond buttons and blue satin trim, over a fine gold brocade waistcoat. He wore his rings again, heavy, archaic gemstones that glittered distractingly on his long, elegant fingers, concealing their true strength.

She recalled the rough grace of those hands on her bare skin, the sparkling magic of them that seemed to flow from his very essence into hers, binding them together more than mere touch, mere sex.

Clio shook her head, trying to drive out those memories, those needs. Lady Riverton's crowded drawing room was no place for her lustful feelings. No place to start any new whispers circulating.

She watched, feigning only casual interest, as Lady Riverton's brittle smile lightened into radiant welcome. Trailed by Mr Frobisher, she hurried across the room to greet this long-awaited guest of honour.

The rest of the company also seemed to turn as one towards the door, once they realised who had arrived. A soft web of awed hush fell over all the loud chatter, the clink of crystal and china. A duke—and not just *any* duke, but the elusive, handsome Duke of Averton!—had joined them. A new kind of glamour-glitter fell over their little party.

And, if she was honest, over Clio, too. When he stepped into the room, even if they did not look at each other, she felt overcome by a flushed, giddy awareness that was not at all like her. He *did* bring a sort of magic with him, something that everyone felt. But it was the deceptive magic of the underworld, and she could not give in to its alluring, pomegranate-laden trap.

'What is *he* doing here?' Marco muttered roughly.

Clio glanced at her friend to find a dark glower on his face, his shoulders tensed under his elegant dark green coat as if he would rush forwards and attack the Duke, right in front of everyone. Rush forwards to avenge what had happened in Yorkshire all those months ago, when they had lost the Alabaster Goddess. Marco and Cameron both had this violent reaction to Edward, then.

Clio laid a gentle, restraining hand on his arm, holding him at her side. Every muscle in his body was taut with anger, yet he stayed with her. For the moment.

What would he do if he learned that the Alabaster Goddess, Artemis, was possibly here in Santa Lucia? Or did he already know? Perhaps that was his reason for being here in the first place. To finish what had begun in Yorkshire.

But there was genuine surprise in his aspect, in those fireworks in his eyes. So, if it was not for Artemis, why was he here?

Why had they all converged at this one moment, in this place?

Clio's head suddenly ached, and not from the wine.

'I don't know why he is here,' she said quietly. 'Probably just sightseeing, like the rest of us.'

'Sightseeing? Dear Clio, surely you do not believe that. He is here to make mischief.'

Unlike you, of course, Clio thought wryly. She watched as Edward raised Lady Riverton's gloved hand to his lips, as that lady laughed, blushing a glowing pink. Mischief just followed them—all of them, Marco, Edward, herself, even Thalia—wherever they went.

'Well, he will have to escape Lady Riverton's clutches before he can hope to make any trouble for us,' she said. 'And that won't happen any time soon. Shall we sample some of those stuffed mushrooms? All this confusion makes me quite famished.'

Marco still did not look at all happy, but he went along as she led him across the room to the trays of refreshments. She held firmly to his arm, talking resolutely of the superficial charms of lobster and white soup. Thalia joined them, and, as usual, her fairy-like beauty distracted male attention from more martial concerns. Once Marco was focused on charming Thalia, Clio glanced surreptitiously at Edward, who was being seated by their hostess near the front row of gilded chairs set up before the stage.

Even as he smiled politely at the viscountess's flutterings, Clio could tell he watched *her*. Her and Marco. His green-gold gaze beamed across the room, and it was as if they were alone in the very midst of the noisy crowd.

She still remembered the gallery at Acropolis House in London, the Alabaster Goddess and her steady bow. The crackle of the air, so heavy with fury and passion and raw need as he grasped her arms in her green silk sleeves. As he dragged her closer, closer, until she could not breathe…

Clio choked on a bite of mushroom, gasping as Thalia thumped her on the back. 'Clio! Are you quite well?'

'Signorina Chase, have some wine!' Marco cried, thrusting a full glass of Marsala into her hand.

'Thank you, I'm quite well,' Clio gasped. If she drank any more wine, she would have to be carried home. At least it was not Paolo's grappa. *That* stuff would send the night spinning completely out of control. 'Just too greedy for the mushrooms.'

'Well, there is no time for that now. The theatricals are about to begin,' said Thalia. She frowned up at Clio, as if she suspected her sister would be taken ill again at any moment. Felled by those pernicious mushrooms. 'Are you sure you are well?'

Clio gave her a reassuring smile. 'Very sure.' The rest of the guests were indeed taking their seats, and the young Manning-Smythe couple were preparing their *Romeo and Juliet* tableau. A papier-mâché balcony, twined with artificial ivy and roses, simulated Renaissance Verona.

'We should find some empty chairs, then,' Clio said. 'Some that are quite close. But aren't you meant to be changing into your costume, Thalia?'

Thalia shrugged carelessly, but Clio noticed her fingers nervously plucked at a fold in her pink satin sash. 'Oh, no, I'm the last performance. Besides, I'm not going to wear my costume. The drama will have to come from the *words*, you see.'

'No fear of that, Signorina Thalia,' Marco said gallantly. '*Antigone* is highly dramatic, and you, I can tell, will be perfect for the role of the doomed princess.'

Thalia tossed him a suspicious glance. 'How can you tell that, Count di Fabrizzi?'

'Because I have made a study of ancient theatre, and you have Antigone's great passion, her great capacity to do what is right—even when it is not easy.' He looked at Clio. 'Your whole family is like that, yes?'

Thalia peered between Clio and Marco, her lips pursed as she nodded. 'I suppose we are, in a way. Complete nuisances, the lot of us. But you say you are a student of theatre, Count? How very fascinating, and useful…'

Thalia took Marco's arm in a light clasp, turning with him towards the chairs with a most determined look on her face. Clio followed, sure of one thing now— she would soon see Marco on the amphitheatre stage, Haemon to her sister's Antigone.

But that was really the only thing she knew. The rest was still obscured by shreds of silvery mist, a disguising shroud that only allowed her fleeting glimpses. Like Etna on a stormy day. Soon, though, like the clouds parting, she would discover all.

* * *

"'O City of Theba! O my country! Gods, the fathers of my race! I am led hence, I linger now no more. Behold me, lords, the last of your kings' house—what doom is mine, and at whose hands, and for what cause—that I duly performed the dues of piety.'"

Edward watched as Thalia Chase finished her dramatic scene, her arms folded and gaze cast forwards towards eternity. She was really quite good, he thought. Despite the fact that she wore a stylish pink-and-white muslin gown and jewels of pink pearls and diamonds, he had forgotten where they were for a moment. Forgot the modern world outside, transported by her simply spoken words, her solemn, dignified mien to ancient Greece. To a land of warring principles, of strict gods, high-minded maidens, unbending kings, and love destroyed by it all.

And he was not the only one so moved, either, to judge by the taut silence in the room. The breathless pause before everyone broke into effusive applause. Thalia made her curtsy, her eyes shining. It was really too bad she was a Chase, a baronet's daughter, he reflected as his applause blended with the others'. If not for her position, she would reign supreme on the London stage.

He watched as Clio turned to say something to her father, clapping madly. Her face glowed with pride for her sister, and for an instant Edward felt a strange, wistful pang. How must it feel to know you belonged with someone, with a family? That you were part of something larger than your own solitary self, that no matter where you went or what you did someone cared about it. Supported it. Loved it.

It sounded like a dream to him, a bright fantasy-world he had never actually seen except in Clio and her sisters. Nothing could break their loyalty and love for each other. He could only admire it, protect it, from afar.

He glanced toward the man who stood along the wall, alone. The dark, far-too-handsome Italian Count who had been Clio's cohort in Yorkshire. He was a gypsy-thief no longer, but a polished, well-dressed gentleman who had all the ladies sighing. He and Clio had seemed to take no notice of each other during the performances, but Edward had seen them talking quite cosily together when he had arrived. As if they made secret plans.

Blast the man, anyway! Blast him for his easy charm, that comfort and understanding between him and Clio. The Count's appearance in Santa Lucia was yet another shadowy fold in a mystery.

Edward had known when he set out for Sicily that his task would not be an easy one. Too little was known of the treasure. But the secrecy of the local townspeople, the determined sociability of the English visitors, and especially Clio's involvement, made it all that much harder. Matters were seldom simple where she was concerned.

So, progress was slow, but it was early days yet. And he was a very determined man.

Lady Riverton took the stage as Thalia exited. 'My dear friends!' Lady Riverton said. 'Miss Thalia's performance was, alas, the last of this evening's theatrical scenes. Yet I think you can agree we have a wealth of rare talent here in our little community.' There was more applause, and Lady Riverton made a pretty curtsy, as if she alone was responsible for that 'wealth of talent'.

But then, poor old Viscount Riverton, though an ex-

cellent judge of ancient coins, had been no keen judge
of females. A pair of pretty eyes had quite blinded him
to a certain lack of good sense.

Not that Edward was in any position to judge
someone else's choice of love!

'There is, however, a supper waiting for us in the
dining room,' Lady Riverton continued. 'If you would
all care to join me?'

A great rustle and commotion arose as everyone made
their way out of the drawing room, gilded chairs pushed
back, the stage abandoned. Edward kept to the edges of
the crowd, hoping to evade their hostess's attention for
a moment. She soon gave up looking for him in the press,
and took the Italian Count/gypsy's arm instead.

The Chases, he noticed, also lagged behind, lingering among the chairs.

'Lady Rushworth has a headache, and I said I would
see her home,' Sir Walter was saying, as Edward
listened in the sudden quiet. From the open double
doors of the dining room could be heard the clink of
china, the rise and fall of laughter. But the Chases were
an island to themselves.

'And,' Sir Walter added, 'I must admit I am quite tired
myself. These social evenings are quite fatiguing. I don't
know why I come.'

'Are you ill, Father?' Thalia asked in concern.

'Not at all, my dear. Merely tired. I would like to get
an early start at the villa tomorrow, also.'

'We will go with you, then,' Clio said.

'No, no! Thalia must stay and enjoy her theatrical
triumph. I will send the carriage back for you…'

'Forgive me, Sir Walter,' Edward said, stepping
forwards. 'I could not help but overhear. If Miss Chase

and Miss Thalia would care to stay longer, I can see them home after supper. My house is not far from yours, and it is the least I can do to repay Miss Chase's kindness in showing me the castle.'

'Ah, Averton!' Sir Walter said happily. 'Very good of you, I'm sure. It would certainly make me feel more at ease to know they were with you. So late to be out and about.'

'Father,' Clio said, shooting Edward an unreadable look, 'we really should go home with you, I think.'

'Yes, indeed,' Thalia agreed, but her glance towards the noisy dining room was wistful.

'Nonsense, Clio,' Sir Walter said. 'You young people should have your amusements. Averton will see you home later, and I will no doubt be tucked up safe and sound long before then. Goodnight, my dears! Enjoy your supper.'

With no further to-do, Sir Walter took Lady Rushworth's arm and strolled out of the drawing room. Thalia, with a mischievous smile at her sister, hurried off to supper, no doubt to 'enjoy her triumph'.

For an instant, Clio seemed uncharacteristically non-plussed. She turned one way, then the other, as if seeking some recourse from his company. Finding none, finding indeed that they were quite alone for the moment, she turned back to him, her arms crossed.

'What did you do that for?' she asked quietly.

'Did you not want to stay for supper?' he asked, mock-innocent. At the castle, it had seemed as if they had come to a new understanding. Now, it was as if they had moved back two steps. Maybe a drawing-room party was not the right place for them. They belonged on that tower, or in a clover-dappled meadow, where there were no boundaries. No expectations.

'I would rather go home and finish some reading,' she said.

'I doubt your sister would agree,' he answered. 'And going home to read would be such a waste of your beautiful gown.' He offered her his arm, and she slowly slid her gloved fingertips into the crook of his elbow, letting him lead her towards the dining room. 'Also, I wished to take advantage of the time to ask you a few questions.'

'Questions about what?' she asked warily.

'Oh, this and that. Most particularly about your friend. The Count di Fabrizzi, is it?'

Clio stiffened, but did not pull away. Neither did she look at him, as a slight pink flush stained her cheeks. 'I hardly know him. Indeed, I did not know he was in Sicily at all until we met at Lady Riverton's tea.'

'Hardly know him? Ah, yes, I suppose you know only a gypsy nomad named Marco. A fellow most adept with a crowbar and lockpick.'

'I don't know why he's here,' she said stubbornly. 'But I do know he has given up his former ways.'

'Like you?'

'Yes. In fact, your Grace, his motives in coming here are as unknown to me as yours are.' She looked directly at him, a bright green stare that burned away secrets and lies, laying them both bare. 'Unless he is part of the "danger" of which you spoke. But you seem to be the only one who would know about all that.'

She broke away from him, making her way to an empty seat at the end of the long, food-laden dining table. Edward followed her slowly, reflecting that it had probably been a mistake to give her even the merest hint of why he was here. They were too much alike, curious and determined. They were like an inferno when they were together, burning all before them.

He would have to be far more careful in the future.

Chapter Eleven

Clio wandered the length of Lady Riverton's terrace, her sandalled heels slapping on the old white marble. Behind her, the tall glass doors were half-open, releasing patches of amber light, the hum of voices as the others gathered for an after-supper hand of cards. Before her was a row of terracotta pots, blooming with fragrant flowers and herbs that blended their bright colours with the darkness, the silvery glow of the waxing moon. Beyond the well-manicured garden was the village, quiet and peaceful—outwardly, anyway.

But, as Clio knew, quiet façades often concealed the greatest tumult.

She leaned her gloved palms on the cold stone balustrade, peering out into the night, the dim concealment and silence that had always seemed her friend. In only a few days, according to Rosa, the night would be torn by the music and illuminations of the springtime *feste*. A time to celebrate that fattening moon and the end of winter's chill, to hope for a good harvest and prosperous year to come. Once, it had been a feast of

Demeter and her daughter. Now it was an excuse for a party.

What would *she* celebrate, hope for? What would the rest of the year hold for her?

Clio sensed she was at a crossroads of sorts, a turning of what had been and what was to come. She couldn't go on as she had, yet she could not go forwards, either. The Lily Thief was done, but not the ideals that drove her to such an extreme in the first place. What was she to do?

Clio heard the squeak of one of the glass doors opening, the soft sound of a footstep on marble. She knew who it was even before she turned, could smell his spicy-clean scent on the evening breeze, feel his beckoning warmth.

Edward placed a glass of ruby-dark wine on the balustrade by her hand. 'I thought you might be thirsty,' he said.

'Thank you,' she answered. She sipped at the sweet brew, half-turning to study him in the moonlight. His blue coat was dark as the sky itself, but his bright hair shimmered like a beacon, luring unwary ships on to deadly rocky shores. 'You don't have any yourself?'

He shrugged. 'I don't care for wine any longer.'

'Nor cards, either, it would seem,' Clio said, gesturing toward the doors, beyond which piquet and loo went on.

'I got my fill of such things when I was young.'

'Yes. I suppose we all have to give up that which is bad for us eventually.'

'Or be killed by it.'

Clio took another fortifying sip of the wine. 'I did give up my bad habit, you know. I promised my sister I would, and my work with antiquities has been strictly aboveboard ever since.'

She did not know why she felt such a need to assure him of that, but she did. She needed him to know that, why ever he had come to Santa Lucia, whatever he was trying to discover, she had nothing to do with it. She wanted only to work on her farmhouse, to be with her family.

'I know,' he said simply. 'I also gave up the bad habits of my youth. Yet sometimes our actions follow us far into the future, have consequences we cannot foresee.'

Clio studied him in silence, turning the glass in her hand. She ached to know what he meant, what had happened to him when he was young. She certainly knew he had got into the usual trouble of rich, titled young men—drinking too much, gaming. Frequenting women of dubious morals, no doubt. But for all the things about him that angered her now, common vices were not among them.

What she wouldn't give to find out the whole truth, why Cal's husband hated him. But Edward was not a person to give up his inner self so easily. And neither was she. Thus they circled each other, not entirely trusting, not certain, but attracted beyond all sanity.

'I really don't know why Marco is here,' she said. 'Any more than I know why you are here. I don't understand anything at all, it seems.'

Edward laughed. 'Then we have something in common, for I am as perplexed as you are. Perhaps your friend has come for the *feste*, eh? An acolyte of Demeter?'

'As you are the acolyte of Hades?'

'Indeed, my dear, you wound me. I have long sought to serve Athena, to absorb some of her cool wisdom. Yet she eludes me.'

'Was it Athena who sent you here? Or someone, something, more prosaic? The Antiquities Society, maybe.'

'Clio, I am a seeker, just like you. I travel here in search of scholarship. New sites, new works of art.'

'New ways of thinking?'

'That, too, my dear. And with you I find that every day.'

Clio finished the last of her wine, placing the empty glass back on the balustrade. 'You are not going to tell me why you are here, are you? Not beyond vague warnings of "danger", like infuriating Delphic riddles.'

'I have told you all I can, all I know. But you would be wise to take others with you to your farmhouse.'

Take others with her? When her quiet hours at the farmhouse were the only things that belonged only to her? 'Oh, Edward. Surely *you* are all I have to fear there.'

He gave her a strange smile. 'Clio. Have I not shown you that you have nothing at all to fear from me?'

From beyond the open door came the sound of chairs being pushed back. The voices and laughter were louder. The card games must be ending, which meant someone would soon come looking for her.

Clio glanced toward the doors, and when she turned back that smile was gone from Edward's lips. He was the Duke again, all calm arrogance. How many other masks did he possess?

'Shall we go in?' he said, gesturing to the palazzo. The jewelled rings on his fingers glittered.

Clio nodded, hurrying past him before she could do something truly foolish—like kiss him again. Clasp him so tightly he could never escape her, never hide from her, and she could lose herself in the essence of him for ever.

The drawing room was filled with clusters of people, conversing, studying Lady Riverton's collections as the servants set up tea. The chatter was quieter than earlier in the evening, but everyone was still clearly reluctant to disperse, to yet give up the amiable company of their own countrymen. Clio saw Thalia by the pianoforte with her swain Peter Elliott and some of the other young people, and she made her way towards them. Perhaps she could persuade Thalia it was time to return home. *Without* the Duke's escort, if it could be arranged.

Behind her, she heard Lady Riverton hail the Duke, latching on to him again. 'Oh, Averton, there you are! You are just the one to help me lead everyone in a new game.'

'Lady Riverton, I fear I am a hopeless fool at party games,' he protested lightly. 'My friends all quite refuse to have me on their teams for charades.'

'I vow this is *not* charades!' Lady Riverton answered. 'It is far more amusing. A little pastime I hear is all the rage in Paris. Gather around, everyone!'

Clio took Thalia's arm. 'Thalia, dear, should we depart? It grows rather late.'

'Oh, no!' Thalia protested, still obviously flushed with her thespian success. 'Not yet, Clio, please. Let's just see what this new game is. If it's not amusing, we can go.'

Clio found she could not disappoint her sister, not when Thalia was having such a good time. She nodded reluctantly. 'Very well. Just one game, though. An old lady like me needs her rest.'

Thalia laughed, and drew Clio with her into the crowd gathered around the fireplace, where Lady Riverton presided from her great velvet armchair. Clio and Thalia sat together on a couch, with Peter Elliott still staying close to Thalia. Edward stood beside Lady Riverton, his jewelled hands on his hips. His face was set in lines of cynical amusement, yet Clio saw tense suspicion in the set of his broad shoulders.

She, too, was suspicious. Party games were such a vast waste of time.

'Now, the title of this game is "Truth",' Lady Riverton announced. 'And it is perfectly simple. Everyone will surely be able to grasp it,' she added, with a glance at the giggling Susan Darby. 'Dear Mr Frobisher told me about it after his recent voyage to France.'

Mr Frobisher, seated on Lady Riverton's other side on a measurably lower chair, laughed. 'Yes, and it is *vastly* amusing! One discovers the most shocking things about one's friends.'

'*That* doesn't sound boring, Clio,' Thalia whispered.

No, not boring. Just potentially hazardous. Clio was certainly glad she had not overly indulged in the wine tonight, as it was clear that others had. Flushed faces and overly loud laughter flooded the drawing room.

Not with Edward, though. He folded his arms across his chest, looking quite as wary as she herself felt.

'Now, as I said, it is a simple game,' Lady Riverton said. 'We will go around the circle, and each of us will tell one truth we have never before revealed. The best truth of all, the most shocking, will receive a prize.'

'Oh, how delicious!' Susan Darby cried, clapping her hands even as her mother tried to restrain her. 'May I go first?'

'Of course, my dear Miss Darby,' Lady Riverton said, exchanging amused smiles with Mr Frobisher.

'I bought *two* ribbons at Signora Cernelli's shop yes-

terday, instead of only one. It was *red*,' Miss Darby said
in a hushed voice. 'I hid it in my dressing-table drawer.'

Mrs Darby rolled her eyes, and Clio bit her lip to
keep from laughing. It was a good thing her father had
left early; his intellectual heart would cry out in fury at
such twaddle! Ribbons had never interested him in the
least, despite all his female offspring.

'I hardly think that will win the prize,' Thalia
murmured in Clio's ear. 'Perhaps everyone would like
to know how we used to swim in the pond at Chase
Lodge, wearing only our old chemises…'

'Don't you dare!' Clio whispered back. 'Though I'm
sure the tale would liven up the proceedings consider-
ably.'

As the circle moved outwards from Miss Darby, the
'truths' followed much the same vein. Pilfered teacakes,
items lost and lied about, the time Peter Elliott told his
parents he was going to Bognor Regis but instead went
to Weymouth.

Clio suspected it would be a far more interesting
game if only the older, married people were present
without their offspring, with the wine and brandy
flowing. But there were young ladies here, supposedly
including herself and Thalia, and things could not get
too out of hand. Though Clio was fairly sure Thalia had
a whopper or two up her sleeve.

And Clio's own 'truth', of course, was a very great
one. The Lily Thief, after all, had once made off with
the Elliotts' own red-figure krater depicting the labours
of Hercules, and sent it back where it came from in
Tuscany in the care of Marco di Fabrizzi.

Marco's 'truth' was a romantic one. The girl he loved
madly as a teenager had been forced to marry another,

leaving him brokenhearted and sure he could never love anyone else. All the ladies in the room were left sighing.

Their hostess followed with yet another romantic 'truth', one that could have been easily predicted. 'I have had only one love, as well,' she declared, more dramatic than Thalia's doomed Antigone. 'One great, great love, my Viscount Riverton. Quite astonishing in these libertine days, I know, yet truly no one could ever compare to him.'

After her sniffles subsided, it was the Duke's turn. Clio watched him with great interest. Surely he, too, had a wealth of secrets he could share! His entire being was one hidden truth.

But his wry smile never wavered. The veil never lifted from his eyes. 'My truth is much like yours, Lady Riverton. I, too, have had only one love. Yet it was not to be.'

'Oh, Averton!' Lady Riverton cried, her hand pressed to her heart. 'How terribly sad.'

'Did she die?' Lady Elliott asked in a hushed voice, awed by the tale of the so-romantic duke.

'No, but she is far too good for me. Now, Lady Elliott, you must tell us your own secret.'

By the time the circle came to Clio, she had some fara-diddle about how once, when she was a girl, instead of attending to her Latin lessons, she read one of her friend Lotty's horrid novels. *The Tragedy of Madame Marguerite*, she believed. And she enjoyed it. Very much.

But all the time she did not stop thinking about Edward and his 'one true love'. The perfect angel who was too good for him. Clio did not know the lady, of course, did not even know her name. But she was fairly certain she did not like her.

'Too good', after all, was a prickling reminder of how far she herself had fallen short of feminine perfection, in all ways.

Chapter Twelve

The next few days were quite busy, and Clio could not make it to the farmhouse site as the Chases were in an uproar preparing for the Santa Lucia *feste*. Sir Walter, at Lady Rushworth's urging, had agreed to host a small dinner party, and Thalia was occupied in planning for the costume ball that would occur in the town piazza.

She spent much time with visiting modistes, often calling for Clio's opinion, so Clio found herself running from kitchen to drawing room and back again, overseeing menus, examining fabrics and sketching seating charts. Not to mention answering invitations, as it seemed everyone in town insisted on holding some kind of event. The small local *feste*, celebrating favourite saints and the old worship of Demeter and her daughter, was overflowing its bounds.

But all the domestic commotion did serve one purpose. It kept her from brooding over the Duke. From wondering at every minute what he was doing. Most of the time, anyway. Well, *some* of the time.

* * *

On the morning of the first day of the *feste*, which would open with the masked ball that night, Clio went out early to buy fresh vegetables at the market. Usually the kitchen maid, a niece of Rosa's, went, but Clio longed for a breath of fresh air. A moment of quiet, for the bustling market *was* quiet compared to Thalia and her last-minute costume alterations. When she returned with her basket of provisions, she avoided the tumult of silks and tulles altogether and crept down the backstairs to the kitchen.

Rosa was working at twisting long strands of bread dough into ornate plaited loaves, painting them with olive oil until they gleamed. Over the fire, the kitchen maid slowly stirred a pot of something delicious-smelling, all herbs and preserved tomatoes. All along the walls were piled baskets and crates, containing delicacies for tomorrow's dinner party.

'I thought it was meant to be a small gathering,' Clio teased, hoisting her basket on to a work table. 'Not a Florentine delegation.'

'When a person eats at *my* table, they eat only the very best,' Rosa said, clearly pleased she would finally get to properly use her culinary skills in the Chase kitchen. 'Paolo has gone to find the right fish for my *tonno alla siciliana*. And for dessert, there will be *cassata*.'

'Cassata?'

Rosa shook her head at English ignorance of good food. 'Ricotta cheese with orange peelings and chocolate shavings on sponge cake. If Signorina Thalia does not drink up all the chocolate first.'

'She is too busy trying on her new finery, I think. She

does so love a disguise, almost as much as she loves chocolate.' Clio gestured toward a brace of fresh rabbits, hanging from the beamed ceiling. 'I see Giacomo has been here.'

Giacomo was the only one of Rosa and Paolo's children who seemed not to have a vocation, beyond hunting—or poaching—Clio never asked. But he sometimes popped up with offerings, often chatting with Clio about antiquities and local mythology. He had a great knowledge of such things. She didn't ask where he had got *that*, either, for fear of discovering he was one of that dread breed of *tombaroli*. Men who raided undiscovered sites for antiquities to sell, and were not above murder and rape.

Rosa just grunted, not looking up from her bread. 'I will braise the rabbit with a marsala sauce for tomorrow's dinner.'

Clio nodded, sensing Rosa had no desire to chat at the moment. Not about Giacomo, anyway. She never wanted to talk about him. Clio went back upstairs to check on Thalia's couture progress.

The drawing room was scattered with lengths of silks, velvets and muslins, spools of lace and ribbon. Clio looked around, but could not see her father or Cory. They had probably taken refuge at the villa.

Thalia stood on the dressmaker's stool, undergoing final alterations on her costume. She had finally chosen the garb of a Venetian Renaissance lady, Clio saw, a high-waisted gown of gleaming ivory-coloured satin shot through with shimmering gold thread. Gold ribbons trimmed the tight sleeves and crisscrossed the bodice. Her blonde hair fell over her shoulders, crowned with a small gold satin cap trimmed with pearls.

'What do you think, Clio?' Thalia asked, fidgeting with the ribbons.

'You look like an angel,' Clio answered truthfully. '*You* should have been Juliet at Lady Riverton's theatricals, not Mrs Manning-Smythe.'

Thalia laughed. 'I have enough trouble being Antigone! Or even just trying to be Thalia.'

What if a person didn't know who they were at all? Clio wondered, as she sorted through a basket full of masks.

The dressmaker put the final touches on Thalia's hem. 'There you are, *signorina*! I think you are quite finished. Do you like?'

'I love, *signora*!' Thalia cried, hopping off the stool to spin around in an exuberant circle, a blur of white satin and floating ribbons.

'Now, Signorina Chase, shall we try yours?' the dressmaker asked Clio. She reached for another basket, drawing out a spool of black thread. 'There is much work to be done if the gown will be ready for tonight.'

'Oh, yes, do, Clio,' Thalia urged, slowing in her spins. 'I haven't yet seen your costume at all.'

'That is because I don't have time for fripperies like my beautiful little sister,' Clio teased. But the truth was she did love a disguise, just as much as Thalia did. Probably more. Was that not what life was, a series of disguises?

She slipped behind a screen set up in the corner, and quickly changed from her simple muslin morning gown to the basted-together costume. Her dress was the opposite of Thalia's, a creation of glossy black satin and cobweb-fine black lace that turned her into a Dark Queen. An empress of the night. With a jet-beaded black mask covering her face, and her hair drawn back under a tulle veil, surely no one would ever recognise her.

She would melt into the night itself, and discover the truth of all the puzzles that plagued her here in Santa Lucia. Even Edward could not hide from her tonight.

The town square was quite transformed after the sun set, with all the shops and booths shuttered, their façades draped with spring garlands and wreaths, all tied with fluttering streamers in green and white and gold. The full moon, amber-gold in the dusty purplish sky, shone down on the revellers, who spun and twirled over the cobblestones to old country-dance tunes. Tables of refreshments and wine were laid out under a portal, while on the cathedral steps presided the painted ivory statue of Saint Lucia. She was not usually brought out until her own feast day in December, but tonight she watched the celebrations with bright blue glass eyes, hands outstretched to receive offerings. At her feet were heaped fruits and flowers.

Around the perimeter of the 'dance floor' were set flickering torches, reflecting in the waters of the fountain, the closed shop windows, the eyes revealed behind beaded and feathered masks. Dancers wove in and out of the light, fantastic wraiths in black dominoes, rustling satin gowns, antique doublets, creations of brilliant fantasy. Saints and devils, Greek gods, dragons, princesses, butterflies.

Thalia clutched at Clio's hand in excitement, and Clio felt her own heart beat faster with anticipation. This was not like London masked balls, where everyone was meant to be incognito, but the world there was so small that each person was clearly identified. Here, it really was a great unknown. Behind that mask could be Mr Frobisher, or Peter Elliott or the Sicilian baker. Or someone else entirely. An exotic stranger. Or one of the deceptively lazy men who lounged about the piazza, watching, always watching.

'Oh, Clio, it is so beautiful,' Thalia whispered.

'Indeed it is,' Clio agreed. 'Most beautiful.'

Thalia was swept into the dance by a young man dressed as Harlequin in black and white silks. And Clio saw her father, dressed as Socrates, strolling toward the refreshment tables with Lady Rushworth in an elaborate Elizabethan gown. They would surely find friends aplenty, and talk about the work at the villa all night, just as Thalia would dance until dawn, as she was utterly inexhaustible. They wouldn't look for Clio for hours.

Clio turned and made her way toward the cathedral steps, keeping to the edges of the rowdy crowd. The music was intoxicating, spiralling higher and higher, carrying the noise and happiness on a great wave to the sky. She laughed as an Apollo tried to coax her into the dance, shaking her head until he whirled away.

She did want to dance, she realised with surprise. Dancing was not often her favourite pastime, and she was not graceful at it as Thalia was. But tonight the music, the torchlight, the beautiful masks, even the night itself, so very deep and dark and full of great possibilities, conspired to fill her with restless excitement. She wanted to whirl and whirl, until she was giddy, until everything blurred and faded.

But she only really wanted to dance in *one* man's arms. To find that mad passion only one man evoked in her.

Clio rubbed at her eyes through the mask, suddenly dizzy. Why had Edward come here at all, to remind her? When she was away from him, he haunted her thoughts, yet she could slowly find her balance again, come back to some sensible semblance of herself. Pretend. When they were together, nothing else seemed to matter. She was pushed off that precipice into a world where nothing at all made sense.

Clio hurried past the cathedral, the steps heaped with harvest offerings, and she could vow Saint Lucia's blue glass eyes followed her, seeing all. Knowing her every sinful thought. She fended off more invitations to dance, taking refuge behind the church.

The narrow street that ran along there was quieter, hidden from the party. She could still hear the music, the thunder of dancing feet and wild laughter, could see the torchlight flickering on the slick cobblestones under her feet. There was no one near, though, just a stray cat on a low wall and the flaking white stucco of the cathedral at her back. The glow of stained glass high above her head.

And, just a little further along the lane, the gates of Averton's palazzo. Clio peered closer at that arched shadow, the wrought iron slightly ajar in invitation to the garden beyond. One window was lit. Was that the room where the Alabaster Goddess resided?

Clio remembered that other masked ball, that other evening of champagne-fuelled revelry and strange disguises. She remembered taking refuge in the silent gallery, with Artemis. Remembered his hands reaching for her, and the longing, the terror she felt. Would it always be thus with her?

She shrugged her black tulle veil back over her shoulder, dragging in a deep breath of the smoke-tinged night air. This night was not that one; she was not the same person now. Edward wasn't the same, either, yet she could not say if it was he himself who had changed, or only her perceptions of him. But she would never go back to *that*.

She heard a slight sound in the shadows behind her, and spun around to find a cloaked figure standing by the wall. Despite the enveloping midnight-blue cloak, the chalk-white leather mask, she knew it was Edward. She faced him in silence, waiting with her breath caught in her throat to see what would happen.

'Does the Queen of the Night not care to dance?' he asked lightly.

Clio swallowed hard. 'I fear she lacks the grace for it.'

'And no doubt she is far too busy to practise. She has stars to rearrange, dreams to invade…'

Clio stepped closer, one tiptoe movement then another, her heavy black skirts and veils trailing behind her. She couldn't help herself, she had to be near him. He drew her, like a dark magician, that underworld god, luring her with shadowy promises of passion and freedom. 'Does she invade *your* dreams?' she whispered, suddenly bold. For she did know one thing now—she was not alone in this spell.

He reached out to touch the edge of her veil. 'Every night.'

Clio trailed her fingertips along the corner of his mask, down a loose lock of bright hair. His skin was warm and golden as sunlight, so alive—just like him. She could almost feel that powerful force of life, that flaming passion, flowing into her, coaxing her frozen heart to beat again. To want to know every part of life, every burning, fleeting, perfect moment.

She went up on tiptoe as he kissed her, twining her

arms around his neck to hold him to her. She felt his own touch at her waist, drawing her even closer.

They fit so perfectly together now, their mouths, their hands, their bodies, as if made for this moment. Clio parted her lips, feeling the tip of his tongue touch hers. Their kiss was frantic, full of need, full of the hot desire to forget all the past and know only *now*. To fall into each other and be lost for ever, to be as one.

Edward pressed her back against the wall, his hands hard and hungry as they slid over her shoulders, tracing the curve of her breasts in her tight satin bodice. Clio moaned at the delicious friction, the sensations that shivered through her, fire and ice in the same instant. She forgot herself, her place in the world, her reputation, everything but the way he made her feel.

The way he always made her feel when they were together like this.

Vaguely, through the silvery haze of desire and need, she felt his fingertips trace the line of her bodice, drawing the thick fabric down to caress the bare curve of her breast. She twined her legs around his hips, holding him to her, not letting him escape until he gave her what she craved. She did not know what that was, only that she needed him more than air or water. He was like the warm flood of grappa in her blood, drugging, delightful.

Her head fell back against the wall, her hands tightening on his shoulders as she urged him ever closer. Her eyes drifted shut, blotting out everything but his touch on her naked skin. The warm, callused fingertips, the cold brush of his rings, the feel of his breath against her, mingling with hers.

He pressed a hot kiss to her neck, the sensitive spot

just below her ear. She shuddered as his lips trailed along her collarbone, the curve of her bare shoulder, like a silky ribbon of fire, of molten Etna lava. Finally, finally, he placed a single soft, longed-for kiss on the upper curve of her breast.

The tip of his tongue lightly traced a circle on that soft, trembling skin, closer, ever closer, to her hardened nipple, just barely covered by her gauzy chemise.

Clio groaned again, tightening her grasp on his hips, drawing him deeper into the arc of her body. Through his velvet breeches, she felt the heavy length of his manhood, hard as iron with a desire that echoed her own.

She buried her fingers in his hair, holding him to her as his mouth finally touched her nipple, drawing it in deep to his kiss. She sobbed at the intense feelings, at the connection that was still not quite enough for her. At the desire that burned higher and higher.

As if she were indeed in a dream, a vision conjured by some goddess of the night to torment her. To drive her mad with crazy desire.

Through that haze of passion, she felt him draw back. Felt his kiss slide from her breast, leaving the skin cold as ice, felt him ease away from her until she stood on her own feet again. But he did not leave her entirely; his hands were still at her waist, tense, his forehead braced on her bare shoulder. Their rough, uneven breath mingled, their heartbeats pounding together until surely all the world could hear it.

Clio caressed his tumbled hair, her hand trembling. Oh, when, *when*, would this end? This terrible weakness, this painful yearning. She was not happy with him or without him.

'Oh, Clio,' he muttered. 'What you do to me…'

What *she* did to *him*? Clio almost laughed aloud. But then she just pressed one lingering kiss to his temple, to the life-pulse that beat there, clinging to him for as long as she dared before she let him go. She half-turned from him, adjusting her gown, drawing her veil forward to hide her flushed face. She sucked in one deep breath, then another, until she felt her trembling slow and stop.

'Clio,' he growled. 'I—'

'No,' Clio interrupted. Truly, she could not bear it if he apologised! If he made this all into something conventional and sordid. 'Masquerade balls do seem to cast some strange spell on us, don't they? Maybe we should avoid them in future.'

'Not *just* masquerade balls,' he answered wryly.

True. There were also castles, and ruins, and drawing rooms and meadows. Clio dared not look at him for fear she would jump on him again. So, she just laughed, and hurried on her unsteady feet back to the well-lit, welcoming noise of the piazza, and of real life.

Chapter Thirteen

Edward braced his palms against the rough wall, his eyes closed as he forced himself to breathe in deeply, slowly, trying to calm the fiery riot inside him. But he could still smell the fragrance of Clio's lily perfume in the air, still feel the warmth of her lingering on the cold wall. She was all around him, part of him.

His hands curled into tight fists as he thought of her, of all the times they met and clashed—and kissed. Her passion ignited needs he thought long buried; it inflamed his own lust until they were both consumed in the bonfire. He so longed for her that every part of his body ached from it—his heart, his flesh, his very soul.

It distracted him from his purpose here, blinded him to all but her, all but what they were when they came together. Something so strange and elemental, something that refused to be constrained.

The man he used to be would not have let himself be restrained. He would have taken what he wanted long ago, would never have denied himself. He was not that spoiled youth any longer. His heedless, impulsive actions had hurt others terribly. His family, his discarded mistresses, people who had tried to be his friend—and one sad-eyed young woman who haunted him still, a maidservant whose unwise love for that insufferable boy had led to her downfall.

He could not be that person now. Not with Clio. Even if the ache of it, of all that desire, killed him in the end.

Edward laughed ruefully at himself. Who would have imagined, ten or even five years ago, that he would be so constrained by honour? By his own version of courtly love? How astonished his parents and his long-lost brother would be to see it! They thought he would be a useless wastrel all his life.

He rubbed at the small, jagged white scar on his brow, the stark reminder of what happened when he forgot his resolve. He would not forget it again.

Clio made her way shakily back to the *feste*, strolling slowly around the edges of the dance. She watched the twirling, kaleidoscopic patterns through her veil, feeling far removed from all the music, the drunken laughter, as if she saw it all in a dream, a play.

Which was so very odd. This party should be the real life, so full of light and noise, and those frantic caresses in the shadows the dream. A tangle of emotions half-understood in the snare of darkness, but lost when daybreak came. Dispersed like so much smoke and fog.

Yet, more and more, the fleeting moments she spent with him *were* the reality.

Something would have to happen soon. Something would have to change. She could not stumble on like this for ever, wanting him with such a furious desire and yet so afraid of that wanting at the same time. Afraid of losing herself for ever.

Yes, she would have to take action. But what? She had never so longed for Calliope's sensible presence, her calm advice! She had never felt quite so alone.

Clio took a goblet of wine from one of the tables, sipping at it beneath her veil as she watched the crowd. Her father and Lady Rushworth sat with some of their friends under the shelter of a portal, conversing animatedly as they passed a platter of cheese and olives. Unlike at Lady Riverton's theatricals, he would have to be dragged away at the break of dawn. 'Old and tired', indeed!

Clio scanned the rainbow of brilliant colours, the masks and feathers and ribbons, searching for Thalia. At last she glimpsed her white gown, the gleam of torch-light on her pale hair. She was not dancing, but sat on the cathedral steps, laughing with a man in a red-striped cloak. They leaned together as they talked, and the man pushed his mask atop his head in one graceful, absent-minded gesture, his gaze close on Thalia's face as she spoke.

Clio was startled to see it was Marco. He leaned one elbow on the step above them, gazing up at Thalia as if she was the only person there. The only one whose voice he heard, whose smiles he saw. And Thalia laughed again, her cheeks a pretty apple-pink under the edge of her gilded mask.

Clio frowned. Marco charmed dozens of other women just so, from gypsy camps to Lady Riverton's drawing room. She had watched him like this before. Thalia was not easily charmed, never easily fooled. Yet she *was* young, and she had the Chase quality of being headstrong and curious. And Marco was handsome, as handsome as Thalia was beautiful. If he hurt her sister…

He would certainly live to regret it. Clio would see to that, if Thalia did not unman him first!

Clio turned away as Thalia and Marco rose and moved back into the dance, hand in hand. Edward had not reappeared, and Clio was finally able to breathe again. She eased her veil aside a bit, strolling around the party, trying to guess who the various masks concealed. The shepherdess in bright pink brocade and diamonds was surely Lady Riverton, and the gentleman in the white fur cloak and painted sheep mask could be Mr Frobisher. The angel was Susan Darby, giggling with the Harlequin who had danced with Thalia when they first arrived. Was he Peter Elliott? For shame, to be transferring his affections from Thalia to Miss Darby so quickly!

Clio laughed, and took another sip of her wine. As she lowered the cup, she noticed a furtive movement just at the edge of the bakery building. A tall, muscular man in a rough brown cloak and white skull mask glanced back over his shoulder, his head swivelling quickly one way and then another before he ducked into the alleyway between the bakery and a shuttered vegetable stall.

It was only a flash of movement, unnoticed by any passer-by, but Clio knew all too well what an air of illicit activity looked like. Felt like. She could practically smell trouble in the breeze, more pungent than any perfume.

She set down her goblet and drew her veil back into place, creeping to the mouth of the alleyway. It was very dark here, darker than even the lane where she had met Edward. Yet her vision, filtered by the black tulle, grew accustomed to the dimness, and she saw a small patch of light at the end, emanating from one of the bakery's back windows. The man in the skull mask stood just at the edge of its glow, talking quietly with someone else, someone shorter and muffled in a hooded black cloak.

Clio felt her pulse quicken in excitement, with the tingle of danger and secrecy. Holding her skirts close to still their satin rustle, she backed away before turning and dashing back around the vegetable stall. Hidden behind it, behind a pile of abandoned crates and the stench of rotting produce, she could barely make out their voices.

'But where can the objects be found?' one of them said, in a low, hoarse voice, muffled by a hood or mask. Clio could not tell if it was a man or woman, but the desperation was palpable.

'I told you, we don't know yet,' the skull mask said, rough with impatience. He spoke in English, but with a heavy Sicilian accent. Clio frowned in concentration, almost sure she had heard it before.

'But we have the bowl! Surely the rest must be near where it was found.'

'That piece must have been separated from the rest of the collection,' the impatient Sicilian said. 'We'll find the rest soon. We're digging whenever we can. It's close, I can feel it!'

'It had better be. This English customer was most pleased with the bowl, and is willing to pay a great deal of money for the rest. The silver is a rare find. It will set us up for life. Why can you not work faster?'

'You know why!' the Sicilian said angrily. Clio heard

a rustle, as of a hood or mask being pushed back. Clio peered cautiously around the corner, and found that she had indeed recognised that voice. It was Giacomo, Rosa's rabbit-poaching son.

She felt a startled, sad pang for Rosa and Paolo, for the bitter realization that he *was* up to no good, and not just poaching. That he was one of the great plague of *tombaroli*. How dare he hurt his kind-hearted parents in such a way! How dare he destroy his own family's heritage? As Lily Thief, she had fought so hard against such terrible ills. She didn't want to fight again, not here.

'Those tomb frescoes last year were much larger and more complicated, and yet you delivered them in half the time,' the other person said querulously.

'No one was lurking around that tomb every day,' Giacomo answered, sullen. 'And the ghosts keep workers away.'

'That has never stopped you in the past. Take care of it. The English wants the silver, or nothing. If *you* want the money...'

'Of course I want the money!'

'Then do as I say. Take care of the site, and find the rest of the silver. No matter what you have to do. It must be there somewhere! All the indications say so.'

There was a snap of papers being unfolded, and the cloaked person said, 'This is what the English wants, the pieces in these sketches. Find it all within a fortnight, and there will be a fat bonus in your purse. Fail, and the consequences could be dire—for all of us.'

Clio stretched up on tiptoe, peering closer as the person hurried away, leaving Giacomo alone. He lowered his skull mask back into place, staring down at the sheaf of papers in his hand. Strangely, that hand

trembled. She heard him mutter in Italian, something
more about 'ghosts'. In her eagerness to hear him, she
leaned too far forwards, accidentally nudging a crate
with her toe. Startled by that scraping sound, she drew
deeper into the shadows, not daring to breathe.

Giacomo spun around, scanning the alleyway, as
nervous as a cat. She could smell his acrid fear. *Tombarolo* he might be, but perhaps not a very good one.
Thievery required nerves of steel.

'*Chi è là?*' he called, glaring frantically one way
then another. A slip of paper fell from his shaking hand.

'Ghosts,' he muttered, rubbing at his face with a
shaking hand. He hurried out of the alleyway, tugging
his cloak around him as if to ward off those ghosts
everyone here seemed so afraid of.

Clio waited, perfectly still, until she was sure he was
really gone. Then she tiptoed forwards, scooping up the
lost paper.

As she peered down at it in the dim light, she saw it
was a sketch of a small incense burner, the drawing
carefully detailed and measured. It was carved with an
elaborate relief of Demeter. An exquisite piece, even in
the pencil sketch, and Clio had never seen anything like
it except in the British Museum, which held the
remnants of a Greek altar set.

She frowned as she tucked the paper into her sleeve.
Giacomo had spoken of a bowl, a part of a great hoard
of silver. Also temple pieces, probably, to judge by the
fine style of the incense burner. It was a piece a collector, this *English* Giacomo and his cohort spoke of,
would indeed pay a great deal for. Where were they
digging for these pieces?

And who was the 'English'?

Clio had a sickening feeling that all the puzzles of the past few days were coming together, and they were centred on this silver. Was it the reason Edward had suddenly showed up in Santa Lucia? Was *he* the English who was after the stolen temple hoard?

She felt dizzy, remembering the long gallery at Acropolis House, packed with antiquities of every description—Greek vases, Roman statues, an Egyptian sarcophagus, Minoan snake goddesses, all jumbled together. She remembered the Alabaster Goddess, reigning over it all. He had vowed then that he had reformed his ways, that he worked for the Antiquities Society, that his task was to stop the Lily Thief and others of that ilk.

But perhaps the silver was too much of a temptation. Perhaps he had fought against his old ways and lost.

Clio shivered, suddenly icy cold and deeply sad. She crept back around the stall the way she had arrived, slipping back into the party. The moon was lower in the sky now; soon the night would give way to dawn. Yet she sensed that *her* darkness was only just beginning.

She sat down on the steps where she had glimpsed Thalia and Marco earlier, suddenly feeling so very old and tired. The music was louder than ever, but she seemed to be wrapped in silence.

From the crowd emerged a tall figure swathed in dark blue velvet, red-gold hair loose on his shoulders, like an angel. Everyone else moved in drunken, haphazard patterns, yet he was all predatory grace. She watched, still feeling that cold, dream-like distance, as he sat down on the step below hers.

Silently, silently, he leaned back against her legs, his head resting on her knees, heavy and sweet and reassuring through her skirts. She laid one hand lightly on his tousled hair, feeling the rough silk of it under her touch, the familiar rush of his pulse with hers. They sat there, wrapped in quiet, in that deep gulf between them, as the night spun on around them.

Oh, Edward, she thought sadly. *How can you be a villain?*

Or was it merely her heart who was the great betrayer?

Chapter Fourteen

The dinner party seemed to be going quite well.

Clio gazed out over the company from her place at the foot of the table. 'Hostess' was not her favourite role to play, but since Calliope's marriage it had fallen on her. Only until her father wed Lady Rushworth, of course. Luckily, Sir Walter did not often like to entertain in a formal way, and her domestic duties were not onerous.

And, she had to admit, there was something quite satisfying when a gathering came together so neatly. The conversation hummed along, assisted by the cosy number of guests, all with similar interests. Rosa's delicious food was much complimented, even though Lady Riverton threatened to steal her away for her own kitchen. The flowers, artful displays of local wildflowers designed by Thalia, were most lovely. And her father seemed happy, with the attentions of Lady Rushworth on his right and Mrs Darby on his left, both avid to hear about his newest discoveries at the villa.

Yes, it was all going very well indeed. The servants, relatives of Rosa and Paolo, hired for the evening, moved smoothly and quietly around the table. They made sure no one's plate or glass was empty, and left Clio with very little to do.

Except think. Which she had done ceaselessly since the *feste*. Her mind whirled until she thought she would scream with it all, and still she could make no sense of anything. The silver hoard that might or might not be real. The *tombaroli* and the 'English' who was going to pay them untold riches for their loot. The Duke—how did he fit in? It could be no coincidence he was in Santa Lucia just now, with a vast stash of illicit antiquities in the offing. Was he on another errand for the Antiquities Society, or had he fallen back into his old, unscrupulous collecting ways?

Did anyone, *could* anyone, ever really change? Or was the temptation sometimes just too great?

That was a conundrum she found herself wrestling with, far too often of late.

She nibbled at the cassata, studying the occupants of the table carefully. They were almost all 'English', all interested in antiquities and collecting. Which of them, behind their smiles and fine clothes, their polite chatter, would deal with thieves? Would steal and hide away what did not belong to them, but to the people of this island? To history?

Marco would surely know. He must have heard *something* about a discovery as rich and rare as a stash of temple silver. Yet they had had no chance of private consultation since he had come to Santa Lucia, and he had kept up his guise of light-hearted, flirtatious nobleman beautifully. Quite the actor, Marco was.

He sat next to Thalia, the two of them talking quietly over the dessert. Clio wondered what they spoke of after their little scene at the *feste*, their dances together. But their voices were too soft for her to overhear more than scattered words and laughter.

Edward was across the table from them, listening to Susan Darby's awed prattle with a polite smile on his lips. He had not touched the wine, Clio noticed, and barely eaten, though his compliments on the cooking seemed most sincere. He had not glanced at Clio since bowing over her hand at arrival.

She could tell nothing from his expression, his eyes, his oh-so-polite conversation. Even if they were alone, she knew she could not ask him about the silver. Could not confront him outright, as someone like Thalia surely would, an Amazon with no fear of attacking from the front. She would learn nothing, and the outcome of any battle would be uncertain indeed.

Despite their desperate intimacy, their kisses and caresses in the dark of the night, there was still a gulf between them of doubt and suspicion. A gulf she didn't know how to bridge, not with her own caution and reserve.

'I still have hopes, too, that Miss Chase will join us,' Mrs Darby said. The sound of her name shook Clio from her brooding, and she looked down the table to where Mrs Darby chatted with her father.

'I beg your pardon, Mrs Darby?' Clio said.

'I was just telling Sir Walter of our planned tour to Motya. The Phoenician sites, they say, are really quite worth seeing, especially the necropolis. The excursion would be so much more delightful if *you* were with us!'

'That is very kind of you, Mrs Darby,' answered Clio. 'I enjoyed accompanying you to Agrigento so much. But I fear I am too taken up here with work.'

'You should go, my dear,' her father urged. 'Mrs

Darby tells me it is only an excursion of a few days, and the change of scenery would do you good. You have been working too hard of late.'

'Miss Thalia and I would be sure to take good care of your father while you're gone,' Lady Rushworth added. 'They do say the sea air is most bracing and reviving.'

Sea air? Did she look so much the pale invalid, then, that they all wanted to bundle her off for a salt-water cure? Clio felt the weight of Edward's gaze on her.

'I will certainly consider your kind offer, Mrs Darby,' Clio said.

'Excellent! We will not leave for a couple of days yet, plenty of time to make arrangements,' Mrs Darby answered. 'We plan to head home to England directly after the tour, so it will be the last time we can spend time with you until you yourself return to London.'

'You must come!' Susan Darby cried. 'Or I will be the only young person on the tour.'

'A great inducement indeed,' Clio said with a smile. 'We will be sorry to lose your society here in Santa Lucia.'

'And we shall be sorry to go,' said Mrs Darby. 'But my husband wants to seek a London publisher for his book. Is that not so, my dear?'

The conversation turned to Mr Darby's manuscript, and Clio sat back in her chair, gesturing to the servants to begin clearing. The Motya excursion *was* tempting, she had to admit. To run away from the confusion Santa Lucia had become, to just be a simple tourist for a few days, with her guidebook and the pleasant, undemanding company of the Darbys.

To be away from Edward.

Yet surely even miles of land, the vast sea itself, could not erase the way his kiss felt on her naked skin.

The desire that trembled through her whenever he touched her.

No, she had to stay, to face whatever this was between them. To discover what was happening here in sleepy, suddenly sinister Santa Lucia.

The ladies soon departed the dining room, leaving the men to their brandy and no doubt more talk about Sir Walter's villa. Clio made certain the tea tray was laid out in the drawing room before sitting down next to Thalia.

'You were having quite the coze with Count di Fabrizzi,' Clio whispered teasingly.

Thalia's eyes gave a quick lightning flash, veiled by her long lashes as she took a sip of tea. 'I have merely been attempting to persuade him to take part in my play.'

'Oh, indeed? So, it is merely for the sake of theatre that you spend time with him?'

'Of course.'

'It has nothing to do with his handsome eyes?'

'Clio!'

Clio laughed. 'You teased me about him before. It is my turn now.'

Thalia bit her lip, but Clio could see a smile threatening to break through. 'True. Very well, I admit he does have—handsome eyes. But I think his affections are already engaged.'

'Indeed?' Clio asked in dawning curiosity. She studied the ladies in the room: silly but pretty Susan Darby; her still-lovely mother; Lady Elliott with her bright red ringlets; and Lady Riverton, who was chatting loudly about some new jewellery she had just purchased. Who could it be? Or maybe it was a dark-eyed *signorina* back in Florence! Marco had broken so many hearts, surely turn-about was only fair. 'Has he confided in you? Who is it?'

Thalia shook her head. 'Oh, Clio. Do you not know?'

Before Clio could answer, Thalia rose and strolled over to the pianoforte. Soon the tempestuous notes of Beethoven filled the room, and the other ladies gathered around the instrument. Lured, as people always were, by the siren song of Thalia's music.

Clio put down her own teacup and went to the window, gazing out at the garden beyond their little terrace. Thalia meant, presumably, that Marco was in love with her, Clio, but that was simply absurd. They were friends, allies, that was all. Despite his unearthly good looks, despite the ideals they shared, there had never been the spark of passion between them. Never a physical awareness, such as that which flowed between her and Edward whenever they saw each other.

No, if Marco was falling for anyone, it was surely Thalia. Clio saw the way he looked at her sister, so fascinated despite himself. She could not say she liked it. She knew what Marco was like, knew his hidden life, and she also knew that her beautiful, impulsive sister needed someone steady and calm. Not a wildly patriotic Italian count.

Likely it would come to naught, just like Clio's own passion for Edward. Clio was going to keep an eye on the situation, though. Starting, apparently, right now. Marco had appeared on the terrace, his chiselled features illuminated for an instant by the flare of a match as he lit a cigar. He seemed to be alone, having escaped from the dining room by one of the tall windows leading outside.

Clio glanced over her shoulder. The ladies were still gathered around Thalia as she moved into a Mozart sonata. Thalia loved an audience, and would thus surely keep everyone entertained for quite a while. Clio wouldn't be missed for a few minutes.

She slipped quietly out the door to the terrace, joining Marco where he stood by the steps leading into the garden.

'*Cara!*' he said with a wide smile. 'How very scandalous of you to join me out here, all alone.'

Clio grinned. 'Save your charm, Marco. It does not work on me, you know.'

He gave a dramatic sigh. 'Alas, I know it only too well.'

'Nor do my charms, such as they are, work on *you*. My sister suspects you are in love.'

Marco took a long draw on his cigar, wreathed in a disguising cloud of silvery smoke. 'Ah, yes, the beautiful Thalia, Muse of Comedy. She is indeed delightful. But also quite imaginative. I do not know why she would think such a thing.'

'Perhaps I am also overly imaginative. For I have been hearing such wild tales of late. Ghosts, curses, looted pieces of ancient temple silver.'

Marco smiled wryly through the smoke. 'That does sound like a novel, *cara*. Are you a writer now, like Mr Darby?'

'Are *you*? Otherwise I cannot quite account for your presence here. I am sure it cannot be on "business".'

'Your doubts wound me. Of course it is business, of the most vital kind.'

'Antiquities business?'

Marco nodded. 'I think so. What do you know of this silver?'

'Not very much. I know our cook's son is involved,

I overheard him talking with someone at the *feste*.
They spoke of a bowl, of finding the rest of the hoard
to sell to some "English" collector. This buyer has apparently offered a great deal of money, if the pieces can
be found soon.'

'So, they have not yet found them all,' Marco
murmured. 'They must be getting desperate.'

Just like her! Clio felt quite *desperate* to know what
was happening. She clutched at Marco's coat sleeve.
'So you *do* know! Tell me, I can help.'

Marco covered her hand with his. 'I know you can.
There was none better than the Lily Thief. Yet I fear at
present I know little more than you do. There have been
some rather unusual pieces appearing on the market
recently, and some of my—friends have traced them here.
Enna is full of sites, both discovered and still buried.'

'What sort of pieces?'

'Coins, jewellery, finely carved grave steles. Silver.'

'Libation bowls, maybe? Incense burners?'

'Bowls, yes, but not yet anything like an incense
holder. Have you seen one?'

'Just a sketch. Giacomo, our cook's son, dropped it
at his meeting. Where—?'

She was interrupted by a sudden burst of fireworks,
a shower of red and green and white that lit up the
night sky in a crack of noise and fire. More celebrations in the village.

Surely the illuminations would quickly draw the
other guests to the windows. She didn't have much time
left. She squeezed Marco's arm and said, 'Send me a
message saying where we can meet. I want to hear more
about this.'

He grinned at her. 'And would you bring your lovely

sister to our meeting? I have seldom seen such beauty *and* such spirit in one lady.'

Clio smacked his arm with the flat of her hand. 'Don't you dare turn your Florentine charm on Thalia! I don't want her involved in anything at all dangerous.'

'Oh, *cara*, I doubt you could stop her getting involved in anything she chose. She seems quite as stubborn as her sister. Perhaps more so.'

'That is all too true. And all the more reason for me to protect her. Promise me you will not embroil her in any of this!'

Marco sighed. 'I promise. And we will meet very soon. Perhaps I will have more to tell you then.'

Clio impulsively kissed his cheek, and spun around to hurry away. Another burst of sparkling light showed her they were not entirely unobserved. Edward stood at the dining room window, watching her. His expression was like a Roman marble statue, perfectly still and calm.

They stared at each other for one long, frozen moment before Edward turned away. Suddenly freezing cold, Clio dashed into the house. She drew her Indian shawl closer about her bare shoulders, but even its warmth could not ward off the chill that had invaded her world.

Clio paced the length of her bedchamber floor, first one way then back again. Books on the Punic War era were open on her desk, along with a new volume on late Hellenistic silver, but she could not concentrate on studies. Her mind was racing, her pulse thrumming with the need to *do* something. To move to action.

She stopped at her window, staring out over the

rooftops of Santa Lucia. All seemed quiet enough now; even Etna was muffled in sleepy clouds. What seethed beneath such a surface?

The Picini palazzo was also silent, except for one lighted window beckoning in the gloom. Was the Duke awake, too?

Clio took in a deep breath. She had to think now, to be calm, not go off on a shower of emotions as brilliant as tonight's fireworks. That was what always happened when she was with Edward, and it would not help her now. Where was the silver, if it was indeed real? Where had it come from? And who sought it with such intensity? What meaning did it have?

She stared at that distant lighted window. There were many 'English' in Sicily, most of them collectors who vied to outdo each other. Surely any one of them would love to find a rare collection of temple silver.

Yet none of them cared about the art itself, about the history it represented, quite as passionately as the Duke of Averton. Once she had thought him the most rapacious of collectors. His holdings of antiquities were vast, and he did not seem to care from where he obtained them. The Duke of 'Avarice', some called him, and she had assumed it to be the truth.

Then she had found out that his guise of insatiable collector was a ruse. He actually worked for the highly respectable Antiquities Society, a group his revered scholar father helped found. And his task was to stop the Lily Thief, which he did—with the unwitting help of her sister Calliope.

What was his game now? Was he the thief-hunter, or the thief? If the silver was real, it could be a great temptation to anyone. But then, Edward was not just *anyone*.

Clio frowned in thought. Giacomo and his cohort had mentioned a bowl. If she could just find that one piece…

She shivered in her thin muslin nightdress, trying to calmly list her options. She could confront Giacomo, of course, lecture him about his loyalty to his parents, to his homeland. If she could find him, and if he didn't stab her through with his rabbit-poaching knife. Men like Giacomo, lower-level *tombarolo*, were usually desperate and unpredictable. She was good with a dagger and a pistol herself, but no match for such desperation. She might be a fool in truth, but hopefully not as big a fool as all that.

She could ask Rosa what she and Paolo knew. Yet Clio could see they would not tell the truth about their son's activities. They liked her, but that was nothing to the iron strength of their family loyalty. Not only would they tell her naught, they would warn Giacomo. That was the code of their village.

She could also confront Edward directly. No one was a better actor than he was, though, not even Marco or Thalia. He played the spoiled, eccentric duke and collector to perfection, fooling everyone, even herself.

No, she had to find that bowl. If it was in Edward's house, she would make her move. If not, then she would need yet another plan.

The Lily Thief would have to rise again, just this one last time. Clio felt a bitter pang at the thought. She had promised Calliope she would not do that any longer, but surely this was different. She would take nothing but the bowl, if it was found, and that only for evidence.

Even as she justified her plan, she shivered again in trepidation. Something *was* happening out there in the quiet town, something that sizzled and bubbled deep inside the tranquil surface. And she intended to discover exactly what it was.

Chapter Fifteen

'Shall we go the Manning-Smythes' waltzing party tonight?' Thalia asked over the breakfast table, as she shuffled through the stack of new invitations.

'Hmm?' Clio said, distracted. She had a book open beside her plate, but had not read more than two words together. Dances were as far from her thoughts as a subject could be.

'It is last minute, I know, but Mrs Manning-Smythe says in her note it will all be quite informal,' Thalia said. 'Just some dancing, a few hands of cards. You would enjoy the cards, Father, even if Lady Rushworth could not persuade you to waltz!'

Their father chuckled. 'Perhaps she could not get me to waltz, yet she will no doubt insist I be there. She says I need to get out in society more often. Live in the present sometimes, not always in the ancient past.'

'That is excellent advice, Father,' Thalia said.

'If only the present didn't move so very fast.' Sir Walter sighed. 'Always changes, changes. You can't rely on it, like you can the past. It won't stand still to be studied.'

Just like certain people, Clio thought. Just as she imagined she had a grasp on them, on their essence and motives, they changed on her.

'A waltzing party is not a mathematical equation, Father,' Thalia said. 'It will be most diverting. Everyone will be there, I'm sure.'

Everyone? Clio took a thoughtful bite of her toast. Surely that included the Duke. And while he was dancing at the Manning-Smythes', his palazzo would be empty.

'I think I must cry off,' Clio said. 'All these parties of late have made me neglect my studies.'

'Quite right, my dear. We cannot forget why we are here,' Sir Walter replied, his tone wistful.

'But *you* must come, Father,' Thalia reminded him. 'I need your escort.'

'Of course. It will be an early evening, though?'

'We shall see,' Thalia teased. 'I have so many people I must speak to.'

'People you must dance with,' said Clio, pushing her chair back. 'Excuse me, Father, Thalia. I'm off to work at the farmhouse today.'

'Do be careful, Clio,' her father said.

'I'm always careful, Father, I promise.' Clio quickly collected her shawl and knapsack, changing her slippers for her work boots before leaving the house.

The village was quiet so early in the morning, just a few shops and stalls opening their doors, a few merchants sweeping out their doorways as they yawned. The tattered remains of the *feste* littered the square, bits of faded confetti and torn ribbon, empty and abandoned bottles. The smell of smoke from the fireworks still clung to the breeze, but there was no one lurking in the shadows today.

Clio hurried along the path to the valley, following the well-known trail only by memory as her thoughts were far away. She had not planned to make her move so soon, but the Manning-Smythes' party was too good an opportunity to miss. She would find out if the Duke was attending, and if he was she would do what she had to do. A swift raid, a search for only the one item, and then she would be gone. She wouldn't be distracted by the Alabaster Goddess again.

Edward would never know she had been there.

The only problem was, what would she do if she *did* find the bowl? How could she fight against him?

She glimpsed the farmhouse walls with relief. *This* she understood. This was rational, open to study. It was knowable, if she just worked hard enough. She climbed the steps down to the old cellar and took her spade out of the knapsack. Work was all she had right now.

Another blasted party.

Edward tossed the Manning-Smythes' invitation on to the desk along with all the others, rubbing his hand over his scarred brow. It was almost as bad as London. Everyone wanted to lure a duke to their gathering, to write to their friends of his presence there. Everyone wanted *something* from him.

Except for Clio. She seemed to want nothing at all from him, except in the dark of a masked ball. Yet she was becoming the only one whose presence he craved. Whose opinion he cared about.

He glanced at the card. He would go, of course. His task would never be completed if he followed his own inclination and stayed home by the fire. An alluring vision suddenly flashed across his mind—he and Clio sitting by the fire in his chamber, laughing companionably over their books. Her smile warm as she reached for his hand. *You see*, she said. *Staying home together is so much better than any party...*

Edward laughed wryly at his own daydream. Erotic visions of Clio naked were one thing; dreams of domestic bliss with her were even more impossible. More insidiously attractive.

Even if Clio would care to sit with him by the fire, there was no time for such things now. The robbers who gathered at the secret house were growing more desperate, which meant their foreign customers were, too. The only way to find out who those customers were was to mingle in society. If they all thought him just an indolent, extravagant duke, they might be careless around him. They might even infer that he, too, was looking for stolen antiquities to buy.

And if he had the chance to waltz with Clio Chase in the moonlight—well, that would be a perk indeed.

Chapter Sixteen

It was a perfect night. Completely black, with just the waning moon for light, covered and then revealed by the drift of lacy clouds. Any passer-by would attribute a flicker of movement to those shifting shadows.

Everyone was dancing at the Manning-Smythes', but Clio knew she did not have much time. Soirées in Santa Lucia did not spin on until dawn, as they sometimes did in London, and the Duke was not the unobservant looby some of the Lily Thief's previous 'victims' had been. They had not missed their treasures for days, in a few cases. He would know something was missing immediately, and who was responsible.

But then, she didn't really intend to steal anything, unless it proved necessary. She just wanted to *know*.

Clio crouched low in the hedges outside Edward's palazzo, clad in black breeches and shirt, her hair covered by a black cap. She stared up at the façade, studying the windows, their narrow ledges, the loops of old ivy. Where would he stash a piece of ancient silver? Where would he hide something so valuable and dangerous?

Many of his antiquities were held in his own bed-chamber, according to Rosa via her son Lorenzo, who was a footman here. Clio would have to start there, and hope she found quick success.

She crept around the side of the house to the back garden, which sloped down to a dramatic cliff and soared out to the sea far beyond. Her soft boots were silent on the overgrown lawn, and she saw to her relief a tall old tree near the house. Its gnarled limbs spread to balconies and darkened windows. No light or noise disturbed the silence, so hopefully that meant the servants were congregated belowstairs with their supper and gossip.

With a master like Edward, gossip and speculation would surely keep them busy for hours.

Clio caught hold of a low-hanging limb and swung herself up into the tree, climbing lightly, higher and higher, concealed by the fresh spring leaves. Despite the danger, and her own trepidation, she felt a new exhilaration as she left the earth far behind. It was like a cool, crisp wind after being locked in a stuffy room too long.

She hadn't realised until this moment that she had been chafing so at her respectable, polite life. She felt like the eagles who sometimes flew out over the valley, her wings spread as she leaped into freedom.

She knew it could not last long. When she found what she sought and climbed back down again, this freedom would be lost and for ever. She had to make the most of this fleeting moment, this one last breath of air.

And, strangely, the one person she wanted to share this rare joy with, the one who would understand its intoxicating transcendence, was Edward. For was he, too, not bound with plush ducal chains? Being subversive was sometimes the only way to break them.

Yet that understanding, that bizarre kinship, was also what made him her enemy tonight.

Clio finally reached a balcony she could catch on to from the tree, and she leaped over its wrought-iron railing, landing softly on the tiled floor. Once she caught her breath, she tried the latch on the tall, narrow door. It was unlocked, of course. Who would bother with security so high up, in such a quiet town? But Edward of all people should know better.

The room was indeed a bedchamber, probably the grandest one in the palazzo. It was dark, but Clio could make out a vast bed, swathed in elaborate draperies, the looming hulks of oversize dressing tables and chairs. An elaborate fireplace gleamed pale as ice. Yet as her vision adjusted to the gloom, she saw the room was not inhabited, for most of the furniture was still draped in holland covers. There were no trunks or cases, no personal objects.

She hurried out of the chamber, opening the door a crack to peer cautiously into the corridor. A few branches of candles flickered there, but no servants bustled about on their errands. Not even a mouse stirred. Clio slipped out, keeping to the edges of the carpet runner as she tiptoed from room to room. She listened at each door before looking inside. Every chamber was cold and musty with disuse, either empty or swathed in more ghostly covers.

Not a man for houseguests, obviously, Clio thought. In London, that was part of what made him so talked about, so sought after in his elusiveness.

But it was one of the things that utterly maddened her.

At last she found what she sought, a chamber that was inhabited. A colza lamp burned on the dressing table, as if waiting to welcome someone home, and it illuminated a room that was luxurious but small. The satin bedhangings were tied back, the bedclothes turned down invitingly, while a brocade dressing gown and slippers were arranged at its foot.

And the small space was full of breathtaking treasures. Some of the loveliest things she remembered from Acropolis House—vases and kraters, carved caskets, obsidian cats, jewelled goblets. The Alabaster Goddess.

Artemis stood by the fireplace, pale and serene, her bow calmly levelled on some unseen foe. Clio stared at her, entranced. She remembered too well the last time she had seen her, in Yorkshire, as she and Marco had tried to lever her from her base. She remembered, too, the masquerade ball at Acropolis House, when everything came, quite literally, crashing down.

Clio shook her head. This was no time to get lost in the past! She had no moments to lose. She quickly turned her back on Artemis and set to work.

The armoire held only clothes, rows and rows of the finest-cut coats and rich waistcoats, stacks of soft linen shirts, perfectly white starched neckcloths. They all smelled of Edward, of that clean, crisp spiciness that was only him. She sifted through it all as fast as she could, shutting the carved doors firmly, as if she shut them on *him*.

He would never be so easily dismissed, though. She knew that well.

Drawers and crates also yielded nothing. Just antiquities she knew were already his, piles of history books, notes written in some odd shorthand she could not decipher. Letters from his stewards in England.

Clio sat back on her heels after examining a valise found under the bed, sighing in frustration. Now she would have to try to find a safe, and there was no time for that! A clock on the mantel loudly ticked away the moments, reminding her of that frantic fact. Why did Edward have to be so blasted cautious about this, when he left his balcony doors unlocked?

She scanned the room one last time, and her gaze alighted on the dressing table. She had not yet examined it, for the piece had no drawers, just a surface arrayed with brushes and bottles, a leather shaving kit. And a small, carved wooden box with a most intriguing lock.

Clio made her way to the table, drawing a thin wire lockpick from the pouch at her waist. The lock was more intricately made than most; it took her several minutes to find the mechanism with the tip of the wire and pop it free. But when she did she was rewarded.

There were more papers written in that baffling shorthand, heavy bags of coins. But the box was too small for its outside measurements. She found the false bottom and lifted it out, revealing one tiny silver bowl. It was a thing of rare beauty indeed, intricately decorated with hammered patterns of acorns and beechnuts. Clio turned it over in her hand, feeling the old metal turn warm against her skin as if it were alive.

On the bottom were crudely etched Greek letters spelling out 'This belongs to the gods'. Just like the sketch of the incense burner.

Still clutching the bowl in her gloved hand, Clio peered into the depths of the box. She half-hoped, feared, to see more silver. A hoard, as Giacomo had put it. What she found was even more disquieting.

A scrap of emerald green, ripped at one end, sewn with green glass beads. Torn from the sleeve of her Medusa costume from the Acropolis House masquerade.

She lifted it out, holding it to the light of the lamp. Along the very edge she could see tiny, rust-coloured stains. Blood and silk, binding her and Edward together. Why would he keep such a reminder of that night, locking it away so carefully?

Clio forced herself to put it back in its place, forced herself not to think of what had happened. After all, she had found what she came for, proof that Edward was somehow involved with the silver. If only she had not found so much more as well.

So absorbed was she by the bowl and the silk, she forgot her own first rule, always be cautious. Always be aware. She did not hear the soft click of the door until it was too late.

She spun around, the bowl still in hand, pressed back against the edge of the table as she faced Edward. Though her heart pounded, her palms turning cold in their gloves, she was somehow not surprised. It was as if the whole night had been spinning to this one moment, their gazes meeting across the room.

Edward leaned lazily against the door frame, his arms crossed over his chest. He still wore his evening clothes, a cloak shrugged back from the shoulders of his black satin coat.

He gave her a bitter smile. 'Well, my dear,' he said, his tone one of affable sociability, 'if you wanted an invitation to my bedchamber, you had only to ask.'

Chapter Seventeen

Clio backed away until she felt the hard edge of the dressing table against her hips, trapping her in place. She tightened her fingers over the bowl, staring at Edward, unable to look away. She was truly caught, like a helpless fly covered over in sticky, irresistibly beautiful amber.

Somehow, she was not even surprised to see him there. The whole hazy, unreal scene had the cold air of inevitability about it. The feeling that the two of them had played this through before and would again, on and on into eternity.

'Where did you get this?' she whispered, holding up the bowl.

'I think a more pertinent question for the moment, my dear, is why do *you* have it?' he answered. He moved slowly toward her, graceful and intent as a predatory tiger. He reached out and clasped her wrist in a lover-like caress, yet Clio found she could not move. His touch was like a velvet-lined iron manacle.

He plucked the bowl from her numb fingers, holding

it up to the lamplight. The flickering golden-red flames shimmered on the old silver. 'Have you gone back to your old ways, perhaps?' he said. He did not watch her, his veiled gaze never leaving the bowl, yet Clio could not turn her stare away from him.

What was his intention? What would he do? Clio swallowed hard against the sudden cold wave of uncertain fear and growing excitement. The very unreadable quality she hated about him was also one of the things that made her feel so very *alive* when she was with him.

The infuriating man!

'I have not resurrected the Lily Thief,' she said, her voice tight.

His glance flickered over her black garb. 'Indeed? Just out for a lark, then?'

Clio flexed her fingers and twisted her wrist hard, breaking free of his grasp. She edged away from him until she stood with her back to the wall. She knew she could never escape from this room, not until he chose to let her go, but at least when they were not touching she could think more clearly.

Could remember why she was here. To find out the truth about the silver. To find out if he was the 'English' collector who would pay any price to possess it. The fact that he had the bowl at all pointed to 'yes'.

The question was, what was she going to do about it? What *could* she do, caught here as she was?

'I heard a rumour in town,' she said. 'Strange tales of a cache of fabulous Hellenistic silver, lost for hundreds of years. About people who would pay vast sums to keep that silver to themselves, no matter where it rightfully belongs. No matter who they hurt.'

'If such a treasure exists, I would say its "rightful" owners are long dead,' Edward said calmly. He laid the bowl back into the box with the silk, closing the lid over it. 'But I have heard such tales myself. Santa Lucia—indeed, all of Sicily—is rife with such things.'

'Is that why you came here, then? To follow Sicilian tales of treasure?'

'Why have any of us come here, Clio?' He turned to face her, his back to the box. His expression was still that veiled, blank look. Calm and faintly contemptuous as any classical statue hewn in marble. 'I am not the villain in this scene.'

'Then why do you have that bowl? Where did you come by it? Where is the rest of the silver?'

'So many questions, my dear. But I do not feel inclined to indulge someone who has broken into my home and rifled through my possessions—again. And after all your assurances that your life of crime was over. Tsk. What would your sister, the oh-so-proper Lady Westwood, say?'

Clio felt a lava flow of bubbling, sparkling anger rise up inside her, red-black and irresistible. She flew toward him, beating at his shoulders and chest with her fists, furious at his calm, at that little half-smile on his beautiful lips that hinted he just might be enjoying this little confrontation.

That smile vanished at the fury of her onslaught. He caught her shoulders in his iron clasp, holding her immobilised, a tiny, angry vein throbbing in his hard-set jaw. A ragged sob escaped Clio's lips, born of fear and frustration, of not seeing, not understanding. Not being in control.

'Tell me why you have that bowl!' she cried. 'Why are you here?'

Edward gave her a small shake, as if to awaken her, awaken them both, from the enveloping spell of their mutual anger and need. 'I have told you why I'm here,' he said hoarsely. 'I can help you, if you will let me. But, blast it, Clio! You make it hard indeed. Creeping around at night, climbing in windows…'

'How are you helping me? I *have* to climb in windows, to discover for myself what is happening when no one will tell me.'

'I cannot tell you, Clio.'

'Cannot, or will not? Because you think I am a mere weak female, who must be protected for her own good?'

'You are hardly a "mere weak" anything, Clio Chase. You are the most fearsomely courageous person I have ever seen, not to mention the most stubborn.'

Clio swallowed back the bitter knot of tears, more confused than ever. 'Then you know I am stubborn enough to not give up, to discover what is going on here on my own. Why won't you just make things easier for us both, and tell me?'

'Because, my dear, I do not yet know myself. You have been a terrible distraction.'

A distraction from buying the silver? '*I* have been a distraction? What of you? I have not been able to see to my work since you arrived here. My studies, the farmhouse, all neglected.'

'Perhaps that is all for the best,' he muttered.

Clio unclenched her fists, her palms flat against his chest. She felt the rich silkiness of satin, the crisp linen of his evening clothes, the strong, primitive beat of his heart beneath. The pounding of his life's blood, mingled with the fevered rhythm of her own. 'What do you mean?'

His touch gentled on her shoulders, sliding around

her back. 'I mean that your precious farmhouse has something to do with the silver.'

'How can that be? The people who lived there were prosperous enough, but they could never have afforded pieces like the silver. I have seen nothing like it at the site. Besides, the *tombaroli* would have looted anything of value long ago.'

'Despite the curse of the angry spirits?'

'I don't understand,' Clio said. She didn't know if she meant the silver, or the strange, crackling energy pulsing between them. The invisible power that bound her to him wherever she went.

'Just please listen to me for once in your life, Clio,' he said, his touch tightening along her back, drawing her closer to him. 'Give up the Lily Thief, stay away from the farmhouse, and watch your back wherever you go. Forget about the blasted silver. It might not even exist.'

Clio shook her head. 'I *do* watch my back, Edward. But if that silver exists, if it is indeed a cache of lost temple pieces, it's too precious and sacred to let disappear. To see it vanish into some greedy collector's vault.'

She glanced over at the Alabaster Goddess, still poised in her eternal vigilance. Clio had let *her* down, had lost her to Edward. She couldn't lose the silver, too. How could she trust him when he hid the bowl away?

She turned from Artemis, staring up at Edward as if she could read the truth in his eyes. His face was half in gloomy darkness, lit by the flickering caress of the low-burning lamp. It was all sharply sculpted angles, smooth, sun-touched skin, the map of some undiscovered country.

He watched her, too, with a wary hunger to match her own.

'What will you do to me, then?' she whispered. 'You have no dungeon here, as you do in your York-shire castle.'

'I'm sure there must be one somewhere,' he muttered roughly. She felt his caress move up the arc of her spine, felt him remove her cap. Her hair, loosely pinned up, tumbled down over her shoulders. His fingers twined lightly in the strands, holding her his prisoner as surely as any dungeon.

'All those Normans and Bourbons,' he continued. 'They had to hold their captives somewhere.'

'Not to mention the Romans and Saracens,' Clio said. 'The Spanish mercenaries…'

'Perhaps there is a nice, quiet little oubliette some-where in the castle,' he said, pulling her closer and closer until there was not even a ray of light between them. Clio slid her arms around his neck, closing her eyes to breathe deeply of his warm scent, to let herself be surrounded by him. To forget, for just a moment.

'An oubliette?' she murmured.

'Oh, yes,' he answered softly, his breath stirring her loose curls, moving over her aching skin like a cool breeze. 'A nice, quiet, dark hole, just big enough for two people to fall into and hide there for ever.'

Clio was sure she *was* falling, tumbling end over end into him and how he made her feel, leaving all else behind. Sense, practicality, even identity—they were all as nothing when she was with him. 'So, there are two prisoners, then?'

'Oh, Clio,' he said, his voice so rough and sad. 'Of course there are.'

And he kissed her, a kiss full of all the need and longing Clio could not express, could not even understand. Her fingers tightened on the nape of his neck, holding him to her, leaning into him. He tasted of lemons, of the night, of ancient mysteries, of all she had ever wanted and yet was forbidden. He was all she fought against, yet he felt like her only haven in a stormy world. She couldn't stay away from him.

Their lips slid away from each other, from the desperate melding of their kiss. He leaned his forehead to hers, and they stood there in heated silence, wrapped in a longing that could not be broken. They could not move forwards, yet neither could they snap that bond and move away.

'What will you do with me?' she asked, her words like a whipcrack in the quiet. A lash that tore at their tenuous control.

Edward laughed harshly. 'Right now, I am going to take you home, before I forget who we are and carry you to that bed over there. Tomorrow, the day after? I have not yet decided. But I want you to stay away from your farmhouse, at least for a while.' He drew back, cradling her face between his hands as he studied her closely. As if he could read all her secrets in her eyes. 'Listen to me, Clio. Stay away.'

'So, I must still watch my back, eh?' she said. She reached up and closed her fingers around one of his wrists, holding him to her.

'Did you not say you always do that anyway?'

'I do, and my vigilance is usually rewarded. No one has ever caught me, except you.'

'I could say the same about *you*.' Edward scooped her cap up from the floor, handing it to her before he turned away. Their touch was broken, yet Clio still felt him wrapped tightly around all her senses. Like a beautiful, drugging dream that made her forget all else, made her want to bask in its glow for ever.

She, too, turned away, toward the dressing-table mirror. She looped up her hair, tucking it into the cap again. In the unforgiving glass she saw that her cheeks glowed a brilliant pink. Her eyes were fever-bright, glittering with desires and fears she dared not yet name. Even to herself.

The closed box lid was before her, concealing the silver and the scrap of green silk, hiding all that they meant. For a while, a moment, she could pretend they did not exist. That there was only her and Edward, and their kiss in the night.

But soon the sun would come up, and shine its mercilessly revealing rays on the world, on reality. She would still have to find the truth about the silver, try to save it, because it was in her nature to do so. Just as it was Edward's nature to stop her however he could, for reasons known only to him.

She would truly have to watch her back, as she did not know which would prove more dangerous, the *tombaroli* or Edward. Or even if they were one and the same.

She tucked the last wayward strand of auburn hair into her cap, and spun around to find Edward holding out his own black velvet cloak to her.

'It has a hood,' he said, draping the soft folds over her shoulders. His hands lingered there for a long, sweet moment, as if he would not, could not, let her go. 'In case we should pass anyone on the street.'

Clio gave a ragged laugh, drawing the cloak closer around her. The fabric smelled of him, still held his lingering warmth. 'Which would be worse, to be thought a thief, or to be thought your paramour?'

'Why not both?' he said roughly.

'Why not indeed?' Clio drew up the hood, retreating into its satin-lined concealment. It made her feel rather like a ghost herself, able to flit around ruins dispensing curses.

'Well, shall we go the way you came?' Edward said, gesturing to the windows. 'Or shall we be dull and take the door?'

'The door, I think,' Clio answered. 'I am not so young as I once was, and clambering in windows is harder than I remembered.'

'The door it is, then.' Edward took her arm firmly through the enveloping layers of wool and velvet, leading her out into the silent corridor. 'Just out of curiosity, my dear, how *did* you manage to gain entry to my house?'

'I am not sure I ought to give away all my secrets,' Clio said, as they hurried out of the door and into the hush of the sleeping town. They were alone for a few minutes more. 'But you will no doubt discover it anyway. I climbed the tree in your back garden and found an unlocked window to one of the bedchambers.'

'Very clever of you,' he said. 'You are a veritable Artemis of athletic prowess.'

She glanced at him suspiciously from under the hood. 'Are you making jest of me?'

'Not at all, my dear. Your ingenuity never fails to astonish me. You find your way into places that seem quite impregnable.'

Clio laughed quietly. 'Indeed, I rather pride myself on that. But you are lucky I am not Artemis in truth.'

'And why is that?'

'Surely you remember Actaeon? He committed the unpardonable sin of watching the goddess while she bathed. Then she turned him into a stag and shot him full of arrows.' Clio saw her house just ahead, dark and dreaming in the night. It appeared no one had yet missed her. She hurried towards it, turning back at the gate to find him watching her.

'Goodnight, Edward,' she called softly. 'I will watch my back, I promise.'

And guard against *him*, above all. As always.

Edward stood outside the Chases' gate, observing the house intently until at last he saw the glow of a candle in one of the windows. For the merest moment, Clio appeared behind the glass like an apparition, clad in a white dressing gown, her hair loose over her shoulders. He wondered if she saw him, if she even looked for him there, staring up at her window like a love-struck supplicant. If she would fly down and land in his arms once more, so fleeting and precious.

But she merely drew the curtains, leaving him with just the reflection of light through silk, the diffusion of brightness and warmth that was all their relationship could ever really be.

Assured that she was safe in her chamber, that her street was quiet, he turned back toward home. A chilly wind had blown up from the valley, stirring the leaves over the walkway in rustling fits. Edward raised the satin collar of his coat to deflect the cold, or perhaps to hide from the world. From what he knew he had to do.

Edward had realised from the moment he arrived in Santa Lucia that keeping Clio away from the silver would not be easy. The Chases were famous for their strong wills, their free-spirited natures, no doubt inherited from their bluestocking French mother. And Clio was by far the worst of all the Chase Muses. Who else would have devised the whole Lily Thief scheme?

It was all only because she cared so very deeply, he knew that. Cared about history and knowledge and art, about doing what she thought was right and damn the consequences. It was one of the things he admired about her, that shining, warrior spirit. She was a passionate woman, and passionate people were seldom malleable. But his stubborn streak was surely at least as wide as hers, and he would not see her hurt.

Edward paused at the turning of the street, glancing back at Clio's house. The light still glowed in her window, but all else was dark and silent. Santa Lucia slept under the blanket of the cloudy night sky, a picturesque ancient village. Yet he knew that under all the beauty, under the peaceful visage, lurked something quite menacing. A shadow just beginning to form its shape.

Yet Clio was not alone. No matter how she pushed him away, how she fought against him, he would keep her safe. No matter what.

Chapter Eighteen

Clio stabbed at the dusty earth with her spade, anger and frustration in every furious dig. It was a warm day, the sun a merciless hard yellow orb overhead, and even the birds and insects were silent in the heat. Clio was all alone at the farmhouse, surrounded by the vibrating silence, the rich, organic smell of the dirt and the clover. She didn't mind, though, for she was unfit for human company that afternoon. The only remedy was to roll up her sleeves and *work*.

She wiped at her damp forehead with her wrist, staring down at the deep trench she was digging along the perimeter of the crumbling wall. She didn't know what she was looking for. Something, anything, to confirm or deny what Edward had said about this site, that it had something to do with the silver and she should stay away. But she found nothing, not even the pottery shards and coins she had come across before. The trench was empty.

Clio took off her spectacles, rubbing at the bridge of her nose. She hadn't slept at all the night before, lying in her bed until dawn going over and over her escapade at Edward's house. The hidden bowl, Artemis—their kiss. Why was it that whenever they met, no matter what the strange circumstances, she could not keep from touching him? From falling into his arms?

She tossed her spade down, relishing the loud 'thunk' it made as it landed point down in the dirt. If only she could throw it at Edward's handsome head! At least that would be one way to end the emotional storms they constantly battled. She didn't seem to have the will-power to end it herself. She couldn't even stay away from him.

Clio sat down under the meagre shade of a tall cypress tree, reaching into her knapsack for a bottle of water. There wasn't much left, and she sipped at the last warm drops, thinking back over all she had learned last night. It wasn't a great deal. Only that the silver existed, or at least some of it, the offering bowls. Supposedly it had something to do with her beloved farmhouse. And Edward was trying to tell her what to do—again.

Why did he want her out of here? Because he saw her as a weak damsel to be protected? Or because he wanted the silver himself?

Clio sighed as she tucked the empty bottle away. Life here in Santa Lucia had certainly been far less complicated before Edward had showed up. But not nearly as interesting.

She laughed aloud. Yes, she must truly be insane to prefer theft, curses and stolen kisses to quiet study, but there it was! She could never be the fine, proper lady Calliope was, and she needed mysteries and causes in her life. But she *didn't* need Edward to make her feel so frustrated!

Clio stretched her legs out before her as she leaned her head back against the rough bark of the tree, gazing out over the remains of the house, her new series of trenches and pits. Lack of sleep made everything shimmer and shift, until the present ruins seemed to fall away, revealing the place as it had once been. Bustling and full of life. Full of happiness and joy, sadness and grief, the flow of daily living.

Until it was all destroyed in a moment. A victim of senseless war.

'You have been in Sicily too long,' Clio muttered. She was becoming too affected by the sun, by the talk of curses and spirits. She needed to go back to grey, sensible London.

Except she knew that even in England she wouldn't be safe from magic. It followed her everywhere, in the form of Edward—whether he was with her or not.

'Maybe I should go to Russia, then,' she mused. 'It is cold and icy there, no room for sunstruck dreams.'

Though surely the fact that she was talking to herself meant the madness was permanent.

And she knew she *was* mad, for she saw Edward himself coming into the valley, riding his black horse along the narrow pathway. He had shed his coat in the heat, and wore only his white shirtsleeves and plain black waistcoat with his buckskin riding breeches and high boots. His hair fell to his shoulders, the same colour as the sun.

Had she thought him a dark, brooding Hades? Well, she was wrong. He was surely Apollo, one with the sky and the light. But Apollo, like Hades, also had a tendency to grab what he wanted and damn the consequences.

Was he really here, then, or was he a figment of her

imagination? Clio climbed to her feet, watching guard-
edly as he dismounted from his horse. He also seemed
to watch her closely, as if unsure what she would do.

Not that she could blame him. In the past she had
done everything from hit him with a statue to jumping
into his arms for a passionate kiss. She wasn't sure
herself what she would do any more.

Edward walked slowly toward her. 'Hard at work, I
see,' he said.

'Yes,' she answered. 'And I have not yet encountered any vengeful spirits.'

'Perhaps they are very tiny, like pixies, and hide in
crevices. Ready to jump out when least expected.'

'It doesn't take a tiny pixie to do that. Large dukes
are equally adept at taking people by surprise.'

He laughed. 'I did try very hard not to sneak up on
you today. I asked Zeus here to be as loud as possible
on the trail.'

And yet, in her dreaming, she had not heard him until
he was right upon her. So much for 'watching her back'.
'Will you sit with me in the shade for a while, then, as
long as you insist on being here?' she said. 'Though I
fear I have no refreshment to offer.'

'No matter. I brought my own,' he said, turning back
to draw a flagon and two goblets from his saddlebag.
'A sort of peace offering, if you will.'

'A peace offering? It should be *me* giving that, considering I was the one to break into your house,' Clio
said.

They sat down together by the tree, and Edward
poured out the deep red wine. 'But I was the one who
provoked you to it. I should have known you would not
be content with vague warnings.'

'True. We Chases are not known for patient docility.' She sipped at the wine. It was cool and sweet, welcome refreshment on a warm day no matter who offered it.

'No, indeed. You are women of action, and I should have planned for that.'

'You have a plan, then?'

'Not yet. But one is forming.'

And would he let her be part of that plan? She could be of help, she knew it, if he would only trust her. She knew how to catch villains, knew how they thought and acted. Unless Edward *was* the villain. Then she would have no idea what to do.

He didn't seem a villain today, lounging beside her in the shade. They sat together in companionable silence, letting the sunny Sicilian afternoon wash over them.

Clio finished her wine, turning the goblet around in her hand. Suddenly, the heavy glass vessel felt like iron, weighty, her wrist and fingers weak with numbness. As she stared down at her hand, bright spots danced before her eyes. Her limbs also turned heavy, her thoughts scattering as soon as she formed them.

What was happening to her? Frightened, she forced herself to her feet, clinging to the tree for support. The world tilted around her.

She sensed Edward standing up beside her, felt his hand on her arm. When she tried to focus her gaze on him, the sun behind his bright hair dazzled her. He seemed surrounded by shimmering heat.

As she tried to back away from him, her booted foot kicked at the fallen goblet. She stared down at it, one thought suddenly fearsomely solid.

'The wine,' she gasped. 'You poisoned me!'

'No, Clio,' he said insistently. His hands reached for

her again, holding her upright, and this time she could not even try to fight him. 'Not poison. Just an herbal tincture to help you sleep. You will wake in a few hours with no adverse affects, I promise.'

Clio couldn't quite believe him. She struggled with all her might to stay awake, to move, to get away. But she felt bound with iron shackles. 'Why would you do that?' she said, her words slurred. Her vision was turning dark.

'To protect you,' he answered. He sounded so very far away. 'You wouldn't stay away from this place, so I had to do it. I'm sorry, Clio.'

Her knees buckled beneath her, and she felt him catch her up in his arms. He held her easily, as if she weighed no more than a feather, yet she felt weighty as a boulder. As she slipped into unconsciousness, she heard him say again, 'I am so sorry it had to be this way.'

Not half as sorry as he was going to be when she woke up…

Edward laid Clio gently on the waiting bed, his heart troubled. The horrified accusation in her eyes as she realised what was happening, the way she believed he could poison her—it wounded him.

But this was the only way he could think to keep her safe. She would not heed his warnings, would persist in breaking into houses and going alone to isolated valleys until she found what she sought. Or until trouble found *her*.

Keeping her out of the way for a few days was the only way. One day she would understand. Or, knowing Clio, she would never understand, but she would be alive.

He gently removed her spectacles and her boots, tucking the soft linen sheets and velvet counterpane around her. The potion was strong; she would probably sleep until morning. And when she awoke…

'It is only for a few days,' he whispered, smoothing her tangled hair back from her brow. In sleep, she was so peaceful, so lovely, a gentle smile on her lips. If only she could always be like this—but then she would not be *Clio*, the fiery, stubborn Clio he had come to care about so.

'Just a few days,' he repeated. 'You will be safe here. And then you can hate me for ever if you like.'

He turned the lamp on the bedside table down to a faint glow before he left the chamber, locking the door behind him. It was dark when he stepped out into the fresh air, the heat of the day banished by cool mountain breezes, by a cloudless blue-black sky.

When he had found this place on such short notice, it had seemed a godsend. A small stone cottage high in the hills, miles from Santa Lucia along bad roads, hidden from everyone. Old Baron Picini, who had been dead many years, had used it for his romantic liaisons, far from the wrath of his wife. It was almost windowless, quiet and solitary, perfect. He had brought in comfortable furniture, books, a quantity of firewood and food.

Surely a few days would see the resolution of the matter of the silver, and then he could let Clio go. Release her back into the world, like a fierce goshawk.

Edward rubbed hard at his eyes, pushing the loose strands of his hair back from his brow. It was a terrible plan, he knew that. But he had no time to come up with a better one, no way to persuade Clio to do as he said. Kidnapping was all he could think of.

He went back into the cottage, and settled by the fire to watch and wait. It was silent now behind the bedroom door, the silence of sleep, dreams, peace. That would not last long.

Not long at all.

Chapter Nineteen

~~~

Clio felt as if she were swimming, fighting her way upwards through a thick, warm liquid, like when she used to dive into the pond with her sisters as a girl. Something dragged at her feet, pulling her back down into waiting darkness. She wanted to go back, wanted to fall into the waiting snare of silent unknowing, but something urged her to fight. She kept struggling upwards, battling against the bonds until finally she burst free into the light.

And into pain. Her head throbbed, as if she had been drinking too much champagne or reading without her spectacles. Or both, like that silly evening she and Thalia stole a bottle of brandy from her father's cellar and then tried to act out all the roles in *Electra*.

Had they done such a thing again? Clio was sure they had not, but she couldn't quite remember. She forced her gritty eyes open, blinking against the sudden cold rush of reality. Where was she? Not in her own chamber, either in Santa Lucia or in London, she knew that.

She pushed back the bedclothes that were tugged up around her chin, and she saw that the counterpane was of soft, rich dark red velvet. The sheets were lace-trimmed linen, thick and luxurious. Her own sheets were nice, but not *that* nice.

As she sat up against a pile of bolsters and cushions, she noticed red brocade bedcurtains looped back from a carved bedstead, like a medieval bower. The only light, a fuzzy ray of chalky white sun that pierced her aching head, fell from one tiny window set high in a whitewashed wall. She squinted against its glare, studying her new and strange surroundings.

The room was small but very well appointed, with dark red-and-green Turkish rugs on the polished wooden floors and several paintings on the walls. There was a mirrored dressing table, laden with brushes, boxes and jars, and a large desk. It was piled with more books than she had ever seen outside a library, their fine leather bindings glowing jewel-like in the faint light. A wardrobe with carved doors lurked in one corner next to a small fireplace.

It was like a chamber in some old fairy story, a bower in a thicket where the princess could hide from the witch. But she was surely no princess! Was she dreaming this place? Had she really been drinking too much wine with Thalia again?

Then it hit her, like a rock tumbled from a hillside to land right on her head. Edward had drugged her! He had drugged her, and snatched her away from the farmhouse, and now she was here. In an enchanted castle.

Clio groaned, falling back onto the pillows. That horrid *fiend*! And to think she had begun to like him. Well, perhaps not *like* exactly, but definitely to think

better of him. And she had kissed him! Let him see her
naked breasts. Given in to her lust for him like a love-
struck fool. Like the silly, romantic females she always
prided herself on not being.

And just look what disasters had ensued! She ended
up kidnapped.

Well, not for long. Clio rolled out of bed, her limbs
aching and weak, and assessed the situation. Her spectacles rested on a bedside table next to a burned-out
lamp. Her boots were lined up neatly by the bed, and
she still wore her loose brown muslin work dress, now
sadly crumpled.

The door was stout wood, bound with thick iron
hinges and pierced by one tiny, barred window, a perfect
prison door. It was, as she had suspected, firmly locked.
But this seemed to be an old place, and old places often
hid such things as trapdoors and secret passages.

Clio searched every inch of the floor and walls,
finding nothing. Not even so much as a crack or
knothole. The wardrobe had no false back or bottom,
and held only some of her own clothes. The villain had
planned well for his crime.

She dragged a chair over to the wall beneath the
window. Standing on it, stretched on tiptoe, she could
just peek outside. And all she saw were trees. Rocks and
trees. She seemed to be in a clearing of some sort, and,
no matter how her ears strained, she could not hear a
single sound.

She slowly lowered herself into the chair, feeling
profoundly alone and lost. Trapped. As she wrapped her
arms around her chest, she noticed a bowl of fruit on the
desk, glistening red and gold and purple, like a Dutch
still life. There were no pomegranates, but she thought

of Persephone all the same. She, too, had been snatched away from her life by a scoundrel on a black horse, borne down into the shadowy underworld just because some arrogant *man* felt like it.

A sudden flame of fury swept through Clio, burning away the chill of loneliness. How dare he! How dare Edward, the well-named Duke of 'Avarice', just lock her in here? How dare he—how dare he make her care for him? Want him!

'Idiot!' she shouted. She didn't know if she meant herself, or the Duke, or even the whole insane situation. Imprisoning her, as if they were caught in one of her friend Lotty's silly horrid novels. She reached out in a flash, shoving books and fruit and candlesticks into a clattering mess on the floor.

She pounded her fists on the table, relishing the ache of it because it was *real*. She didn't know why Edward had done this, though really she should not have been surprised by it. He was a strange man. But she did know he would not get away with it. Not this time. She was just as determined as he was. She would escape, and then she would…

Well, she didn't know yet what she would do. But it would be something terrible. Something to equal Artemis and Actaeon. Edward would be sorry he ever encountered her at all.

As she sat there, fuming, she heard a muffled noise from outside. Clio stood up on the chair again, peering into the clearing. Ah, there he was at last. Her Hades, astride his black steed. He studied the house cautiously for a moment before he dismounted, taking a package from his saddlebag.

'You *should* be cautious,' she muttered, watching

with clenched fists as he approached. 'It will avail you nothing in the end.'

Tense, every nerve alert, she heard a door open somewhere below her chamber, heard the click of his boots on stone floors. On tiptoe, hardly daring even to breathe, she crept off the chair and scooped up the empty fruit bowl. It was bronze, light and thin, but she was stronger than she looked. Maybe if she took him by surprise, she could knock him unconscious and run away. Steal his fine horse.

Oh, yes. She would like that.

Holding tightly to the bowl, Clio took up her position by the door. She held her breath, listening tensely as his footsteps made their slow way up some stairs. Her heart pounded, and she couldn't breathe. He was almost there; she heard the metallic rasp of keys.

She raised the bowl high…

Chapter Twenty

❧❧❧

Thalia knocked softly at Clio's bedroom door, leaning close to listen for any hint of sound. She didn't expect an answer, but half-hoped anyway. All she could hear was the echo of her father and Cory talking together downstairs.

She pushed open the door, slipping inside. It was dim, the curtains drawn over the windows, the bed neatly made. Even after only a day, there was the dusty air of disuse, of abandoned places.

Or maybe playing actress had only made her fanciful. Made her see drama and mystery where there was none.

Her father thought there was certainly no mystery. When they returned from a day's work at the villa to find a message saying Clio had decided to go to Motya with the Darbys after all, he had taken it quite in his stride. Clio had done such impulsive things before, going off to Agrigento, for instance, and he considered that it would be good for her to leave Santa Lucia for a while.

But Thalia was not so convinced. Yes, it would be good for Clio to get away, to be far from the Duke of Averton, and she did like to do things on the spur of the moment. Yet she never went away with only one hurried message.

Something was going on, something Thalia didn't understand, but a deep-seated feeling told her that all was not right.

Calliope and Clio had often concealed things that were unpleasant from her, trying to protect her. To shield her sensibilities, because they saw her as their baby sister. A silly little blonde who could be trusted to do nothing but play the pianoforte and dress up in pretty clothes.

She had had *enough* of that. Enough of being shielded and protected, of holding secrets. She was nineteen now, not a baby, and not a fool. Clio was up to something more than sightseeing, and Thalia wanted to find out what it was.

She quickly searched Clio's dressing table and wardrobe, finding that her brushes and perfume bottles, her soap and bath salts, and many of her clothes were missing. Just as if she *had* gone on a voyage. Her knapsack, which she carried to her farmhouse site every day, was also missing, which was a bit strange. It held picks and spades, not usually needed for a spot of genteel tourism. Her books and notebooks were still on her desk.

It did look as if Clio had gone on a short holiday, but Thalia was not convinced. Her sister had been acting oddly, ever since that Count di Fabrizzi had appeared in Santa Lucia.

Thalia went to the window, drawing back the curtains to peer down at the street. It grew late in the day; the walkways were full of people hurrying home to their supper, to the cosiness of their own hearths. A young

Sicilian couple strolled past, the man carrying the woman's market basket, their heads close together as they laughed at some secret joke. How they *fit* together, Thalia thought as she watched them. How assured they looked in their belonging.

She wondered wistfully how that felt, to know that you belonged somewhere, with someone. To find a true safe place. It must be glorious indeed. It must be something worth fighting for.

She thought of the Count's dark eyes, of his teasing, dimpled smile that hid so very much. He had tried to flirt with her, had danced with her all night at the *feste*, a round of wine and laughter and giddiness that still revealed nothing of him to her. Even as she longed to know more, to know everything, she could tell he was not like other men of her acquaintance, English men who gave her what she wanted with one pleading glance from her cursed blue eyes. One coquettish flutter of her fan.

The Count was not like that. He was wise to her wiles, as she was to his. But she was certain he knew Clio, knew her from before that tea at Lady Riverton's. Thalia had one great skill from all her theatrical studies—she could read people. Could tell when they had secrets, good, bad, guilty. She saw when they tried to hide those secrets behind polite smiles and pretty compliments.

Count Marco di Fabrizzi had secrets. Many of them. Thalia admitted she had almost been blinded by his charm, his fine looks, by the heady way she felt when he took her in his arms to dance. But not entirely. He was not here just on 'business', not just to call on his old friend Lord Riverton's widow. She was sure of that.

To Deceive a Duke

Was he here because he was in love with Clio? Thalia narrowed her eyes on the whispering couple below the window, remembering how Clio had flushed when the Count had entered Lady Riverton's drawing room. Was Clio in love with him?

Had she eloped with him?

Thalia sighed. How complicated things became, when one was never told the truth about anything! It consumed so much time having to snoop around, ferreting out secrets. But it could also be vastly rewarding.

It was a valuable thing at times, being thought a pretty bonbon. No one ever guessed at her treasure trove of scandalous discoveries. If she wanted to give up music and theatre, surely she could make a fortune as a novelist!

But before she could become the next Maria Edgeworth, she had one more discovery to make. She had to find what had really become of her sister—before it was too late.

Chapter Twenty-One

The scraping of the key in the lock sounded as loud as cannon fire in Clio's ears. She couldn't even breathe, her throat was so tight. Her arm muscles ached as she held the bowl high above her head. Time hung suspended.

Then it sped up in a great, roaring blur. The door swung open, and she lunged forward, bringing her 'weapon' down in a swinging arc. She aimed for his thick, stubborn head, but even her agile quickness was not enough. He was a fraction faster, grabbing her wrist just before she could make clanging contact.

His grip tightened until she dropped the bowl, and he kicked it away. She tried to kick *him* in turn, forgetting that she was not wearing her boots until her toes crumpled achingly.

'Ow!' she cried, startled. He pressed her back against the wall, his hands on her shoulders deceptively light. They felt like the merest caress, feather-soft, but Clio knew she couldn't get away even if she tried. She leaned her head back, staring at him tensely. The air hung heavy and static between them.

She couldn't speak. Her throat was still tight and aching, and she feared if she started shouting at him she would never stop. Her fury would bring the roof down on top of them.

He, too, stared, his face white and strained, his lips set in a hard, determined line. 'I'm sorry, Clio,' he said hoarsely. 'I didn't want things to come to this.'

'To *this*?' she answered, finding her voice at last. 'To kidnapping? I think that is a crime, even for dukes.'

'After this is all over, after I know you're safe, you can do whatever you like,' he said. 'Go to the authorities, denounce me, have me transported—shoot me. But for now I will do what I must.'

'And I'll do what *I* must!' Clio cried, her temper beyond all control. The arrogant blackguard! She twisted in his grip, breaking his hold so she could shove him away. She couldn't bear the heat of his nearness, the piercing green light of his all-seeing eyes, for another moment.

She dashed to the other side of the room, gripping at the bedpost until she thought she would snap the thick wood in two.

'You have done crazy things in the past, your Grace,' she cried. 'But you must be mad indeed to think you can get away with this! My family has surely missed me by now.'

'I think not, my dear,' he said, still so infuriatingly calm. 'They think you've gone to Motya with the Darbys, and I know that family plans to go directly home to England after their excursion. It will be a few weeks before you are missed.'

Clio opened her mouth, then closed it again, nonplussed. It was a rather good ruse, she had to admit.

Everyone knew she had gone off on impromptu jaunts before. Her father and Thalia would be busy with their respective projects; they wouldn't question her whereabouts for a while.

'How did you get my clothes and things?' she asked.

He gave her a gentle, disquieting smile, more fearsome than any shout. 'I have my methods.'

Of course he did. The man could surely coax the very birds from the trees, if not with his title and money, then with his fine looks. The intense charm that affected all women, even Clio, no matter how she fought against it. Denied it.

She fought against it even now, when she was his prisoner.

'Do you think to compromise me?' she asked, more and more puzzled. 'Why would you do that, when dozens of women would happily be your wife or mistress?'

Edward laughed wryly. 'No one will know you're here, so you won't be "compromised". I would be a fortunate man indeed to have you for my wife *or* mistress. But I'm not fool enough to think that will happen.'

'Of course it won't, after this ridiculous escapade! I don't understand it at all. I don't understand *you*.'

'Then we are even, my dear, for you are a mystery to me as well. Why could you not have heeded my warning, have stayed away from your blasted farmhouse?'

'You surely know me quite well enough to know I never do what I'm told, unless I am given a good reason. Why did you want me away from there so very much? So you could send in your *tombaroli* unobstructed?'

'I am no thief, Clio. Remember what happened last time you suspected me of such crimes?'

Clio remembered all too well. She had been caught in her own thievery. The one failure of the Lily Thief.

She shook her head, not able to look at him.

'I should ask what sort of scheme you and your good friend, the so-called Count di Fabrizzi, are up to,' he said. 'So convenient, him turning up like that in Santa Lucia. I must say he is more convincing a count than he was a gypsy.'

'You won't distract me like that,' said Clio. 'We aren't talking about my sins now, but yours. At least I have never kidnapped anyone.'

'Perhaps, then, I could distract you like this?' he said. Before Clio could tell what he was about, he swiftly crossed the room, reaching out to clasp her by the waist. His lips descended on hers in a quick, crashing kiss.

Clio arched back, startled, still angry. But all her fury and confusion, her frustration, flashed out, colliding with her desire for him like alcohol meeting a flame. It burned away all rational thought, all memory of their tangled, complicated past, and left only pure emotion. Pure need.

She threw her arms around him, her fingers wrapped tightly in his hair, holding him to her as her lips parted for his kiss. He groaned, a primitive sound of need to equal her own, his tongue meeting hers, their mouths and bodies and even thoughts enmeshed. He was caught as surely as she was, bound by this push-pull, cat-and-mouse game they could never be free from.

He did terrible things, but then so did she. Kidnapping, theft. Would they each be into such irredeemable mischief without the other? Clio didn't know, and at the moment she didn't care. She only knew, only wanted, his kiss. His touch. How could he make her forget, with only a glance, a touch, how very bad they were for each other?

Pulling him with her, Clio stumbled backwards until she fell across the unmade bed, sinking into its feathery softness. She drew him down on top of her, their kiss frantic. She wrapped her legs tightly around his hips, kicking her skirts out of the way. Her stockings abraded against his soft breeches, and she felt the heavy proof of his fierce desire against her thigh. But it wasn't enough, not nearly enough. Not any longer.

Clio let her head fall back against the tumbled sheets, revelling in the shivery sensation of his lips against her jaw, the arc of her throat. The hot rush of his breath, his heartbeat, all around her, part of her. How *alive* he was, how vital and real! She had lived too long among ancient artifacts, lives long over, and now she wanted his heat and life. His passion. No matter how angry he made her! No matter what happened after.

When she was with him, she knew real emotion, the true urgency of existence and craving and passion. When she was with him, no matter if they argued or kissed, she was alive herself. She couldn't give that up.

Her eyes still tightly closed, absorbing every feeling and sensation, she slid her touch over his tense shoulders, his taut chest, until she found the buttons of his waistcoat. She made quick work of them, pushing the heavy cloth back so she could unfasten his shirt. The lacings grew tangled under her desperate touch, and she sobbed in frustration. She had had *enough* of half-measures, of broken kisses furtively snatched. She wanted to touch him, feel his bare skin under her hands.

Now!

She caught at one of the knots and tugged hard,

breaking it open. She parted the placket of the soft linen, shoving it away from his shoulders. Edward groaned, his face buried in the curve of her neck as her fingers traced the naked skin of his chest.

Clio had only ever seen the nude male form in cold marble statues or flat paintings, had only been able to wonder how Edward would compare to them. How real, living flesh would feel. The curiosity and fantasy had sometimes been quite—intense. But it could not compare with the reality. Not even close.

Her fingers traced over hot, smooth flesh, roughened by a sprinkling of coarse hair. His heart pounded under her caress, his breath quick, yet he did not move away, no matter how much he might want to. He did not try to snatch control from her. He lay wrapped in her caress, his lips against her shoulder, and let her explore.

She smoothed her palm over his flat nipples, the sharp arc of his collarbone, his muscled shoulders. She would have thought an English duke, waited on slavishly, swathed in ease, would be soft. But his skin was taut over lean, powerful muscles.

Clio tightened her clasp on his shoulders, rolling him to the bed as she rose above him on her knees. She could hardly breathe, hardly think! All she could know was him, the unbearable need that had been building inside her for so long. She had tried so hard to deny it, to push it away, fight against it.

She just could not do that any longer.

Her dress was loose, and she grasped it by its rucked-up hem, pulling it off over her head. Her chemise quickly followed, and she knelt above him clad only in her stockings, gartered above her knees. She shrugged off the temptation to hide behind her hair, pushing the long, tangled strands down her back. She held her breath, staring down at him in what was suddenly a crackling and profound silence.

Edward's bare chest, sun-golden and touched with the red-blond of his hair, rose and fell with the force of his own breath, the heartbeat that stirred the small amulet on a thin chain. She saw it was a tiny cameo, Clio the Muse of History's scroll, on ebony.

She knew that he wanted her, as she wanted him, could see the proof of it straining his breeches, but he lay still. His green eyes, dark as a primeval forest, watched her closely.

'You see, Edward,' she whispered, 'I have no weapons. I give in. I surrender.'

He stared at her for a long moment, still wrapped in that heavy silence. Clio started to feel cold, to feel the strongest urge to cover herself. To run for her old shelters of anger and reserve. Was she hideous, then? She was tall and thin, she knew that, and her breasts were small. But she had always assumed that men were not so picky as all that—a naked breast was a naked breast, after all. And Edward *did* seem to want her. Had he not kissed her in London, at the farmhouse, at the *feste*?

But maybe now that she was naked before him in all her thin boniness, now that she offered herself to him, he had changed his mind.

She felt the itchy prickle of tears behind her eyes, and tilted back her head to hide them. *Men*—they were absolutely incomprehensible!

Then she felt the slide of his touch around her bare waist, easing her away so he could sit up. So they were eye to eye. Clio wrapped her legs tightly around him.

'On the contrary, Clio,' he said roughly, 'it is *you* who demand *my* complete surrender.'

'And do I have it? Do we have a truce between us, if only for today?'

'You have every part of me. You know that.'

Clio tipped her head back, laughing in a sudden rush of utter exaltation, hotter and wilder than her anger had ever been. 'Oh, Edward. I only want *one* part of you right now. Now, do be quiet and kiss me.'

He claimed her lips again, their mouths meeting in a desperate clash that held nothing of artful romance or subtle seduction. Only a deep, primitive need that had been too long repressed. Too long denied.

Clio could certainly deny it no longer. Love him or hate him—or both—he was a part of her. They were like two halves of an ancient coin, mirror images too long separated.

They couldn't be parted now.

She broke their kiss only to pull off his shirt, then wrapped her arms around him again, leaning into the sharp curve of his body to feel the press of naked skin to naked skin. Heartbeat to heartbeat. They tumbled down to the bed, limbs entangled.

'Clio,' he gasped, rearing back from her. 'You are a lady, and I'm—we shouldn't do this.'

'I don't think we really have a choice,' Clio said, suddenly desperate at the thought that he might leave her now. Walk away from what they both needed, and had wanted for so long. They *had* to exorcise each other from their blood, or they would never be free.

'This has been coming for a long time,' she said. 'We can't stop it now. No one will know, and I—well, I know how to prevent complications. You see, I might be young, and, yes, a virgin, but I am not such a *lady* as all that. Now, be a gentleman, and finish what you started!'

He gave a startled laugh, and she dragged him back on top of her, silencing his words with her kiss. Soon there were no words at all, not even rational thought, just emotion, feelings, hot sensation. The joy of being inevitably joined at last.

He quickly shed his breeches, sliding into the welcome of her parted legs as if he was always meant to be just there. Their bodies *fit*, their movements perfectly coordinated like the most beautiful dance. Clio closed her eyes, revelling in the feel of his mouth at her breast, the delicious friction of their damp, hot skin, the frantic need that built and built inside her.

Through that white-hot haze, she felt the press of his fingers against the seam of her womanhood, parting her for the heavy slide of his penis as he entered her. She tensed at the slight burning, the unfamiliar stretch and ache of it. Her breath caught in her throat, and she gave a tiny whimper.

But even as he drew back she arched upwards, sliding him even deeper inside her, so deep she could vow he touched her soul. As she held him there, the ache subsided, and there was only the deep satisfaction of being part of him. That delicious joy building up again.

'Oh. That *is* nice,' she whispered.

Edward laughed roughly. He drew slowly out, then back again, faster and deeper, that wonderful friction expanding, growing, until Clio felt she was soaring up into the sun itself. Surely no one could survive such intensity, such overwhelming, frantic ecstasy!

She held tight to Edward, calling out to him incoher-

ently as at last she touched that sun, and flew apart in a
million flaming fragments. A shower of bright release
that sent her tumbling back to earth, weak and trembling.

He caught her as she fell, holding her safe in his arms
as she suddenly, inexplicably, burst into tears.

'Oh, Edward,' she sobbed. 'That was—marvellous.'

He cradled her against his chest, and she felt the
deep rumble of his laughter as he kissed her hair, her
temple. 'Marvellous, my dear,' he muttered, 'doesn't
even begin to describe it.'

Chapter Twenty-Two

'**Y**ou are such a *duke*,' Clio said, laughing. She sat on the worn brocade couch in the cottage's only parlour, wrapped in her dressing gown and watching Edward attempt to light a fire. She had just finished drinking her infusion of smartweed leaves and rue—vile, but Rosa had solemnly assured her it would prevent pregnancy—and Edward's efforts were an excellent distraction from the bitter taste.

He glanced back over his shoulder, grinning at her. He wore nothing but his breeches, his hair carelessly tied back, and he looked—happy. Happiness was certainly not something she ever associated with him, yet it certainly looked good. His eyes, his smile, the golden glow of his skin, it was so very beautiful. Her bright Apollo.

She felt quite happy herself, light and giddy, as if her feet floated right off the ground. Despite being a prisoner here, she couldn't remember ever feeling quite so carefree.

Sex certainly wasn't overrated, then.

'I've been called worse,' he said, trying again to light his haphazard pile of wood and kindling. 'What about me is particularly duke-like right now? My fine raiment?'

'The way you can so handily kidnap someone, yet you can't light a fire,' she said.

'Would you care to try, then, madame? Not that *you* live daily with a houseful of servants, of course. I'm sure you have far more experience with domestic chores than I would...'

'Oh, here, give me that!' Clio pushed him out of the way, taking the flint from his hands. She studied it carefully. She had certainly watched the maids light fires dozens of times—surely it could not be so hard?

Edward leaned back against the abandoned couch, his hands behind his head as he watched her with smug satisfaction. It made her all the more determined to build the best fire ever seen!

'Surely I am not so completely useless,' he said. 'Even dukes have their advantages.'

'Oh, yes? Like what?'

'Did I not carry in vast quantities of water, just so you can have a bath?' He gestured toward the buckets lined up on the hearth.

Clio laughed. 'So you did.' And he had also brought a shining brass hip bath, piles of fluffy towels and her own lily-scented bath salts and soap. All the finest *ducal* luxuries. Yet it would do them no good if they could not heat the water.

At last she got the flint to catch, and lit some of the kindling. She pushed it under the wood with the poker, watching with a great sense of accomplishment as the flames caught and built.

'I'm exhausted.' She sighed. 'And famished! What have you brought for my supper?'

'So very demanding,' Edward teased. 'Build me a fire, find me some rue, give me supper.'

Clio laughed, snuggling back into his welcoming arms as the fire heated the room. His embrace surrounded her, warm and safe, and she felt his chin nestle atop her hair. She thought she could surely stay there for ever, curled up next to Edward with a good fire and a soft bed. They seemed to be the only two people in all the world.

It could not last long, she knew that. It was far too sweet, too perfect. She would have to escape soon, to find out what was happening in the wide universe outside their little cocoon. But not yet. Not tonight. It had taken her and Edward too long to come to this moment of understanding; she had to enjoy it to the fullest.

While it lasted.

'As a matter of fact, I did bring supper,' he said. Not letting her go, he reached out with his bare foot and hooked a covered basket, dragging it close. 'Bread, cheese, olives, prosciutto. Some fruit and lemon cakes. Wine.'

'Hmm, so there *are* advantages to being a duke,' Clio said, rummaging in the basket until she found a loaf of bread. She tore off a soft white bite, popping it into his mouth before eating the rest herself. 'Delicious.'

'A true ducal repast, one worthy of you, my dear, would have at least twenty courses.'

'Served on golden plates?'

'Of course. And ruby goblets.'

'With an orchestra from Vienna to serenade us while we eat our roasted swan and lobster patties.'

'And doves to soar overhead, carrying banners embroidered with your name, "Clio the Most Fair", as they dropped diamonds and pearls into your lap.'

Clio laughed at their silliness as she poured out the wine, not into ruby goblets but into plain pottery. 'Knowing doves, it would *not* be pearls they dropped, but something far less glamorous.'

'Not ducal doves.'

'So, even birds do your bidding?'

'Certainly. The only creatures who don't are Muses.'

'We don't do anyone's bidding, I fear.' Clio dug about among the food, laying out the meat and cheese, the glistening lemon cakes. At the very bottom of the basket was a small nosegay of Sicilian wildflowers, gold and purple and sage-green, tied up with white satin ribbons.

'For "Clio the Most Fair",' Edward said quietly. 'I wish they were diamonds.'

She shook her head, inhaling the crisp, clean scent of the flowers. They smelled of nature, of wildness, of freedom. Of everything she had found here on this ancient island, with him. 'Flowers are surely far better than any diamonds.'

'I knew you would say that. So I sent those earrings back to my jeweller…'

Clio laughed, falling back into his arms. 'Oh, Edward. I can see now that even dukes might make good husbands, given the proper training.'

He held her close, his breath stirring the loose curls at her temples. She felt the quick press of his kiss on her ear, and it made her smile. 'You could find a hundred better husbands than me, Clio.'

'Oh, undoubtedly. A kind husband who would do my

bidding without complaint, and not lock me up in funny little cottages with no servants to prepare my bath.' Men who weren't somehow involved in shadowy antiquities deals...

'Italian counts with handsome faces and hand-kissing manners?'

'My goodness, Edward, are you jealous? Of Marco?' For some reason, the thought that he might be just a little bit jealous gave her a twinge of satisfaction. Edward had surely been in love, or at least in lust, many times in the past, whereas she had only him. But he didn't have to know that just yet.

'Marco and I are merely friends,' she said airily. 'Colleagues, I suppose you could say.'

'And where did you find this *colleague*? Skulking around a gypsy camp in disguise?'

'Of course not,' Clio said, laughing. 'He wrote a very stirring pamphlet, on the sad fate of some Italian antiquities, stolen from Florence and Tuscany and hidden away in foreign private collections. He's very passionate about such things, about culture and heritage.'

'And you approved of his views right away, I'm sure.'

'I did. I had often despaired of many of the more, shall we say, unscrupulous collecting habits I saw in some of my father's acquaintances. I just had no idea what I could do about it. So, when I read Marco's pamphlet, I wrote to him about it.'

'You wrote to a strange man?' Edward said incredulously.

'It wasn't a romantic letter at all! And really, Edward, are you surprised I would disregard propriety in such a way?'

He gave a rueful laugh, his arms tightening around her. 'I suppose I should not be. Nothing you do ought to surprise me any longer.'

'No, it should not. I have ceased to even surprise myself.' Though, in truth, she was rather surprised at herself at this moment. Sitting alone with Edward in an isolated cottage, half-naked, chatting casually about her most closely held secrets. A month ago, even a week ago, she couldn't have imagined it. 'But that is how I came to be friends with Marco. And when I devised the idea of the Lily Thief, I knew who to turn to for help.'

They were silent for a long moment, nibbling at their repast to the crackle of the flames, the whistle of the night wind outside their cottage refuge.

'You're really not in love with him, then?' Edward said at last.

Clio laughed. 'Not at all. He is far too charming for me.' She turned in his arms, looping her hands around his neck. He watched her cautiously, and she pressed tiny, light kisses along his jaw and cheekbones until he smiled at last. 'I much prefer mysterious, taciturn dukes.'

He held her against him, cradling her to his bare chest as he buried his face in the curve of her neck. 'Oh, Clio,' he muttered. 'We're two of a kind, whether we want to admit it or not.'

Two of a kind? Before Clio could say anything, could question him or demand that he finally stop being so blasted mysterious, he kissed her lips and she forgot everything else. She just knew that kiss, his breath and skin, the now-familiar way his body felt under her touch. The hot, sharp need their lovemaking had created rose up inside her again, more urgent than ever.

Could she ever have enough of this man? Could her yearning ever truly be satisfied? Clio feared the answer was *no*. Never. The more she had, the more she wanted. She wanted every part of him, his body, his spirit, his secrets. For he surely possessed all of *her*.

They tumbled back on to the floor, the heat and smoke from the fire wrapped around them as they shed their clothes, the last barrier to their touch. Clio welcomed him into her body, into her very heart and soul. Even as she lost herself in their lovemaking, she feared he would stay there, locked in her heart, for ever.

This time out of time, with the world shut away from their secret bower, was a rare and fleeting gift. She wanted to make the most of every second, every touch and kiss.

Because it surely could not last long.

Chapter Twenty-Three

Thalia glanced down at the slip of paper in her hand, then up at the house. It seemed to be the right address, yet she wasn't sure. It didn't look like the residence of a count.

She didn't know what sort of abode she expected for Marco di Fabrizzi. A vast white baroque palace, with stucco flourishes and wrought-iron balconies? A medieval castle, cold and forbidding, bound in ancient stone and overgrown ivy? Whatever she imagined, this wasn't quite it. A tall, narrow town house in a part of Santa Lucia tucked behind the palazzos, inhabited mostly by shopkeepers. Neat and respectable enough, but not grand.

Thalia's estimation of him went up a small notch. He was not a snob, then, like his friend Lady Riverton. But that did not mean she intended to leave him alone. She had come here for answers, and answers she would get.

She drew her cloak's hood closer about her face, staying in the night's shadows. Chase Muses were known for being daring, for being fearless bluestockings, yet coming to a man's house would be too much even for daring young ladies! Luckily there was no one on the street; respectable shopkeepers probably retired early. And there were no lights to be seen in the Count's windows.

If she was fortunate, he would be out and she could rifle his desk in search of secret papers and letters without being hurried. She wanted to discover something, anything, to tell her where her sister really was.

Unless—unless they had gone off together. Eloped. Was there some form of Gretna Green in Sicily?

Thalia knew that Marco was not all he pretended to be. No, he was definitely more. More than a charming, peripatetic, not-too-bright Continental aristocrat who cared only to flirt, dance and acquire artwork. When he had talked to her, in the dark of the masked ball, she saw such fierce intelligence in his eyes. Saw the intensity he tried to hide. He held secrets, many of them. He had a purpose here in Santa Lucia far beyond going to parties. Yet she—and Clio—seemed to be the only ones who saw that.

That was the thing about great beauty, Thalia reflected. It was a blessing and a curse for those who possessed it. A blessing, because most people seldom looked past it to see the ugliness and pain, the secrets and plans, hidden beneath. There was always a certain power to being underestimated, as she well knew. Yet it was a curse, too, because most people also didn't *want* to see past fine eyes and glowing skin. They wanted only the fantasy.

She knew Marco was up to something, something hidden behind the glory of his face. He thought himself well disguised, but he had not reckoned with her.

Thalia hurried back behind the quiet row of houses, counting until she found the right one again. A set of shallow stone steps, set behind an iron railing, led down to the kitchen. It, too, seemed quiet, as if the servants were out. Or perhaps he kept no servants, all the better to hide his secret deeds.

She tiptoed down the steps and carefully tested the door, finding it unlocked. When she peered inside, she found a narrow corridor piled with crates of produce and wine bottles, but no noise or movement. No people. From the gloomy light coming through the open door she dashed through the kitchen to the servants' stairs.

How thrilling it all was, she thought, to be doing something so very *wrong*! She could see now why criminals, like that Lily Thief who had struck London last year, kept on doing it, despite the danger. Thalia suddenly felt so very alive, tingling with excitement and fear all at the same time. It was like a suspenseful play, and she held her breath to see what would happen next.

She pushed open the door at the top of the stairs and found herself on a landing, a high-set window illuminating two partially opened doors. She glimpsed a dining room and a drawing room, simply furnished and dark. The whole place had a chilly air of disuse about it, an abandoned quality that made her think of ghost stories.

Her hand trembled, but she kept moving. She had to; she had come too far to turn away, to miss what the next act might hold.

She crept up the stairs, higher and higher into the darkness. Finally, along another narrow corridor, there was one door with a thin line of light around the edges. She could hear no sound, no murmur of voices, no screams or shouts. Just the enveloping silence of the rest of the house.

Steeling her nerves, Thalia ran forward, shoving open the door with a great bang. At first, she dared not look, dared not see what horrors she might have found. But when she peeked, she saw—well, not much at all.

It was a small bedchamber, well lit by lamps and a cosy fire in the grate. Marco di Fabrizzi sat at a desk by the heavily curtained window, papers and books scattered before him. He wore a brocade dressing gown, his black hair rumpled over his brow, yet as he glanced up in shock his hand shot to a wicked-looking dagger resting on the desk. He held it balanced expertly on his palm, prepared to do battle.

Thalia's gaze darted around the room, but she saw no one else. Marco appeared to be alone.

He came slowly to his feet, still holding the dagger. 'Signorina Thalia?' he said incredulously. 'What are you doing here?'

'I came to find my sister,' Thalia cried. 'Where have you hidden her?'

'Clio?' he asked. He watched her closely, his lovely dark eyes full of wariness, suspicion, and—and laughter? 'Is she not at your house?'

'Of course she isn't, or I wouldn't be here looking for her, would I?'

'I'm sure I could not say.'

'I am not as big a fool as all that.' But she was, Thalia realised with a horrible sinking sensation, something of a fool. Once again, she had dashed into things without pausing for thought. Without thinking of the consequences. Now she was alone in a silent house, with a man in possession of a dagger.

'I thought she had eloped with you,' she said weakly.

He gave a startled laugh. 'I do not believe so.' He

went to the wardrobe, opening the doors to show her the interior, empty of everything but clothes. 'No ladies there, alas.' He knelt to peer under the bed. 'Nor there. Though I must speak to the maids about dusting.'

Thalia watched him, more and more chagrined, as he stood up and smiled at her. It was a beautiful smile, of course, carving unearthly dimples into his whisker-roughened olive cheeks. But it was also careful, as if he humoured the crazy lady who had broken into his house.

Thalia stepped back, pressing her hands to her burning cheeks. 'Then you don't know where she is at all?'

'I fear I have not seen her since your dinner party,' he said gently. 'Has she really disappeared?'

'Yes. No. I don't know.' Thalia groaned. She felt the most ridiculous, childish urge to stamp her feet and sob! But was this whole exercise not another way to make her family see she was grown up now, not a silly child? Not someone to protect? So, she kept her shoes firmly on the floor, determined to stop and think for once in her life. Now that it was too late.

'Here, *signorina*, sit down,' Marco said. He put down the dagger and moved slowly toward her, holding his hands out as one would to a skittish horse. Thalia let him take her arm and lead her to a chair. 'Have some wine, and tell me what has happened.'

'I really don't know *what* has happened,' she said, watching as he poured out a glass of wine and pressed it into her cold fingers. She sipped at it automatically, but it was indeed bracing. It helped her slow her racing thoughts.

'You say your sister has vanished?' he asked, sitting down beside her.

'I thought she had. She sent us a message saying she had decided to go to Motya with the Darbys after all. But things have been so very odd lately…'

'Odd?' He spoke quietly, as if he feared to scare her, but she heard the concern in his voice.

'Yes. Clio has been rather, I don't know, moody. Quiet. Especially since you arrived. I thought perhaps you two had decided to elope, and I was angry she was keeping secrets from me. I decided to find out for myself.' She took another fortifying sip. 'I see now I was wrong.'

He smiled wryly, as if amused she could think him a seducing eloper, even though he himself seemed to want to appear a heartless flirt. 'Why would you think I would run off with your sister?'

'I saw the two of you on the terrace at our party, talking together so intimately,' she said. 'And did you not know each other before?'

'Before?' The dimples vanished.

'Before Santa Lucia. In England, even.' Thalia laughed. 'You needn't look so surprised. There are some advantages to looking like a silly blonde bonbon, you know. I see things my sisters think I do not.'

'I *am* surprised, Thalia,' he said. 'Yet I should not be. I knew you were dangerous the very first time I saw you.'

'Not half as dangerous as you, I'm sure—Count.' She put down the empty glass with a sigh. 'But I am no closer to finding my sister.'

'Is it possible she really did go to Motya?'

'It is possible, of course. She has gone off on such excursions on short notice before, and my father doesn't seem concerned. Yet…'

'Yet *you* are concerned?'

'Yes. It doesn't feel right to me somehow.'

Marco shook his head. 'Nor to me. She would not go now. You are right to be concerned.'

Reassured by the fact that he seemed to take her seriously, and did not just laugh her fears away as her family would, Thalia turned to him, reaching for his hand. 'Tell me. What do you know of the Duke of Averton?'

Chapter Twenty-Four

Edward roused slowly from sleep, a deeper, sweeter rest than he had known in a very long time. A dreamless, healing slumber that seemed to wrap all around him like a soft velvet blanket, bringing such beautiful dreams.

Only the dreams were real. He opened his eyes to find himself lying on a pile of cushions on the cottage floor. The air was warm, scented with woodsmoke, wine and lilies. As he gazed up at the dark rafters high overhead, he heard the splash of water. And a humming sound. Loud and distinctly off-key.

"'It was a lover and his laaaaasss, with a hey and ho and a heeeyyy nonny no",' the voice sang, all warbling and wavering. And very, very happy. "'Nonny nonny no!'"

Grinning, Edward sat up to find Clio in her bath, splashing her feet in the water in time to the song. Steam rose up in curling wreaths around her, dampening her pinned-up hair and flushed cheeks. She was truly the most beautiful thing he had ever seen.

'Thomas Morley would roll over in his grave, if he could hear what you do to his song,' he said.

Clio smiled at him over her shoulder, giving one more great splash that sprayed water over his bare chest. 'I confess I am not the musician Thalia is. But everyone is a great singer in the bath. I'm glad you're awake. You can hand me that soap over there.'

Edward pushed himself to his feet, stretching luxuriously in the heated air. When had he ever felt so very—free?

Never. And surely he never would again. But he would always have this time with Clio. Even if he had had to resort to kidnapping to gain it!

'It is no use trying to tempt me with your body, Edward Radcliffe,' she said teasingly. 'I am taking my bath, and that's that. I can't be distracted. Now, soap please.'

Edward laughed, and scooped up the ball of white soap from the table. It, too, smelled of lilies, summer-sweet, just like Clio. He walked slowly toward her, the soap held out like an offering, to see if she could indeed be tempted.

Her eyes widened, but she shook her head. 'Would you be so kind as to wash my back?'

'With pleasure, madame. I am yours to command.'

'Well, that's a first,' she said, leaning forward in the tub. 'Why do I suspect you are mine to command only in things you already wish to do?'

'You know me too well.' Edward rubbed the soap between his hands, working it into a frothy, scented foam. He studied in fascination the elegant arc of her bare back, the curve of the nape of her neck, the damp curls that escaped their pins to cling to her skin. So beautiful, yet so vulnerable.

'On the contrary,' she murmured, shivering as his fingertips touched her spine, 'I don't really know you at all.'

She knew him, deep-down knew him, better than anyone ever had. 'What do you want to know that you don't already?' he said, tracing a soapy pattern over her skin.

Clio leaned back into his touch. 'Everything, of course. Everything you love, everything you hate. All that has ever happened to you.'

'That's a great deal to know.'

'Of course. So, start at the beginning.'

He laughed. 'From the day I was born? I fear I don't remember it well.' He kissed the nape of her neck, breathing deeply of her lily perfume.

'Then tell me what you do remember,' she whispered.

He ran the flat of his palm over her shoulder, the curve of her arm, the slickness of her wet skin. He felt the pulse beating in her wrist, strong and alive. 'I grew up much like you, I suspect.'

'Not with a passel of sisters!'

'I fear not. Only with an older brother. A perfect older brother.'

'Ah, so you *were* like me. For no one could be a more perfect older sibling than Calliope.'

'William was.' Edward gently urged her forward, slipping into the tub behind her. It was a tight fit, but he wrapped his legs around her, holding her close, and she curved her body back to fit against his, her head on his shoulder. The lily-scented water lapped against them.

It was easier for him to talk about his family, to voice their long-unspoken names if she couldn't see him.

'William was always good at his lessons, and he never, ever got into trouble,' he said.

'As you did?'

'Oh, always. I never could resist getting into mischief. William, though, was my parents' fine classical son. Their Hector, they called him. He followed in their scholarly footsteps, did well at school, at university, at everything. He joined the Antiquities Society, found a perfect lady to become his fiancée.' Edward paused. 'He would have made a fine duke.'

'But you, too, must have learned your classical lessons well!' Clio exclaimed. 'Everyone admires your great scholarship, even my father.'

'Oh, I learned eventually. One could hardly avoid it, with tutors and my parents ramming Plato and Aristotle and Herodotus down my throat every day. Yet I did not care. Not until much later. Only then, when it was too late for William and my poor parents, did I see the true value, the wonder of it all. They knew only my wild youth.'

Clio was quiet for a long moment. Then she leaned over the edge of the tub and caught up their goblets from the remains of their supper. She held them up, hers empty of wine, his still full. 'Does this have anything to do with it? I noticed your glass was full at our dinner party, too.'

Edward plucked the cup from her hand, studying the ruby-red liquid as if it held vast secrets in its depths. He placed it gently back on the floor, and leaned his head on the edge of the tub. 'You asked me once why your brother-in-law hates me.'

Clio thought this seemed as if it might turn into a rather serious discussion. She stood up from the water, reaching for one of the fluffy towels and wrapping it tightly around her torso, as if the thick cloth could be an armour to ward off words. To keep the truth away from their idyll, even as she knew she had to hear it.

'Yes,' she said quietly. 'Cameron is so very amiable, I don't understand his fury with you.'

'Amiable, yes. He always was, even with me. We were friends of a sort, when we first met.'

Clio sat down on the couch, still wrapped in her towel. Edward leaned his arms on the tub, watching her. His hair was damp, slicked away from his handsome features. 'You were friends?' she said, surprised.

He smiled humourlessly. 'You are startled, I see, and who could blame you. People less observant than you, my dear, have noticed the strained manner of our recent meetings. But when we first met at university, he was like no one I had ever encountered before. He had spent his life travelling, seeing places, meeting people all my other friends had thus far only read about. He was serious, serious about his studies and his family, yet also—kind. Always ready for a jest.'

'And you were not? Serious and kind, that is.' She couldn't picture him jesting, either.

'I was not. I was spoiled, always seeking the next pleasure, the next novelty. My friends were the same way, a useless, debauched lot whose lives did no one any good. Least of all themselves.' Edward rose from the bath and reached for the other towel. His breeches were soaked through, his amulet gleaming on his wet, naked chest. The stone floor around the tub was covered with soapy puddles, but he didn't seem to notice. He was far away from her, deep in his own past.

'A friendship with Lord Westwood might have been a good thing for me then,' he continued. 'After all, *he* has come out a worthy husband for a Chase Muse. Yet I was too caught up in drinking and whoring, gambling away any money I had, or didn't have. Showing my parents how little I cared for their scholarly ways, for what was important to them.'

'Did you truly not care?'

He laughed harshly. 'Of course I cared. But I was tumbling downhill too fast to stop myself. I was drunk all the time, living in a haze, in danger of being sent down and disgracing my parents even further. That was when it happened.'

Clio felt a cold, clammy dread creeping over her, yet like Edward she felt she could not stop anything. There had to be truth between them if they were to move forwards. Even if the truth was like daggers. 'What happened?'

'There was this woman. Isn't there always? But she was girl really, she couldn't have been more than seventeen or eighteen.' He sat down on a bench by the fireplace, not close to her, not looking at her. He stared only into the past, to a place where she could not go. 'She worked as maid in a tavern where my useless friends and I liked to go. She was pretty and sweet-natured, and she seemed to like me a great deal. Heaven only knows why.'

Clio swallowed hard, her throat dry. 'You had an affair with her?'

'An affair? I swived her in the alley behind the tavern, if that's what you mean. Several times, if I remember correctly. My—relationships back then were always of that sort.'

'Then what was special about that one girl?'

'Your brother-in-law liked her. Not in the debauched way I did. I think he saw her true vulnerability, in a way I could not. He warned me to leave her alone, but I just laughed at him. Told him who knew the Greeks were really such priggish puritans, insulted his mother in a way I'm ashamed to remember. He was right in the end.'

'What happened?'

'She came to me one night. I was drunk, as usual, and had just lost my entire quarterly allowance on the turn of a card. I was in a foul mood. And she said she was pregnant.'

'With your child?'

'Yes. I did not believe her. I disavowed that the brat could be mine, declared I was sure the father could be any one of a dozen men.' His voice was low, expressionless, but tight with an emotion long suppressed. 'She fled in tears. Two days later she was discovered hanged in her room. And it was Cameron who found her.'

'Oh.' Clio felt she had had the air punched out of her. She crossed her arms tightly over her chest, closing her eyes against the rush of tears. That poor, poor girl.

'Once you told me I could not possibly have been worse than any other young nobleman, gadding about in my misspent youth,' he said. 'Perhaps I was not. I'm sure my so-called friends got plenty of tavern wenches and house maids with child. But I have been haunted for years by that girl. I murdered her, and my own child, and I was too drunk and callous to care. Cameron broke my nose the day he found her body, and he should have done worse.'

Clio shook her head. 'What could he do that is worse than what you have done to yourself? It was a terrible thing, true, but you don't drink now. You don't debauch serving maids.'

He smiled ruefully. 'Only young ladies of good family. After kidnapping them, of course.'

'*This* young lady practically forced you to debauch her! As for kidnapping—I am still not happy about that. But I know you did it because you believed you had to, to protect me somehow. You work for the Antiquities Society; I have heard you are exceedingly generous to charities. You are trying to make amends. And your old friends are probably just as useless as ever.'

'Better late than never, eh?'

'Of course. None of us is a lost cause until we're dead.'

He laughed, no longer the harsh, humourless sound she so hated, but a real laugh. 'Clio, who knew you were such an optimist?'

'Well, I am not a lost cause, either. At least I hope I am not. We all have lessons to learn; yours was harsher than most. It made you see you had to abandon your old ways. Turn your life around.'

'Not *just* that.'

'What do you mean?' Clio wondered if he had yet more terrible secrets in his past, and she shivered. But she, too, had made a choice when she made love with Edward. She had made the choice to let him into her life, for good or ill.

'You remember Lady Riverton's game of Truth?' he said.

'Yes.'

'This is my truth, Clio. After that girl died, I spiralled even further into trouble. More drink, gaming in ever-rougher establishments, even experiments with opium. I told myself it was because of the pain of my broken nose, but that was not so. I loathed myself; I wanted to destroy myself, end what I was doing. Not even my parents could stop me, though they tried.'

'What *did* stop you?' she asked softly.

He came to sit beside her on the settee, reaching for her hand. His fingers entwined with hers. 'A muse. For are they not figures of great inspiration?'

'So I've heard,' she whispered. She touched his bare arm with her other hand, tracing a sinuous line along his tense muscles. 'What did this muse inspire in you?'

'She inspired me to change, once and for all. To seek to alter my course before it was too late.'

'An extraordinary muse indeed. Don't they usually just inspire a sonnet or a play?'

He smiled at her. 'This was a more far-reaching muse. An ambitious one, you might say.' He pressed a kiss to her temple, lingering there as if to savour her taste, her feel. 'That game at Lady Riverton's…'

'Oh, yes,' Clio said, remembering his words that night. 'You said you lost your one true love.' She had been intrigued then by his hinted-at secret. Had even been jealous of that unknown woman.

Could it have been that poor, lost tavern maid? Was that part of his torment? Or…

'I did not lose her so much as she was never mine in the first place. Muses can't truly belong to anyone at all, I am coming to realise.'

'And where did you find this—muse?'

'Where does one find anything important? At the British Museum, of course.'

Clio gave a startled laugh. Of all places, she did not expect that. Gaming hells, brothels, taverns—those fit his story. Not the British Museum. 'When did you find time to go there? Getting drunk and losing your allowance must have been very time-consuming.'

'So it was. But after one particularly lurid night, some of my friends thought it would be amusing to go the British Museum, to scandalise all the high-in-the-instep scholars. I agreed, thinking news of my behaviour would surely reach my parents. But I got more than I bargained for.'

Clio remembered that long-ago day now, surely the very day he talked about. She and her parents, along with Thalia, Cory and baby Urania had gone to the museum to look at a new black-figure vase just donated to the collections. As they went in, she stopped to peer into one of the sculpture galleries, drawn by the sound of raucous laughter.

She had known who he was, of course. Everyone knew the Radcliffes, their great interest in antiquities and philanthropy—and the trouble they had with their younger, prodigal son. Her own parents commiserated about it, laughing about how fortunate they were to have only daughters. But Clio was only fifteen then, still practically in the schoolroom, and she had only seen Lord Edward Radcliffe from a distance, riding in the park or at a play or concert. From that distance, he was terribly handsome. Terribly intriguing.

Up close, he was still handsome. But so very—careless. Looking at him she had felt so terribly angry. Here was someone who had things she, as a female, could only dream of—a university education, the chance to travel, to study, to do important things. And he did not seem to even care. Did not even see the beauty all around him at the museum.

She had been angry that day—and sad.

'You saw *me*,' she said softly. 'That day when I was fifteen.'

'I saw you. And you were so very disdainful, so beautiful. I had lived with my family's disappointment for years, yet I could not bear when I saw it in your eyes. I found I wanted to be worthy of someone like you.'

'Someone like me?' she said incredulously. 'Someone angry and confused, always searching for something that can never be found?'

'Someone sure of themselves,' he contradicted. 'Someone willing to fight for what they care about. *That* is what I admire in you. That's what I wanted to be like then.'

Clio felt that ache of tears behind her eyes, and she fought them back. Fought not to fall into his arms and sob like a lost child. All those lonely months and years of feeling no one understood, no one shared her burning desire for more. More than a privileged, civilised life. And here all along was someone who had shared her wandering spirit. Her quest for transcendence.

'I, too, have done things I regret,' she said. 'But I have found that no one is really lost. Some of us are simply on a different path, a new, undiscovered trail. And redemption can surely be found there in the wilderness, if we seek it.'

'Or if we are willing to accept it when *it* seeks *us*?'

Clio kissed him, their hands still entwined. It was a slow, sweet kiss, a kiss that said what she could not. All her yearning, all the old pain and uncertainty, everything she longed for. She sought to take away *his* pain, too, to give him forgiveness that was not hers to bestow, to ease the ache of the past. She clung to him, to this moment that meant so much. Meant everything.

She drew back, studying the elegant angles of his aristocratic face in the dying firelight. She traced the line of his mouth, the sweep of his jaw, his crooked nose. Memorising every inch of him so she would always, always remember. His eyes were closed, his jaw clenched as if pained, yet he did not move away. Not even when she softly kissed the corner of his mouth, the pulse that beat at the base of his throat.

'I think,' she whispered, resting her forehead on his chest, 'that we should go to bed now. It's late.'

Without a word, he wrapped his arms around her, lifting her high in the air as he stood up. Clio held tightly to his neck as he carried her up the stairs into the darkness of the bedroom. *Their* bedroom.

Once she had fought him, feared him. Now—now she trusted him to lead her anywhere. Even into the fearsome unknown of a game of Truth.

Chapter Twenty-Five

Edward lay propped on the pillows of Clio's bed, *their* bed, among the tumbled blankets. Clio slept beside him, her arm flung over his chest as if to hold him there. She sighed in her dreams, burrowing deeper under the sheets. The whole chamber smelled of her lily soap, the sweet smell of her skin, the warm, dark presence of *her*.

He smoothed her tangled hair back from her brow, wrapping the long, auburn strands over his chest and throat.

It was possibly more than he deserved, yet he savoured it all the same. Beings like muses were mercurial indeed; she would fly away at any moment. But for now, she was his to hold.

He studied the starlight blinking in the small window, growing ever fainter in a sign that night would soon end. But it was a night that had changed so very much. He had never talked of that tavern maid before, of the terrible thing he had done. He never talked of the drinking, the opium, the wild friends, all the things that had carried him so far from what he owed to his family. Carried him away from himself.

It was all years in the past, the work of a heedless, angry boy. The man he was now, the Duke, worked every day for scholarship and antiquities, for charities and his estates, yet it had never been enough to erase the past. Not until tonight, when he had looked into Clio's eyes and seen forgiveness. Seen understanding, and the first rays of hope.

Like all muses, she looked on human folly and weakness and saw everything. Saw what drove people to the desperate things they did, and understood and pitied. Her kiss was an absolution, if he could just accept it.

Clio stirred in his arms. She blinked her eyes open, staring out into nothingness as if still caught in dreams. Then she focused on him, and smiled.

'Are you all right?' she asked.

'Of course I am. Better than "all right", as a matter of fact.' He slid down among the sheets, still warm with her sleep, and wrapped both arms around her as she curled into his body. 'I have never felt better.'

'Neither have I. Who would ever have imagined it?'

'Imagined what?'

'That you and I would be here now, like this. And no one has even been knocked unconscious or pushed out of a window.'

He laughed. 'I think one would be hard pressed to push so much as cat out of such a tiny window. But I must say I'm grateful for the lack of bodily harm. It's more than I deserve, I think.'

'Indeed it is. Kidnapping is a capital offence, and I will certainly get you back for it one day.'

'When I least expect it?'

'Revenge is pointless when it's looked for, isn't it? But you are right about one thing.'

'Just one? And here I've fancied I'm right about many things.'

'So conceited, just like a duke. You're right that this cottage is in need of a cat.'

He gave a surprised laugh. Whatever he expected her to say—and really, Clio could be counted upon to say anything—it was not that. 'A cat? So you can push it out of the window in lieu of me?'

She slapped his shoulder indignantly. 'Certainly not! I have always wanted a cat, but they make my father sneeze. When I was a child, we could only have fat ponies as pets. And a barn owl Cory took in once, fancying herself Athena. This cottage needs a cat, a fluffy grey one. To sleep beside the fire and purr cosily. That would make this place completely perfect.'

'You like this funny cottage, then?'

'I adore it. Can we stay here for ever and ever?'

That was a most tempting prospect. To stay hidden here with Clio, to just be Edward and not a duke for the rest of his days. To forget. To be happy. 'Do you not think we would be missed before "for ever"?'

She frowned, her fingertips tracing light, enticing patterns over his shoulder. She lifted his amulet, studying it in the starlight. The scroll of Clio, Muse of History.

'I suppose we might be missed,' she said. 'My father is absent-minded, but he still might notice if I never came back. So, we just have—how long?'

'I don't know yet,' he answered.

He was afraid she would ask questions about his task, about what drove him to bring her here in the first place. He had no answers for any of that yet. But she just let the amulet drop.

'So, for ever might still be a possibility,' she said.

'What else did you want when you were a child?' he asked. 'Besides a cat.'

'Many things. A library of my very own where I could work, without my sisters running in and out making noise and distracting me. A lake to go swimming in the summer and skating in the winter, though we actually did have that. Oh, and no music lessons. I could never do better than Thalia at the piano-forte and the harp, and I hated that!'

'Ah-ha! One thing the muse can't do.'

'I also can't dance well,' she said, laughing. 'But I can ride, and swim, and pick locks.'

'I have ample proof of that one. I'm surprised you didn't pick the lock on this door and run away.'

'I didn't have time. And now—well, it's rather nice here.'

'Nice enough to stay for ever.'

'Even if there is no cat. And that would be easy enough to obtain.' She was quiet for a long moment, so quiet Edward thought she had fallen asleep. But then she said, 'What happened after?'

'After?'

'After that day at the British Museum. Did you immediately reform? Swear off drink and courtesans?'

'I had to. For when I left the museum I heard my brother had died, fallen from his horse and snapping his neck. My parents' Hector was gone, and all they had left was poor, unsatisfactory Paris.'

'With no Helen?'

'Alas, no. My parents tried to get me to marry

William's fiancée, but I could not. I tried to make it up to them in other ways, by sobering up, resuming my studies. Going off on a Grand Tour to find antiquities to add to their collection.'

'What did they think of your efforts?'

'I don't know. They died of a fever when I was in Rome. I'm sure they had their doubts, though. It must have troubled my father's last hours to know I would soon be the Duke.'

'But if they could see you now, surely they would be proud. They would see that their legacy is in safe hands.'

'Perhaps not if they saw me right at this moment. In bed with one of the Chase daughters, so very scandalous,' he said with a laugh.

Clio laughed, too, pushing herself up against the pillows, the sheet drawn across her naked breasts. 'Perhaps not right this moment, no. But if they saw your work with the Antiquities Society, the monographs you write on your travels and the history of the Punic Wars. The way you don't drink and don't—well, you know.'

'Debauch women?'

A dull pink flush spread across her cheeks, and he almost laughed aloud with the rare wonder of it. Clio Chase, blushing!

'I wouldn't know about that,' she muttered.

'Of course you would. You are the only woman I have *debauched* in quite a while.'

'Oh, Edward. You great, romantic fool,' she said between kisses.

'So, for all that, do I not deserve a reward?'

In reply, she cast off the sheet and pushed him flat on his back to the mattress, climbing atop his naked body. She kissed him again, a hot, heady flurry of embraces that drove away all thoughts and doubts. Drove away everything but the knowledge that he was making love with *Clio*. That he was hers, and she was his.

'Clio…' he muttered.

'Shh,' she whispered, stopping his words with her kiss. 'I'm giving you your reward.'

He fell back on to the bed, his eyes closed as he lost himself in the feel of her lips, her hands. Her fingertips swept lightly, enticingly over his shoulders, his chest, the sharp plane of his hipbones. Her mouth followed, trailing a hot ribbon across his skin.

Her teeth scraped over his flat nipples, and he sucked in his breath. His hands tangled in her hair, the tangled strands gliding through his fingers as her kisses moved ever lower.

He felt the light touch of her tongue over his ribs, her lips on his taut abdomen. He dared not move, dared not breathe, for fear this dream would vanish. That Clio would be just a vision again, a fantasy.

But Clio was very real, and ever surprising. Her hair tugged at his grip as she knelt between his legs. Her fingertips skimmed over his thighs before alighting, ever so delicately, on his erect penis. The merest brush, but it was like a bolt of lightning, flashing with sizzling heat all through his being. She traced its hard, straining length, her nails gently scraping over the tip.

Edward arched up. 'Clio!' he cried hoarsely. Did he protest—or beg her not to stop? He hardly knew; he couldn't think straight at all with her touch *there*.

'Be quiet,' she murmured. Her gaze was rapt on his body, her touch growing more sure. 'I haven't done this before, I have to concentrate.'

He gave a strangled laugh. 'Please, my dear. Concentrate all you like.' He collapsed back onto the pillows, surrendering utterly to her caress.

She lowered her head, her hair trailing over them both in a dark curtain as she kissed his hip, the top of his tense thigh. Her breath was warm on his skin. Slowly, tentatively, the tip of her tongue touched the veined length of his manhood.

'Blast it, Clio!' he groaned. It was almost unbearable.

'Did I do it wrong?' she said worriedly. 'The fresco at Pompeii...'

'On the contrary. You did it far too correctly.'

She laughed and kissed him again, her tongue sweeping down the length of him as she balanced him lightly in her hand. Finally, he could bear it no more. He clasped her shoulders, pushing her away from him as he rolled her to the bed.

'Clio, you are *killing* me,' he said. 'No more trips to Pompeii, I beg you.' She parted her legs, welcoming his desperate lunge into her body. She arched up to meet him, thrust for thrust, her arms and thighs wrapped around him until they were as one being, one person. Everything else vanished.

'Then we'll die together,' she gasped.

'Is that not what romantic fools do?'

'Oh, yes. And I'm the most foolish of all.'

He found his climax, a hot, bright flash of light that obliterated all before it. Nothing mattered but the heat and scent of *her*.

'Clio!' he shouted out. 'Clio.'

'Yes,' she whispered, her own body tensed with the rush of her orgasm. 'I'm here, my darling. Yes.'

Chapter Twenty-Six

'Where are we going?' Clio asked, laughing. Edward held one of her hands; with the other she touched the edge of the silk scarf covering her eyes. The darkness made her very sensitive to the rough ground under her feet, the scratching noise of leaves and pebbles. To the smell of fresh air, warm and tinged with the earth and green, growing things. It was a whole new world.

Edward laughed, too, his hand tightening on hers as he led her onwards. He also seemed new-made after their late-night revelations. Younger, freer somehow.

She did not know how *she* felt. Not shocked or surprised by his old mistakes. Surely she had heard of worse. But sad that he had been buried with the guilt of it for so long, unable to forgive himself. To put the past behind, and move into a future full of possibilities.

She, too, had not let the past go. It was always with her. But it seemed there *was* something magical about this hidden place, their fairy-tale cottage. Something that lifted a blinding veil and allowed her to see new truths at last.

'Where are we going?' she asked again. 'Are you trying to kidnap me all over?'

'I should have kidnapped you long ago, if I had but known what delights my latest crime would lead to,' he said. 'But I won't tell you where we're going. You just have to find out for yourself.'

'I knew it,' she said. 'You're taking me to the underworld!'

He laughed. 'And here I thought I was finally emerging from the darkness! Like Orpheus and Eurydice.'

'That didn't turn out well at all.'

'Ah, but in *my* version of the story, it is Eurydice who does the leading, and they emerge safely into the light.'

'Just like a woman,' Clio said. 'We are far too sensible to look back when told not to.'

'My dear, there are many words I could think of to describe you,' he said. 'But "sensible" is not one of them.'

'Ha! I tell you, I can be quite sensible indeed when needed. Have I not resigned myself to being your prisoner when there was no hope of escape?'

'Only because I bribed you with books, and cakes, and baths.'

'And other things, too.'

'Other things?'

'Come now, your Grace. You must not underestimate your own attractions.' She stumbled over a tree root, and his arm came swiftly around her waist, keeping her from falling.

Clio held on to him, the darkness heightening even her awareness of his nearness, the heat and clean scent of him. The way his muscle-corded arms, clad only in the thin linen of his shirtsleeves, felt under her avid touch.

'So, you think I'm attractive,' he murmured in her ear.

She shivered, despite the warm spring day. Her body knew his well now, craved its pleasures and intimacy. Craved the closeness. 'You know you are.'

'I know no such thing. But I'm glad to know one lady—the most important lady—finds me so.'

Suddenly, he swept her up in his arms. The world tilted dizzily as her feet left the ground, and she clutched at him, laughing giddily. 'Edward!'

'Don't worry, I won't drop you,' he said. 'We're almost there, and then you can satisfy your curiosity. Both about our destination *and* my "attractive" body. If you are so inclined.'

'I hardly think so, with my stomach so queasy,' she gasped.

'It's all those infusions you've been drinking,' he teased. 'Not to mention the vast quantity of bread and cheese you consumed at breakfast. Shocking.'

'I worked up a great appetite last night. All your fault.'

'Feel free to call on me whenever you feel the least bit peckish, my dear.'

She felt his steps turn, heading down a slope, and she tightened her clasp on his neck. The shadows at the edges of her blindfold grew closer, as if they entered a dense grove of trees. She heard the wind sing overhead, rustling leaves and birds stirring into flight. He turned again, the new ring of stone under his boots. They seemed to be descending stairs of some sort.

Then she heard an unexpected sound, the soft lapping of water.

'Is it the River Styx?' she whispered.

Edward laughed, and lowered her gently to her feet. 'See for yourself,' he said, untying the scarf.

For a moment, Clio's gaze was unfocused from being in darkness. She blinked hard, and found that they *had* entered the underworld. An enchanted realm.

She gazed around in wonderment. They were in a cave, rough stone walls rising steeply to a skylight high above that streamed pale yellow sun down to where they stood on the bottom riser of a steep flight of flagstone steps. Below was a pool of clear blue-green water. It shimmered in the faint light, curls of silvery steam rising from its surface.

'It's not exactly a lake,' Edward said. 'And I doubt anyone could ever skate on it. But I thought you might like it.'

'What is it?' Clio murmured, entranced by the water, the rough designs painted on the stone walls. Sheaves of wheat and baskets of fruit, she saw, along with heavily pregnant animals and red poppies, the emblem of Demeter.

'The Grotto of Demeter,' he answered. 'I was told about it when I leased the cottage. They say in ancient times acolytes of Demeter performed rites here, asking for the bounty of the harvest and a fruitful season.'

'It is beautiful.' She knelt down to trail her fingers through the water. It was warm and soft, as befitted a life-giving goddess. She had the sudden undeniable urge to dive into the pool, to feel its essence all around her, its promise of a bountiful future she could not yet believe in. 'Can we swim in it? Or is that forbidden?'

Edward smiled. 'I doubt Demeter would mind. It's *your* grotto today. A new realm for the Muses.'

Clio laughed, and sat down to tug off her shoes and stockings. Her dress and chemise quickly followed, and she eased herself into the welcoming embrace of the waters. The pool wasn't very deep; she could rest her feet on the sandy bottom, letting the waves lap over her shoulders. Her loose hair floated around her, and her limbs felt buoyant, as if the water held her up, above all the cares of mortal life.

'It is wonderful!' she cried, her voice echoing around them. 'You come in, too, Edward.'

He smiled at her delight, kneeling down by the edge. His gaze was tender, and strangely wistful. 'In a minute.'

She eased down until she could float on her back, staring at the sky so far overhead. It was their own underworld indeed, a magical place of old ritual and prayer. A place where all truths were revealed and forgiven. Loves lost and won—and lost again.

But for that moment, she felt only a sweet lassitude, a healing contentment that washed over her with the water.

'When I was a girl, my sisters and I used to go swimming in a pond at Chase Lodge,' she said. 'My mother forbade us to do it, but we would sneak off and do it anyway when she and my father were in town. We couldn't help it, it was the most fun! We would swing out over the water from a tree branch and dive in, pretending to be mermaids and pirates. But it was cold and murky, nothing like this.'

As she floated there on her back, she heard the soft rustle as he shed his clothes and slid into the water. The waves splashed, signalling his swim to her side. She felt his touch on her bare skin, holding her aloft.

'I missed having lots of siblings when I was a boy,' he said. 'Brothers and sisters to swim and ride with, to make up games and tell ghost stories with on rainy nights. William was so much older, and not much for games anyway.'

Clio laughed. 'We certainly did all those things, true, but we also argued and fussed, and pulled each other's hair and called each other names. Well, Thalia and I pulled each other's hair; Calliope was too good. She was our peacemaker. I sometimes wished I was an only child, so I would have time to study in peace.'

'Would you really have been able to do without your family?'

She dove down under the water, getting her feet beneath her before she plunged back upwards. She pushed her hair back over her shoulders, smiling at him. 'No, of course not. I adore my sisters, though they also drive me mad sometimes.'

'Drive you mad?'

'They are always *there*, you see. We aren't our-selves, we're a collective—the Chase Muses. Part of each other for all time. It means we always have each other to rely on, but it also means we are obligated. Always and for ever.' Clio paused. She had never spoken of such things before, never even really thought about them. But somehow, here with Edward in their sacred grotto, she felt she could say anything at all. That all her thoughts and dreams and fears would be understood by him, and him alone.

'I think perhaps that is one of the reasons I decided to become the Lily Thief,' she said.

'Because of your sisters?' he asked quietly.

'Yes. Oh, there were the antiquities, of course—that was the most important. To save them from people who did not care for them, to make sure they went to where they truly belong. But also it was something *I* could do. A cause just for me, a secret. It was wrong, I see that now. I went about my ideals in entirely the wrong way.

Seeing the disappointment in Calliope's eyes was the most horrible feeling. But for a while…'

'For a while you felt truly alive.'

'Yes,' Clio said, surprised. 'How did you know?'

He gave her a wry smile. 'Because I know what it is to feel numb, dead inside, to try to feel something, anything, by doing things we're told are wrong. But it didn't work, not for me or for you. It was as if I watched the world in shades of hazy grey, never vivid, clear colour. Not until now. Your red hair is the first real colour I see.'

Clio feared she might cry. She had gone through years with no tears, only to become a veritable watering pot when she was near Edward! She swallowed hard against the dry, hard knot in her throat and said, 'It is *auburn*, I will thank you to remember.'

Edward laughed, catching her around the waist and lifting her high, twirling her through the frothing water. 'It is red! Everything about you is painted in the most vivid of hues, Clio Chase. Red, and emerald green, and sun yellow. You're all the heat and noise and passion I've ever known.'

Clio laughed, too, giddy with the emotion of it all. She braced her hands on his shoulders, staring down at him as the steam rose around him in a silver veil. She had thought him handsome before, but in that moment he looked so young and free, his beauty positively incandescent. Her golden Sicilian god. 'I *am* noisy, that's true.'

'You are life itself,' he insisted, lowering her slowly back into the water. They stood there entwined, part of each other in the ancient magic of that place. 'You saved me.'

'No, no. You saved yourself.'

'I turned myself from a careless boy to a semblance of a duke, I suppose,' he said. 'I gave up taverns for the dusty halls of the Antiquities Society. Yet I could not have done it without your disapproval.'

'Ah, well, I am good at disapproval. I managed to keep it up with you for years.'

'I know. I still feel the stinging effects of it,' he said, laughing as he reached up to touch the faint white scar on his brow where the Alabaster Goddess had once landed.

Clio kissed that scar, filled with a sudden rush of remorse at the violent memory. 'I'm so sorry, Edward! I never—'

'No, I deserved it. My wooing of you was—rough, to say the least. But do you still disapprove of me? After everything?'

She shook her head. 'It's true that you should not have snatched me away like that. It's surely something the "old" Edward would have done! I know that you have your reasons, but you could have talked to me. Explained things.'

'I only wanted to keep you safe. And time was, is, so short. I couldn't come up with anything else. I'm sorry.'

'No, I don't want your apologies.' She laid her hands gently against his face, holding his gaze on hers. There could be no running away now, for either of them. No more deception. 'I want to know what is really happening.'

'Clio.' He pressed his fingers over hers, holding her to him. 'It is dangerous.'

'Come now. You know me better than anyone ever

has. You know I do not shrink from danger. I want to help you, if I can.' She studied him closely. 'I know it's to do with the silver. Are you here to take it for yourself?'

He shook his head, turning to kiss her wrist. 'Surely *you* know *me* better than that. I have given up adding to my own collection, though pieces like the silver would be tempting indeed.'

'Then what? You're working with the Antiquities Society again, like in Yorkshire?'

'I am trying to.' He was silent for a long moment, as if weighing his options, weighing her words. Finally, he nodded. He took her hand and led her to a stone bench cut into the wall beneath the waterline.

'The bowl that I have,' he said, 'it came to the attention of the Antiquities Society last year, along with the information that there was certainly more where it was found. Could be an entire temple's altar set, the likes of which have never been discovered before. But it was in danger of being lost before it could even be seen.'

'Who discovered it?'

'Mr Darby, who is, as you know, also a member of the Antiquities Society. He is taking a report back to London. Soon before you arrived here, an informant brought Darby the bowl and told him of the search for more.'

'What sort of informant?'

'A former *tombarolo*. He claimed he sought more legitimate ways of making money, but I think he just wanted to play both sides for greater profit. It availed him naught, as he was soon after found dead. But his information seemed legitimate, and I was asked to come to Sicily and help investigate further. We had to hope it was not too late.'

'And did you know I was here?'

'No. I knew you were travelling with your family in Italy, but not in Sicily. I assumed you wanted to be as far from me as possible, after what happened in Yorkshire.'

Indeed she had, Clio remembered ruefully. Had longed to run from him, from what she felt and yet could not understand. Her father's suggestion they go abroad for a time was a godsend. 'Would you have stayed away if you had known?'

He laughed. 'On the contrary. I would have travelled here even faster.'

Clio laughed, too. 'Perhaps you should have! We've wasted so much time being angry. Not—not seeing. But tell me the rest of your tale. Have you found the silver yet? Any piece of it?'

'Not yet, but luckily it seems that neither have the thieves. You have got in their way.'

'Me?'

'Your work at the farmhouse. That is where it's thought the silver will be found. Before your arrival, no one ever went there, and the thieves could work in leisurely peace. When they could find people willing to brave the curse, that is. Now…'

'So, that *is* why you warned me away!'

'Of course. These are ruthless men. They would get you out of their way however they could.'

Clio shook her head, furious that thieves would dare defile her farmhouse! Dare sully the lives of those who had lived there, had buried that silver in fear and frantic hope so long ago. *This belongs to the gods.* 'The English buyer grows impatient,' she said, remembering the conversation she overheard at the *feste*.

'Yes. That's why you are now in greater danger. Why I kidnapped you.'

'Who is the English, then, that has the money to command such a flock of thieves?' Including, it seemed, Rosa's Giacomo.'

'At first we thought Ronald Frobisher.'

'Lady Riverton's cicisbeo?' Clio said, somewhat surprised. She would not have thought of him; he always seemed merely concerned with his neckcloths and planning parties, staying in the good graces of Lady Riverton. She should have remembered appearances were almost always deceiving.

'He seems to have the money, and he's quite an ardent collector, if something of a neophyte. Possessing a silver altar set would gain him attention and respect among other collectors. And with Lady Riverton.'

'Very true. No one else has anything like that, not that I know of.'

'If you *had* known, would the Lily Thief have struck again?'

Clio laughed. 'I told you, my thieving days are behind me. Except for the night I broke into your palazzo, of course. But you said you *did* suspect Frobisher. Do you not any longer?'

'Oh, he is part of it. It seems, though, that he is acting on behalf of someone else.'

'Of course,' Clio breathed, feeling suddenly foolish. 'Someone he wants to impress above any other. Lady Riverton.'

'Indeed,' Edward answered. 'When I first came to Santa Lucia, I did not suspect her, either. Lord Riverton was a great collector, but she never really seemed to share his interest.'

'No. Only hats and parties. I should have known no one could be *that* interested in bonnets without having something to hide.'

'I couldn't understand why she was in a quiet place like Santa Lucia, and not in Naples. Only people with a great interest in history and antiquities come here.'

'I just thought she wanted to play social queen for a while, in a place where no one else has time to throw lavish parties,' Clio said reflectively. 'Father and Thalia enjoyed her entertainments well enough, and I didn't think of it all very much. What a cabbage-head I was!'

'Then we are cabbage-heads together, surely.'

'Are you quite certain it is Lady Riverton?'

'Not completely. But the list of suspects is short, and she and Frobisher are at the top.'

Clio tipped her head back against the stone wall, staring up at the skylight as her thoughts whirled. 'We have to find out for sure.'

'*We?*' He shook his head. 'No, Clio.'

'Yes!' she cried. She turned to him in growing excitement, clasping both his hands in hers. 'You said yourself you cannot lock me up to keep me safe.'

He shook his head again, his lips set in a stubborn frown. 'That does not mean I will put you right on the path of danger.'

'I am not like the silver, you know,' she insisted. 'You cannot hide me away. I may not have seen the truth of Lady Riverton, but I can help you. I have worked with people like that, I know how they think. How they act.'

'No! If you were hurt…'

'I won't be hurt! Did anything happen to me when I was the Lily Thief?'

'Only because you were lucky.'

'Lucky, yes. But also I was not stupid. I won't be stupid now, either! Please. Let me help you find the silver. We can't let it be lost.'

He stared down at her, his green eyes dark and full of stern doubts. She did not turn from him, just held on to his hands, willing him to believe in her. To see that she could be strong, and they could achieve so very much together.

'I am not a porcelain doll,' she said. 'I don't crack easily, and you know that. I *can* help you, if you will just give me a chance.' She pressed kisses to the white scar on his brow, the crooked line of his nose. 'You will be there to protect me, I know.'

Finally, finally, she sensed him wavering the merest bit. He shook his head again, but said, 'Very well. I know that your help will be invaluable. I have seen what you can do. But you must promise me you will be careful, that you will take cover at the first hint of any danger.'

'Thank you!' she cried, kissing him again in a burst of jubilant excitement. 'You will not be sorry. We will find the villain, whether it's Lady Riverton or not, and they will lead us to the silver. You must promise *me* something, though.'

'What is it?' he said. He still looked most wary, but she knew that would soon change. Once he saw the full potential of all they could be together.

'That you will also be careful. For you are quite precious, as well.'

He caught her in a fierce embrace, his mouth finding hers in a kiss full of passion and desperation. Clio wrapped her legs tightly around his hips, feeling his manhood lengthen and harden against her, as he walked up the sloping ground to the dry side of the grotto. Passion born of danger and anticipation blossomed between them, undeniable as a tidal wave. He pressed her back against the wall and entered her, fast and full of need, lust, fear and—and hope.

Clio arched against him, melding him to her even deeper, until she didn't know where he ended and she began. They were, and always had been, as one. And there, in that ancient grotto, she gave him her whole heart. In that moment she was his.

Not that she would tell *him* that, of course. He would only take that as a sign he should marry her and lock her up for all time. And she would make a terrible, miserable captive-duchess.

But for that instant, as their bodies and kisses and souls melded, she loved him. And it had to be enough.

Later, Clio lay at the edge of the pool, revelling in the feel of the warm water lapping at her feet, the broken sunlight that fell over them from high above. Edward's head rested on her naked stomach, and she ran her fingers through his loose hair, smiling at the absolute perfection of that moment, the gentle, sweet lassitude that had stolen over her in the wake of their lovemaking.

She laughed in a sudden burst of irrepressible merriment, kicking out at the water and sending a blue-green spray high in the air. Edward rolled over, grinning up at her.

'I love the sound of your laughter,' he said. 'It's much too rare.'

'No doubt it sounds rusty with disuse,' she answered. 'We are far too serious people, you and I.'

'True. We don't do anything casually. Nothing by halves.'

'All for one, eh?'

'If you would only let me.'

'Hmm. It's—difficult for me, you know. To trust, to share. I'm used to living in my own head.'

'Keeping your own counsel?'

'Indeed. Like someone else we know, *your Grace*.' She splashed water over his handsome head, making him laugh in turn. 'You're infuriatingly close-mouthed when you want to be.'

'Oh, not always. Not now, for instance.' He pressed a warm kiss to her abdomen, the curve of her ribs. 'Or now…'

Clio shivered, tangling her fingers in his wet hair. 'You are trying to distract me.'

He grinned against her skin, leaving a string of yet more kisses just under her breasts, the arc of her shoulder. 'Is it working?'

Of course it was. She could hardly remember her own name when he touched her like that. She tightened her clasp on his hair, drawing him away from her so she could think again. 'You know I am trying to get you to promise not to keep secrets from me any longer.'

He groaned, and rolled over to lie by her side. Only their hands touched. 'I have no more secrets left. You know everything.'

'Not quite everything.'

'Everything that matters. You know more of me than anyone else ever has. But I am not the only one with secrets,' he said.

'I have also told you everything,' she protested. 'You know all. Even about the Lily Thief.'

'Oh, come now, surely I cannot know *all*. You are a very complicated person, Clio Chase. There must be a great deal hidden in the dark corridors of your soul.'

Clio laughed. 'Dark corridors of the soul? Are you perchance a secret novel reader, your Grace?'

'I have been known to indulge in a Minerva Press tome a time or two, if you must know my very last secret,' he said. 'Purely for cultural research.'

'Oh, yes, certainly.' Clio squeezed his hand.

'So, tell me,' he said. 'What would Clio's truth be?'

That she loved him to distraction, of course. Her beautiful, strange, horrible, wonderful duke. She couldn't say that aloud, though, for she *did* still have some secrets she locked away. 'I told you, Edward. You know them all. Every last shocking thing. The wonder is that you are still here with me.'

'I don't scare that easily,' he said. 'The only thing that could have made me run away would be discovering that you are actually an empty-headed débutante. One of those dreaded gigglers in white gowns.'

'No fear of that. None of the Chases are *gigglers*.'

'I'm very glad to hear it. So, giggling is not your secret.'

'Indeed not.'

'A propensity to read fashion papers? Secret tippling?'

'I have enjoyed a grappa on occasion,' she admitted. 'One of our cook's many sons distils it, you see, and it's quite good.'

'Ah-ha! I knew there was something.'

'Now you truly do know all,' Clio said lightly. But the memory of that grappa made her think of Rosa's other son, Giacomo the *tombarolo*, and she felt a deep pang of sadness for people she had come to care about. 'I have been thinking…'

'Oh, no! Never that.' He laughed. 'Terrible things come of thinking, Clio. Thefts, night-time break-ins, things of that sort.'

'Well, you are just going to have to become accustomed to thinking. I do a lot of it, you know.'

'I do know. What are you thinking of right now?'

'Of finding the silver, and ferreting out the thieves.'

'I see.' Edward sat up, suddenly serious. 'Well, surely no one would know better how to go about such things. What are your thoughts?'

'I've been hearing quite a bit about vengeful spirits, curses and such. They often seem to take matters like that seriously here, and it seems my farmhouse is ringed with them.'

'I have heard such tales, too,' he said. 'That your site is guarded by ghosts who keep away interlopers. It's probably one of the reasons the hoard has stayed safe so long.'

'Hmm, yes. The local thieves would be scared of the spirits who guard the silver.' Clio remembered the warning inscription on the bottom of the bowl. 'Silver that belongs to the gods.'

'You think we can use these curses in some way?'

'Not on Lady Riverton, perhaps. But maybe on the thieves who do the actual work. Giacomo for one seemed to be convinced.' Clio frowned in thought. 'Lady Riverton and Mr Frobisher couldn't get the silver themselves. They wouldn't know how to do it. They rely entirely on their hired *tombaroli*. If the thieves thought the curse was upon them…'

'They might lead us to the cache, or at least refuse to dig up any more.'

'Hopefully, yes.'

'How do you propose we implement this curse? Ghosts are notoriously unreliable.'

'Well, for that we may need some assistance. *You* are certainly dramatic enough for anything, but you are so well known. I don't think we two can do it alone.'

'Exactly what kind of "assistance"?' he said suspiciously. 'Your friend Marco?'

'I hadn't thought of Marco! I'm sure he could be of valuable use, though. He's quite good at disguises, and he knows more about local customs than I do.'

'Yes, I know about his disguises. Then, if not the Count, who? We don't want too many people involved.'

'I agree. The more people, the more likely the scheme will be discovered. But Thalia is entirely trustworthy, and always ready for mischief,' Clio said.

'Your sister?'

'Yes. She is an excellent actress; you saw her at the theatricals. And she is also something of a playwright. She would be the best one to help us concoct a play about ghosts and curses.'

'I don't know,' he said, the stern Duke again. 'I agreed to accept *your* help. I cannot put all your sisters in danger, too.'

'It is only one sister! Believe me, Thalia is ideal for such a task. She might look fluffy and fashionable, but she truly is quite talented. And she has even more "dark corridors" in her soul than I do, I would vow. If anyone is ruthless enough to spring a trap on Lady Riverton, it is Thalia.'

Edward was quiet for along moment, then said grudgingly, 'Very well. Your sister, then, and perhaps that blasted Count. That is all.'

'That's all I need,' Clio said, satisfied. For the moment.

'Where shall we "spring this trap", then?'

'Where else, my darling? The ancient theatre. I'm sure all manner of ghosts dwell there.'

Chapter Twenty-Seven

Clio peered through her spyglass at the amphitheatre below her rocky perch. It grew late in the day, but Thalia was still there, her script open in her hands as she paced the length of the old stage. The sun was an orb of shimmering burnt-orange behind her, beginning its long descent below the horizon and casting Thalia's white draperies in stripes of bright colours.

Already Clio felt the fairy-tale magic of her little cottage fading away into mist, dispersed by the cold winds of life and plotting. The soft cocoon that enclosed her in that small bedchamber, the grotto, fell away, leaving her shivering and exposed, aching for dreams she hadn't even realised she possessed. They were all gone now, vanished in the face of the real world.

But even as she lost her idyll, she felt a new, hard-steeled sense of purpose she hadn't known since the end of the Lily Thief. There were treasures to save, and this time she was not alone in her mission. She had Edward.

Edward. She smiled just to think of his name. Months, even just weeks ago, she would have scoffed at the idea that they could work together and not against each other. That they could even see things from the same angle. Yet here they were, joining forces.

Oh, she knew very well he was still reluctant. She could see it in the troubled depths of his eyes, feel it in the tension of his embrace as they had kissed goodbye on the road into Santa Lucia. He still had his silly, wonderful chivalric ideas about ladies and their place, about keeping her safe. But he would see soon enough. Would see that she would not be kept in an ivory tower, or a cosy cottage.

It all hung on the safe recovery of that silver.

Clio gazed through her glass again, watching Thalia as she drew a shawl up over her robes against the breeze. For an instant, Clio saw her sister not as she was, a beautiful, wilful young lady of immense talent, but as she had once been. A golden little cherub, their mother's favourite, who toddled everywhere after Clio and Calliope, screaming to be allowed into their games.

Clio sympathised with Edward's driving desire to keep everyone safe. Thalia was her little sister, the loveliest of the Muses, but also, in many secret ways, the most vulnerable. It had always been her older sisters' task to protect her. How could Clio put her in danger now?

She nearly turned and fled, running home to hide all her secrets away from her family again. To come up with a new plan, one that put no one but herself in danger. Yet even as she glanced back over her shoulder to the open path, she knew she could not. Thalia would not take kindly to being 'protected', any more than Clio had. Thalia would want to be involved, and indeed was truly the best person for the task.

Clio had vowed to let the past go. Perhaps that included letting her sister grow up.

"'I have heard tell the sorrowful end of her, Niobe",' Thalia said, her voice strong, carrying on the wind. The resolute voice of the tragically principled Antigone. "'How strong shoots upgrown like ivy bonds enclosed her in the stone. With snows continuous and ceaseless rain her body melts away…likest to hers the bed my fate prepares".'

To Clio's surprise, another voice joined Thalia's, this one deep and resonant. Touched with the music of a Florentine accent. "'She was of godlike nature, and we are mortals, of human race. And it were glorious odds for maiden slain, among the equals of the gods in life—and in death—to gain a place".'

As Clio watched through her glass, she saw Marco appear from the stony wings. He and Thalia stood together against the brilliant glow of the sun, hands held out to each other, but not touching. Golden day and darkest night.

"'Ah me, unhappy!'" Thalia said. "'Home is none for me. Alike in life or death an exile must I be".'

"'Thou to the farthest verge forth-faring, o my child of daring",' Marco said. "'The cause is some ancestral load, which thou art bearing".'

Clio held her breath. She felt she was not watching Thalia and Marco at all, but ancient Greek figures, caught in unbearable, inescapable struggles. Dragged down by fate. No, she could not protect her sister, no matter how much she longed to. Not from anything. They were all bound by their own 'ancestral loads'.

She put away her glass, scrambling down from the rocks and hurrying along the path to the old agora and theatre. As she moved closer, she saw Thalia and Marco still stood together at the edge of the stage, not speaking, not touching, just gazing together out over the sunset-lit valley.

Perhaps it was her own heightened emotional state, the deep feelings of being with Edward, making love with him, but she sensed a new tension between Thalia and Marco. A shimmering, tenuous tie between them that made the very air taut.

'I still don't think you said it right,' Thalia said suddenly, snapping that tie in a shower of sparks.

'Of course I said it right!' Marco argued. 'You wanted more emotion in the words, and I gave you more emotion. Italians are good at that.'

'But now it is too much emotion,' Thalia insisted stubbornly.

'May the gods save me from obstinate Englishwomen!'

'And may the *goddess* save me from men who think they can act! Marco, I do believe that—Clio!' Thalia cried. She dashed to the edge of the stage, her script fluttering from her hands. She ran down the path to throw her arms around Clio, nearly knocking them both from their feet. 'Clio, you're here! You're alive.'

Clio laughed in surprise, patting Thalia's shoulder. 'Of course I am alive.'

'I was so worried.' Thalia drew back, her gaze sweeping over Clio as if to be sure of her wholeness. 'You're back very early.'

'I turned back before we reached Motya. There's too much work here for me to waste time sightseeing.' Clio glanced over Thalia's head at Marco, who had come to the edge of the stage and watched warily. 'I see you have been busy.'

'Marco, you mean?' Thalia said carelessly. She laughed, but Clio thought it was a tense sound, unlike

Thalia's usual exuberant chuckle. Her sister also wouldn't quite meet her gaze.

What was going on here?

'He has been helping me with the play,' Thalia said.

'Only the play?'

Thalia shrugged. 'He has also been working with Father at the villa. Father is most impressed with his knowledge of ancient architecture.'

'Well, I see you have *all* been busy while I was gone!'

'We had to do something to occupy ourselves. Lady Riverton hasn't been entertaining at all, and the Duke of Averton was gone. To Palermo, they say.' Thalia peered closely at her. 'Did you know about that? The Duke being gone, I mean.'

'I…' Clio instinctively opened her mouth to deny any knowledge of the Duke's whereabouts, but then she shook her head. Had she not determined to stop sheltering her sister? To stop lying, and admit when she needed help. Admit everything.

Almost everything, anyway.

'Actually, yes. I did know,' Clio said. She took Thalia's hand, turning with her back towards the stage. 'I need to talk to you and Marco about something important.'

'I can scarcely believe it!' Thalia exclaimed.

'It is indeed a strange tale,' Clio admitted. Her sister and Marco sat in rapt silence as she told her story, minus the personal bits in the cottage, of course. Now they burst into questions. 'Lady Riverton, the Duke asking for help…'

'Oh, no, Clio,' Thalia said. 'The wonder is that *you* ask for *my* help.'

'Why would I not? There is surely no one else who knows more about putting on theatricals.'

'That is true,' Marco agreed. 'She is a stern stage manager indeed. But how did the Duke come to suspect Lady Riverton in the first place?'

'Did *you* suspect her?' Clio asked him. 'Is she the reason you came here to Santa Lucia?'

Marco shrugged. 'I thought she might know something of the silver. Such a find would be very valuable, and there are rumours she has considerable debts. People say she was in Florence for a time, but had to leave in a great hurry.'

'Probably she owed her milliner,' Thalia said wryly. 'It will be a vast pleasure to help see her come to justice!'

'You will do it, then?' Clio asked.

'Certainly. I already have an idea for a scene we could use. But…'

'But what?'

Thalia glanced at Marco from the corner of her eye. 'Nothing. We should get home, Clio, before it grows even darker. Father will be surprised to see you.'

'You're right, of course. We can meet here tomorrow to finalise our plans.' Clio watched as Thalia gathered up the scattered pages of her script, her white skirts and red shawl fluttering in the breeze.

She noticed that Marco watched, too, his dark eyes solemn as they followed Thalia's pretty figure.

'If you hurt her in any way,' she whispered fiercely in his ear, 'I shall make you very sorry.'

Marco gave a startled laugh. '*Cara*, when it comes to your sister I think the one you should worry about is *me*.'

'I mean it, Marco. Thalia likes to flirt, but she has a

good, kind heart, and she cares so deeply. She's not like you, with your great causes and sacrifices.'

'What makes you think I do not care deeply? I can see the worth of a person, Clio, just as well as I see the value of an Etruscan vase.' He pushed himself to his feet, stalking over to help Thalia gather her papers.

Clio stared after them, feeling suddenly dizzy. A lot *had* happened in the short time she had been gone, in the world around her as well as in her very own heart.

Whatever would she find at home? Her father married? Cory betrothed? She shuddered to think of it all.

Chapter Twenty-Eight

Clio leaned out of her open bedroom window, gazing out over the burnt-red rooftops and white church spire of Santa Lucia. Everything was blanketed in the usual dusty purple-black of Sicilian night, as quiet as ever. No one was betrothed or married, after all, yet something had definitely changed. A new tension in the air, a feeling of waiting, watching for something. She did not yet know what that *something* would be, what would happen tomorrow or the next day. When the peace would be shattered.

Perhaps it was not the town that had changed, she thought, but her. Maybe her too-short days with Edward had altered everything she saw and did.

She drew in a deep breath of the clear, cool air, curling her hands tightly on the windowsill. Before, when she had become the Lily Thief, she had felt no fear. Nervousness, of course, that tight fluttering inside whenever she broke into a library or gallery. Yet never cold fear, like the sense that came over her now. She had much to lose before; now she had everything. She had Edward.

Well, she did not *have* him exactly, she thought with a laugh. He wasn't a statue or ivory box she could tuck safely away, much as she might want to. But he was her lover, her other half, and she knew so well that the work he did was dangerous. He faced people who were ruthless in their pursuit of riches. They would not let art, history, or even human life stand in their way.

She could see now why he had lied to her, why he had tried to lock her up to keep her out of harm's way. To risk one's own life was easy. To see a loved one leap off that cliff was quite a different matter.

And she found that she hated that worried feeling, that cold pit in her stomach. It gnawed at her, making her feel so tense she feared she might jump out of her skin at any sudden noise. At dinner, it had taken all of her willpower just to sit in her chair and listen to her father talk. To look at Cory's new sketches, and pretend all was well. All was the same as it had ever been.

Was this love, then? This deep craving, this hollow feeling when he was out of her sight? Was this what her father and mother had felt all those years, what Calliope and Cameron felt? If so, how did they ever survive?

How would *she* survive?

'Oh, Edward,' she whispered. 'What are you doing to me?'

As she stared out at the street beyond, she noticed a shift of movement, a ripple in the shadows. She straightened, reaching for the nearby table where she had left her dagger. That tension inside her grew and expanded, until she feared she would snap and go shooting off into the night.

She tucked the blade close to her, hidden in the folds of her silk skirt as she peered closer to the shadows. That movement slowly coalesced into a tall, cloaked figure. A thief? Or one of the cursed spirits?

'Clio,' she heard a voice call. A voice as familiar now as her own.

'Edward!' she answered. Her fingers loosened on the dagger's hilt. She had to smile despite her fear, her taut apprehension. Surely all would be well, if they faced the unseen foe together. 'What are you sneaking about like that for?'

He stepped closer to the wall beneath her window, shaking back his hood. The lamplight fell across the tumble of his bright hair, making it shimmer. 'I thought your father might not appreciate me calling after midnight.'

Clio laughed. 'Perhaps not. He does seem to like you, but he also likes his rest. Stay there, I will come down.'

She caught up a black shawl, wrapping it over her head and shoulders before she dashed down the stairs. The house was dark and quiet, except for the soft sound of the piano from behind the closed drawing-room door. Thalia was still awake, too, pouring out her own hidden emotions in Beethoven.

Clio slipped out of the front door, running around to the side of the house where she had seen Edward. He was not there, though, the garden seemingly empty.

Had she just imagined him, then? She spun around, scanning the darkness. Suddenly, a strong arm caught her around the waist, dragging her close to the wall. Her startled cry was buried in a hot, hard kiss. Edward's kiss.

She seized him by the shoulders, holding on to him tightly as she returned that kiss with a desperation of her own. They clung to each other as if it had been a year and not just a day they had been parted for.

'I've missed you,' he said roughly.

'I missed you, too,' she whispered. 'And I miss our cottage. My bed here looks so big and cold…'

He groaned. 'Don't remind me! I should have kept you my captive even longer.'

'But you couldn't, I know. While we basked in our grotto for weeks and months, the villains would certainly escape.' She pressed one more kiss, a soft, alluring caress, to his lips. 'Once the silver is found, feel free to kidnap me any time you like.'

'I will be sure to remind you of that offer later,' he said, laughing. 'Did you speak to your sister, then?'

'Yes, and, just as I suspected, she is up for any mischief. She and Marco will help us. I'll send out invitations to our own little theatrical evening tomorrow. Everyone will surely want to be there, as Thalia tells me Lady Riverton is not entertaining so much now.'

'Everyone?'

'The Elliotts, the Manning-Smythes. All the English visitors. Rosa and her vast family. And Lady Riverton and her faithful Mr Frobisher, of course. We will make it the event of the Season. With a fabulous finale, of course.'

'Not as fabulous as *this*, I hope,' he muttered, kissing her again.

'Hmm,' Clio moaned, arching into his body. 'Nothing could be as wonderful as this.'

'Then let's go back to the cottage,' he said, taking her by the hand and tugging her teasingly toward the gate. 'Right now. We'll hide in bed until this is all over.'

She laughed, shaking her head. 'I would run back to our cottage in a moment, Edward. But none of this can be over without us. We have to finish it, find the silver.'

'Oh, my dear, how sadly, sensibly right you are.'

'I'm always right.' Except when it came to him, of course. There she had been terribly, wonderfully wrong. 'Almost always.'

'I shall have to remember that.' He took her other hand, gazing at her with that steady stare that always seemed to see everything. 'What about after?'

'After we find the silver? I don't…'

'Will you come to the cottage then?' His voice was suddenly serious, deeply so. Clio tensed, yet did not pull away. She couldn't run, not any more. No matter how much she wanted to.

She tried to laugh. 'Why, your Grace. Are you propositioning me? Shocking.'

'I'm asking you to marry me.'

Clio didn't know what she had expected him to say, but it was surely not that. She shouldn't be surprised; all he had told her in the last few days, all she had discovered, made her know he was a changed man. A man with his own sort of honour. They had made love, she was supposed to be a well-born lady, therefore he thought he should marry her.

As she stared at him in the moonlight, at his beautiful, solemn, scarred face, she felt a deep yearning unlike any she had ever known before. A longing to be permanently joined with this man, her other half.

But—but she did not want him like this, she found. Obligated and honourable.

'I would make a terrible duchess,' she said, trying to be light despite the tightness of her throat.

'You couldn't possibly be a worse duchess than I am a duke,' he answered. He held to her hands, not letting her run from him and the inescapable behemoth of the future. 'Yet I have found that dukes are given great indulgence for their eccentricities.'

'Like swimming naked?'

'Like doing whatever we—you and I—like.'

'Edward, I just—I can't think about that now. My mind is too full of the silver, the play, everything.'

He nodded. 'I understand, my dear. I'll give you time. But after this is over, I will come back and ask you again. And I will keep asking, until we are both old and grey, if need be.' He kissed her hands, and let her go to melt back into the night. 'Think about it, Clio. That is all I ask.'

'Yes. I will think about it.' As if she could think about anything else now! She stood there for a long time after he left, leaning against the wall with her shawl drawn up against the wind. Yet she did not feel the chill, or even see the darkness that wrapped around her. She heard only his words, echoing over and over in her mind. *Marry me.*

Yet how could she? How could the magic of their time here, the ancient enchantment of Sicily, ever translate to England? To the reality of their lives there, especially Edward's with his vast myriad of responsibilities.

She would surely end by disappointing him. And that she could not bear.

Clio shook her head, pressing her hands to her aching temples. 'Don't think of that now,' she ordered herself sternly. 'Think of your work here. That is all that matters right now.'

The rest of it—well, it would surely be waiting for her later. Unless Edward changed his mind.

'Clio? Is that you talking to yourself out here?' she heard Thalia say.

Clio quickly wiped at her damp eyes, pasting a smile on her lips before she turned. Thalia was leaning out of an open drawing-room window, still dressed in her pale blue muslin dinner gown, an Indian shawl tossed over her shoulders. Her gaze was curious, and very concerned.

'Are you quite well, Clio?' she asked.

'Of course,' Clio answered. She sounded far too cheerful, even to her own ears. 'I just needed some fresh air.'

Thalia didn't look convinced. She climbed straight out of the window, tugging her skirts impatiently behind her, and hurried over to Clio's side. She didn't say anything, just leaned against the wall next to her. But Clio was suddenly glad of her presence, her silent sympathy.

'You are up late, too,' Clio said.

'I couldn't stop thinking about our scheme. Playing the piano helps me sort out my thoughts, work out the play in my head. I thought I heard voices out here.'

Clio smiled. 'So, of course you had to investigate yourself. No time for summoning the footmen or anything like that.'

'The servants have already retired! Why should I disturb them just because my sister takes it into her head to wander about the garden talking to herself?'

'I suppose we are neither of us behaving as we ought.'

'Do we ever?'

'No. Especially since Calliope left.' Clio paused. 'You have been spending a great deal of time with the Count lately?'

Thalia shrugged, not quite meeting Clio's gaze. 'Not a *great* deal. We have met once or twice, and he kindly offered to help me with *Antigone*. You were gone, so he had to make do with the second-best Chase.' She added in a soft, barely audible voice, 'As usual.'

'Thalia,' Clio said warningly. 'I'm not certain the Count is someone you ought to—'

'Oh, Clio!' Thalia waved away all warnings with a laugh. 'I am not like Susan Darby, I won't lose all signs of intelligence at the sight of a handsome man. I know what Marco di Fabrizzi is. He's fun to flirt with, of course, and an excellent co-conspirator in our little scheme. But I won't take him seriously. I probably won't even see him again when we leave here.'

Clio had seen the way Marco looked at Thalia, and she was not so sure of that 'never see him again' business. But she knew when Thalia was set against discussing something, and her sister had that mulish look in her eyes now. So, Clio merely nodded.

'I am more worried about you and the Duke of Averton,' Thalia said.

'The Duke? Whatever do you mean?' Clio said. But she was not quite as good an actress as Thalia, and she found her bright, innocent tone fooled no one.

'I mean he is working on finding this lost silver, too, is he not? You must have met him recently, become friends even, if he has taken to confiding in you. Asking for your help.'

Clio tugged her shawl closer around her. 'He knows how much the Chases care about antiquities.'

'Hmm, yes. He could hardly miss that little fact, I think. But you two have always quarrelled in the past! And he is so—so strange.'

Clio could hardly argue with that. Edward *was* strange. He was like no one else she had ever known.

'Sometimes we have to put aside past differences for the good of the future,' she said weakly.

'That is very good, Clio. You should write it down,' Thalia said. 'Speaking of writing, I must go begin work on our new play. It will be ready to start rehearsal day after tomorrow, I promise.'

'It will be suitably Gothic, I hope.'

'Of course. Thunder, lightning, quite horrid. Our friend Lotty would love it.' Thalia turned back to her window, eschewing doors. Before she climbed back inside, she glanced back over her shoulder and said, 'Don't stay out talking to yourself all night. It's turning cold.'

'I won't.' As Clio gazed up at the hazy stars, she reflected that even when she felt alone, she never truly was. Someone, somewhere, was always watching. Knowing.

Once, that feeling would have frightened her, made her angry. Now—well, now it was strangely comforting. She was no longer alone in her work, but then neither was she alone in the danger of it. There was Edward, and Thalia and Marco. And *that* knowledge made her shiver more than any cold night wind ever could.

Edward lingered in the shadows just beyond Clio's gates, watching as she talked to her sister. Making certain she went safely back inside.

For was that not what he must do now? Make sure Clio was always safe. That she came to no harm, both here in Sicily and…

And always.

When he had come to Santa Lucia at the request of the Antiquities Society, come to find the elusive altar silver, that was his one goal. All he could see, think about. The presence of Clio Chase was a distraction, a danger. But then, slowly but certainly, it became something else entirely. Something deeper, richer—stranger. She became a partner in his task.

A partner in his life. She said she would make a terrible duchess. But she was wrong.

He watched Clio follow her sister into the house, the windows and doors closed firmly behind them and the lights flickering out one by one. Only then did he turn towards his own house, towards the work that waited for him.

When he had kidnapped Clio, he had wanted only to keep her out of the way, safe, until everything here was finished. He should have known better, of course. Clio was like no other woman he had ever met. Her fierce intelligence, her steadfast independence—the determination that led to the Lily Thief—would always be there. She could not stay quietly at home when action was needed over a cause she believed in, no more than he could. And that was why he had come to love her so very much.

Edward stopped just outside his house, suddenly astonished. Not that he loved Clio, but that it had taken him so long, so many turns, to admit it. He *loved* her! Loved everything about her, even the stubbornness that drove him to madness. She was his other half. His helpmeet. His duchess, whether she believed it or not.

There was just nothing else for it. She would have to marry him, even if she continued to protest. Honour demanded it, after what had happened between them in the cottage. And love…

Love demanded it, too. She would surely come to see that, just as he had.

They *would* be wed, the moment danger was past. And he would keep her safe.

Chapter Twenty-Nine

Clio peered out from behind a screen, hastily erected at the back of the amphitheatre stage to provide effects for their play. The theatricals hadn't begun yet; the audience was just arriving, trickling to their places on cushions scattered about on the stone benches. The sun was setting over the valley, illuminating their fine clothes, the silken gowns of the English ladies, Rosa and her Santa Lucia friends in their best black dresses. They all seemed to be talking and laughing as if it was a normal evening out. No one suspected anything.

'Is everyone here?' Thalia asked.

Clio glanced back, and smiled at her sister. Thalia wore her costume, a fanciful creation of cheesecloth and white muslin. The ragged hem and the ends of the draped sleeves were tinted pale silver, a colour that would catch the flickering lamplight and glow with an otherworldly illumination. She did not yet wear her headdress, and her golden hair fell loose over her shoulders.

Thalia didn't seem nervous at all, Clio thought. In

fact, she seemed far calmer than usual, her blue eyes serene as she mouthed her lines one last time.

Clio, on the other hand, felt all alight with nerves. The anticipation, the calm before the theatrical storm, vibrated all through her. They had had to prepare everything so hastily, she wasn't sure any of it would work. What would become of the silver, of all of them, then?

And what, oh, *what*, would she say to Edward's proposal? That was the greatest uncertainty of all.

She pressed her hand tight to her fluttering, aching stomach. 'No, not everyone is here yet,' she answered Thalia. 'Mr Frobisher and Lady Riverton are nowhere to be seen.'

She peered again past the screen, and saw that Giacomo was not yet there, either. There were a few men from the village she had heard might be involved in a bit of recreational pottery hunting. But Rosa sat with just Paolo, a couple of their daughters and some grandchildren, and a few of her friends. The children scampered up and down the tiered stone steps, scandalising the English guests with their playful shouts. Sir Walter sat with Cory and Lady Rushworth in the front row, where Clio could keep an eye on them.

'Never mind. We still have lots of time before curtain. I'm sure they'll arrive at any moment,' Thalia said. 'Come and help me finish getting ready?'

'Of course.'

Thalia had set up a small mirror in the corner, with a table scattered with an array of brushes, hairpins and theatrical maquillage. Clio had no idea where Thalia had procured those strange little pots and bottles. Probably she had broken in backstage at Drury Lane one night and insisted some hapless actress sell them to her.

'Here,' Thalia said, handing Clio a pot of what appeared to be chalk and a little brush. 'Sweep this over my forehead and cheeks, like so. It will give me a wonderful pallor. I'll look quite dead.'

Clio shuddered, spilling some of the white stuff on the table. 'Don't say such things, Thalia.'

'Clio! Never say you have become superstitious, too.'

'No sense in taking chances.'

'Well, let's hope your *tombaroli* are of the same opinion. No one wants to anger the spirits.' Thalia turned her face up to the fading light, holding still as Clio dusted a thick wash over her skin. The roses-and-cream complexion quickly turned to ashes.

'What is this stuff, anyway?' Clio asked. 'It's quite good.'

'Isn't it? I heard Mrs Thompson uses it at Covent Garden whenever she plays a spectre. I have some lip salve, too.' Thalia reached for a tiny bottle, rubbing a bit of grey over her lips. 'Do I look frightening?'

'Terribly,' Clio said truthfully. She longed to scrub away every bit of the grey and white from her sister's pretty face, to make her alive again, but Thalia spun away from her. She stood before the mirror, fitting on her headdress of more cheesecloth and white feathers.

'Don't worry, Clio,' she said. 'Everything will go perfectly. You won't be sorry you asked for my help.'

'Of course I won't. If anyone could scare the truth out of Lady Riverton and her thieves, it's you. Just promise me you'll be careful.'

'Certainly she will be careful,' Marco interrupted. 'She will be with me, won't she?'

Clio turned to find him emerging from his own

'dressing room' behind yet more screens. He wore the costume of a peasant shepherd, rough russet-coloured wool breeches and waistcoat, a cap on his raven hair. He carried the 'cursed object' his character stole from a tomb, a fake Etruscan vase painted with the large letters 'Belonging To The Gods'. Just like the inscription on the silver.

Thalia rolled her eyes, but Clio could see the shadow of a smile on her grey lips. 'I can take care of myself, thank you very much.'

Clio could tell that Marco longed to argue. Honestly, every time she saw those two together they were arguing! They seemed to take a strange delight in it. But there was no time now. She held up her hand, forestalling any quarrelsome words, and said, 'Go practise your lines, both of you. It's almost dark.'

She peeked around the screen again. The amphitheatre was filling up, as it had not since ancient days, and Giacomo was now with his family, fidgeting in his seat as he glanced nervously around. Ronald Frobisher was also there, holding his little court with the friends who always gathered around him and Lady Riverton. But of the lady herself, there was no sign.

Clio's gaze swung over the audience. Servants were lighting the torches along the stone steps, and the lamps on the stage that served as footlights flickered in the soft breeze. The glow illuminated laughing faces, the sparkle of jewels.

Along the very top row of seats, half-hidden in the darkness so far from the torches, she glimpsed Edward's bright hair. He, too, surveyed the crowd, tense and watchful.

Reassured by his presence, Clio turned back to

Marco and Thalia. 'I think it's time,' she said. 'If we wait too long the audience will become restless.'

'And perhaps throw rotten fruit at us,' Thalia said. 'That would quite spoil the mood, I fear.'

Clio smoothed the skirt of her amber-coloured muslin gown one more time, before she slipped around the screen and stepped to the edge of the stage. As she held up her hands, the audience shifted into expectant silence.

'Good evening, everyone, and thank you so much for being here on such short notice,' she announced, gaining new strength and confidence from knowing Edward was out there beyond the blinding lights. That soon this would be over, and they would have the truth at last.

'As you know, my sister Miss Thalia Chase is very talented at amateur theatricals,' Clio went on. 'What you may not know is that she is also a playwright. We have not before been able to persuade her to share her work, but she has been so inspired by this beautiful place that we were able to convince her to perform this little scene. Because we know that you, too, love Santa Lucia and its intriguing history.'

Clio stepped a bit closer to the lights. 'My sister's tale is based on stories she has heard, *true* stories of a violent past, brave deeds and hidden treasures. Long ago, this Greek settlement was invaded by a Roman army, which laid all to waste and enslaved the people. What had been a prosperous, idyllic town, with a marketplace, baths, theatres and fine villas, was ruined.

'But a few people managed to flee. They left behind them beautiful objects, sacred things. They did not, however, leave them unprotected…'

Clio stepped back behind the screen as Marco took

his place on stage. He began the tale of the shepherd who finds a vase buried behind the walls of a ruined Greek farmhouse, and determines to steal it. Thalia waited in the wings, a truly fearsome sight in her make-up and draperies.

Clio stood where she could continue to watch the audience unobserved. Was Giacomo shifting even more nervously in his seat? Was Frobisher looking guilty? And where was Lady Riverton, the centre of it all?

Yet there was no time to worry now. Action was needed. The plan was in motion. As Thalia glided on to the stage, her arms raised as she crept up behind Marco, Clio reached for her own costume. It was made of cheesecloth and muslin like Thalia's, and with a deep hood to hide behind.

Once covered, she crept out through a hole in the back wall of the amphitheatre, dashing up the hillside and around to where the main entrance led to the old agora. From there, she could peer down on all the activity with her spyglass.

Thalia was cursing Marco quite enthusiastically for taking that which belonged to the gods, the vase that had been buried so long ago and ringed round with spells to keep it safe. Marco's tormented screams were all too convincing, quite terrifying really. Clio wondered if Thalia had pinched him under her draperies. The audience members either looked on in wide-eyed, delicious horror, or giggled nervously. Frobisher peered back over his shoulder, a handkerchief wound tightly in his hand.

And Clio found she was, strangely enough, rather enjoying herself.

As Marco's torment went on, she was so caught up

in the scene that she almost missed what she had been waiting for. Giacomo emerged from the theatre, glancing frantically both ways through the deserted old marketplace. His brow glistened nervously in the moonlight. As he took off running toward the ruins of the temple, Clio followed, glad of all the recent hill-walking that made her sure-footed and fast on the bumpy pathways. *And* glad of the fact that Giacomo's fear seemed to make him clumsy, unsure of his direction.

She scrambled up atop a large boulder that lay by his meandering path, and held her arms up. The breeze stirred her draped sleeves in a gratifyingly eerie manner.

'Halt! Thief!' she cried, in as deep a voice as she could summon. 'You have stolen what belongs to the gods.'

Distracted and frightened by her shout, Giacomo stumbled just long enough for Edward to tackle him from the shadows. The timing on this part of the plan, on the entire plan really, was so delicately balanced. But this bit came off just right. Clio watched in satisfaction as Edward leaped up, dragging Giacomo to his feet and holding him fast even as Giacomo struggled desperately to escape.

Clio clambered down from her perch, crouching behind the boulder to keep a watch on the distant theatre entrance. Surely the other players would soon make their appearance, if all went well.

And if Giacomo's thieving cohorts didn't interfere.

She pressed her palm to her leg, feeling the reassuring weight of the dagger strapped there beneath the muslin and cheesecloth.

'It's very rude to leave the theatre before the final curtain,' Edward said calmly, almost conversationally.

Clio peeked around the rough corner of the boulder to see him holding the frantically twisting Giacomo as if the thief was naught but a rag doll.

Surely no one would recognise the indolent Duke of 'Avarice' now!

'Why were you running?' Edward said. 'Did Miss Thalia's play strike a chord with you, perhaps? Remind you of some previous obligation?'

Giacomo babbled something in quick, rough Italian. Clio couldn't catch it all, something about warnings and how he had 'told them' it was not safe. She could hear the raw edge of cold fear, though. The panicked sense of the line between reality and dream blurred.

Good. Maybe it would keep him away from tomb-robbing in the future, and reassure Rosa at last. But in the meantime they still had to find the silver. And stay out of danger themselves.

'I know you found part of that silver hoard,' Edward said, also in Italian. 'Did you find the rest? Where is it?'

'The altar set, *sí*. We found it.'

'And sold it?' Edward said, his voice tight with fury. Clio certainly did not envy Giacomo his current predicament. 'Illegally?'

'I should not have! I know the legend, the curse. My mother warned me…'

'But ancient ghosts were nothing to modern coin, eh?'

'It said it belonged to the gods, and I should have listened! Like the Count.'

'Count di Fabrizzi? Is he part of this?'

Clio tensed as she waited for the answer.

'No, no,' Giacomo said. 'He knew better. You saw him tonight.'

'Then who did pay you?' Edward demanded. 'Who is your English customer? Frobisher?'

'Of course. He is the one who first approached us. Yet the money does not come from him. He's hired, just as we are. He pretends he is not, but we all know the truth.'

'Lady Riverton,' Edward said slowly. 'She is the one who hires you and Frobisher, then, just as we suspected.'

Before Giacomo could answer, could give them the confirmation they sought, Clio saw Ronald Frobisher himself emerge from the theatre. The play was not yet over; she could hear the echo of Thalia's voice. Yet Frobisher seemed intent on his own errand, hurrying toward the pathway to Santa Lucia. He didn't run or babble, like poor, frightened Giacomo, but he was obviously in a great rush all the same.

Clio cast off her robes, shoving them into a crevice at the base of the boulder before she darted out and grabbed Edward's arm.

'There he is,' she urged him. 'We have to go!'

Edward nodded brusquely. He let go of Giacomo, who sank to the ground with his hands over his face.

'Shame on you, Giacomo!' Clio shouted back at him, as she and Edward ran off after Frobisher. 'What would your parents say?'

'And what would *your* parent say, my dear, if he could see you now?' Edward said. She marvelled that he could go from menacing to teasing in an instant. She was so very excited she was sure she would scream at any moment! 'Running off with a man into the night?'

'He would say we have to save the antiquities, of course. He *is* Sir Walter Chase. Now *hurry*!'

They ran up the path, trying to keep Ronald Frobisher in sight, but he was surprisingly quick for someone who professed complete indolence. Clio's lungs burned, her legs ached, yet she did not slow down. She held tightly to Edward's hand as they dashed through the village gates into Santa Lucia.

The town was quiet, as almost everyone was gathered at the theatre. The evening breeze blew clouds of dust across the square, bits of paper and leaves over the cathedral steps. Frobisher was nowhere to be seen.

'Have we lost him?' Clio panted, dismayed.

'I'm sure we can guess where he's gone,' Edward answered.

'Lady Riverton's palazzo?'

'Where else? I have a guard on his lodgings, though, just in case.' He squeezed her hand, leading her down the street toward the grand palazzos. 'Well, my dear, shall we pay a call on Lady Riverton? A rather unorthodox hour, I know.'

'Somehow, I think we will be expected anyway.'

The house, like the rest of Santa Lucia, was quiet and dark. No sound escaped from the shuttered windows. Without the life and noise of one of her parties, it seemed a gloomy and ominous place. Clio half-expected to see more ghosts, flitting in and out on their ethereal, sinister errands.

'Servants' entrance, I think,' Edward said, as they studied the courtyard. 'Those doors are usually unlocked, and people like Lady Riverton don't think of securing belowstairs.'

They found the servants' door at the side of the palazzo, down a short flight of steps. Clio cracked open the door and peered carefully inside, in case some stray footman or maid was not enjoying their evening off at the play. It was as silent as the rest of the house, though, the stone floors cold with no fire in the kitchen grate.

Hand in hand, they hurried up the steep stairs and through a doorway into Lady Riverton's realm. They stood there for a moment, Clio hardly daring to breathe as she listened for any sound at all. Any clue as to where Frobisher might have gone.

Then, at last, it came. A faint, faraway crash. They immediately followed it, running along a corridor and down more steps to the grand drawing room.

It was far from the lavish, welcoming space where Clio had sipped tea and applauded Thalia's *Antigone*. Only one branch of candles was lit, perched on the marble fireplace mantel and casting a circle of light that didn't reach the corners and high ceilings. But Clio's eyes were used to the dimness now, and she quickly saw Ronald Frobisher.

He stood by a table, its hinged top hanging open, broken and fallen on its side. The large, velvet-upholstered chair Lady Riverton had used to preside over her gatherings also lay toppled on the floor. Its rich cushions were viciously torn open, no doubt by the wickedly sharp dagger now in Frobisher's hand.

He swung toward them, the blade held aloft. 'Don't come any closer!' he shouted. All signs of the foppish, fawning Frobisher had vanished. His entire being fairly vibrated with anger and desperation.

For the first time, Clio thought he might really be descended from the Elizabethan pirate. She reached slowly for a fold of her skirt, ready to draw it up and pull out her own dagger.

But Edward clasped her arm, pushing her partly behind him so that he alone faced that blade.

'We only want to find Lady Riverton,' Edward said slowly, softly. 'We know that she is the one behind this whole scheme.'

Frobisher laughed bitterly. He gave the fallen table a venomous kick. 'I would certainly like to *talk* to her myself. But she isn't here. She's gone.'

'Gone?' Clio said sharply. 'To the theatre?'

'She sent me to your ridiculous play, told me she would meet me there. But she's taken her jewels and several of those wretched bonnets,' Frobisher answered. 'So, I dare say she has gone somewhere rather further away. The *witch*! She said we were partners, she promised me…'

'Promised you what?' Clio said, peering over Edward's tense shoulder.

For a moment, Frobisher was mutinously silent. But then he shook his head, and said, 'I might as well tell you now. She's gone, and I will be the one who pays. She said we would take that silver and go away together, to Naples or Rome. There would be plenty of money then, an easy life for both of us. "Just help me, Ronald," she said. "You're my only friend." And I believed her. Fool!' He kicked again at the poor table, reducing one carved wooden leg to splinters.

Clio nearly kicked out herself, in sheer frustration. Why had she not thought of that, of Lady Riverton fleeing while they were all distracted by their own scheme? She should have set someone to watching this house days ago.

'Now she is gone, and left me nothing but this,' Frobisher growled. He held up a small silver bowl, the twin of Edward's with its fine etchings and embossing, but more battered, its edges dented. 'She took all the rest: the incense burner, the ladles, the other bowls. The *witch*! I hope she burns in hell, I hope…'

Clio watched, appalled, as he raised the bowl above his head, prepared to dash it to the marble floor. She cried out, breaking away from Edward and lunging towards Frobisher, grasping for the precious bowl. All they had left now. She caught it, falling into Frobisher and knocking him back against the wall. His arm came down, the dagger in his hand nicking her in the shoulder.

But she barely felt the sting as she crashed to the floor, clutching the bowl tightly in her numb hand.

Then the pain flooded down her arm, her whole side. She stared down at her torn sleeve, the blood on her shoulder, in hazy shock. She barely heard Edward's frantic shout, the clatter of Frobisher's boots as he fled. She felt Edward's strong arms around her, helping her sit up.

'Clio,' he cried, his voice full of fear and panic. Strange—she hadn't known Edward *could* be afraid. 'Clio, darling, don't faint. Stay with me.'

'Did he open a vein, then? Am I going to bleed to death?' she murmured. She felt the sticky, warm, disgusting trickle of blood along her arm. Her head swam, and she could barely focus on his face above her. Who knew she, the Lily Thief, was afraid of blood?

'Never,' he answered. She heard a ripping noise, then he wrapped a length of soft linen around her shoulder. He had removed his coat and torn a piece of his shirt hem off for a makeshift bandage. 'I won't let you.'

'I've never been wounded before,' she said, bemused.

'Then you are profoundly fortunate, with the damn foolish risks you take,' he said fiercely, tying off the end of the linen. 'What possessed you to leap at a man holding a knife?'

'I was afraid he would damage the bowl. It's all we have now, to help us find the rest.' She gazed down at the bowl in her lap. So tiny to cause so much trouble. 'But he'll get away! What if he *does* know where Lady Riverton and the rest of the hoard is?'

'He won't get far, don't worry.' Edward cradled her gently in his arms, rocking her gently as the sting faded and she felt only weary. Weary—and safe, with him. 'We have to get you home, where you can be nursed properly.'

'And where you can lock me up so I don't get into any more trouble.'

He laughed, and kissed the top of her head. 'My dear, I don't think there are any locks strong enough.'

'But the silver is gone!'

'Clio.' Edward drew back, gazing down solemnly into her eyes. For that moment, there was only the two of them. 'Don't you know? I would never, ever leave you bleeding on the floor to chase after any criminal, any antiquity. I would never leave you at all.'

Clio curled against his chest, inordinately content. She should not be—Frobisher, Lady Riverton and the silver were gone. She was wounded, lying on a cold floor in an abandoned house. But she was wildly happy.

Edward would not leave her. And, for that night, that was all she ever wanted.

Chapter Thirty

'I vow, England is going to be dull after all this!' Thalia declared. Clio sat with her on their terrace, sipping tea and enjoying the sunny afternoon with her arm bound up in a sling.

She stared out over the garden, at the bright spring green turning dry at the edges. Soon it would be summer, and the intense southern sun would blast everything to brown. Days would grow long, drowsing in the heat. But they wouldn't be here to see it.

'I fear you're right,' Clio said. 'Our work here is almost done. Even Father thinks so.' At breakfast that morning, Sir Walter, appalled that his own daughter had been set upon by 'footpads' walking home after the play, declared that they would head to Geneva for the summer. 'But we can look forward to boating on the lake, and perhaps a spot of mountain climbing in Switzerland.'

'Mountain climbing!' Thalia pulled a face. 'That's all right for you, you're half-mountain goat anyway. But what will I do?'

'You could write a new play. An Italian tale of angry gods, stolen jewels…'

'And valiant heroines, wounded as they try to defeat the villains?' Thalia gently adjusted the shawl over Clio's shoulders, careful of the sling.

Clio laughed. 'Your heroine will have to be far braver than to fall apart at a mere scratch. She will have to be *truly* wounded.'

'It is hardly a "mere scratch"! The bleeding would have been quite dangerous if not for the Duke's quick thinking.'

Clio sipped at her tea, remembering last night's haze of pain and confusion. Remembering Edward tearing his own shirt to make a bandage, carrying her home through the night. *I would never leave you*, he had said, and last night she believed him.

'Will there be a hero in your story?' she asked.

'Of course. And a romance. A play must have a romance. Passion and devotion that surmounts all danger, even death itself,' said Thalia.

Clio smiled at her. Thalia's blue eyes gleamed with the birth of a new tale. 'A dark Italian count in disguise?'

'Or an English nobleman with a secret errand! He has been in love with the heroine for years, of course…'

'Yet she, the stubborn chit, has never seen it before.'

'Not until he saves her life, sacrificing that secret errand to do so. Because love is more important.' Thalia nodded decisively. 'You catch on to this storytelling business, I see.'

'Love, danger, sacrifice, all the required elements.'

'Perhaps I will add in some gypsies who steal the cursed object. Bits with gypsies are in all the best plays.'

'Oh, yes. Though I don't recall any gypsies in *Antigone*.'

'The only thing it was missing, I assure you.' Thalia drew a notebook from her workbox and started scribbling away.

As Clio settled back in her chair, Rosa came out bearing fresh tea and a plate of cakes. She didn't say anything, didn't even look at Clio, but she tenderly tucked a blanket over her knees before gathering up the old tea things.

'How is Giacomo today, Rosa?' Clio asked quietly.

'Well enough, *signorina*. He sometimes suffers from nightmares, ever since he was a baby, and he was up with a very bad one last night.'

'I hope there is something that can be done about these—nightmares.'

'*Sí, sí.* He is going to stay with my brother in Palermo, who owns a grocer's shop. We have been trying to persuade Giacomo to learn the trade for years, and now at last he has agreed.'

'I'm sure he will do well there.'

Rosa nodded. 'Don't sit out here too long, *signorina*. You need to rest,' she said, bustling back into the house.

Clio turned back to the garden, to the endless expanse of blue sky. At least someone had found a new beginning out of all this. All she seemed to have was more questions.

Thalia lowered her notebook to her lap. 'I just don't know what will happen at the end.'

'I fear a play's audience would be most unhappy if the tale ends with "who knows what will happen"!'

'True. The actors would likely be pelted with rotten fruit.'

'They have to rescue the treasure, of course.'

Unlike in real life. All they had were two small bowls, and the rest was who knew where with Lady Riverton. 'And love? Will it triumph?'

'It depends. Do I write a comedy or a tragedy? And that reminds me…' Thalia drew a folded letter from inside her notebook. 'This came for us this morning, from Marco. In the excitement over your arm, I almost forgot.'

'What does it say?' Clio. asked. 'Does the Count declare his most tender feelings for you?'

'Don't be silly,' Thalia said, shoving the note into Clio's hand. 'We have no tender feelings, only quarrels. Remember? He says he is leaving, going to Pisa to search for Lady Riverton. It seems he visited Mr Frobisher in the Santa Lucia gaol and discovered that was her first destination. Why would she go to Pisa, of all places? If I was trying to hide a stolen treasure, I would go to Russia. Or maybe India. Somewhere very far away.'

'Why does anyone go anywhere?' Clio muttered. 'I would wager that sooner or later Lady Riverton will wash up on England's shores. And Marco will end up chasing her across the whole continent.'

'How very exciting, to go dashing across Europe on a gallant errand!'

'Indeed.' Clio felt a sharp pang that she, too, could not just dash off after the silver. That she had to stay home while the treasure retreated further and further away.

But then she looked at Thalia, and thought of Cory and their father, Calliope and Cameron, all their little sisters in England. Of everyone she loved. Edward had let Frobisher flee while he stayed with *her*, had declared that she was always more important than any antiquity. She could not do any less. Her family needed her, and she needed them. She would stay with them all, and let Marco do the dashing into danger.

For now.

But would Edward go after the silver, too? Would she lose him when she lost this place?

'But Switzerland will be interesting, too,' Thalia said reassuringly, as if she sensed Clio's melancholy. 'Lots more adventures wait for us there, I'm sure.'

Clio smiled at her, her heart still aching. It was time to begin a new chapter, yet she wasn't sure how. So much had happened here in Santa Lucia, so much had changed. *She* had changed, in ways she couldn't yet understand. It was as if the old Clio had been washed away in Demeter's grotto, been newborn in Edward's kiss. How did this new Clio move forwards?

'Signorina Clio,' a footman said, coming out on the terrace. 'There is a package for you.'

'A letter *and* a package in one day?' Clio said with a laugh. 'We are certainly popular. Thank you, you can bring it out here.'

'I fear it may be too large to fit through the door, *signorina*.'

'Too large?' Curious, Clio tossed back the blankets and shawls and hurried into the house, Thalia close on her heels.

In the foyer stood a massive parcel, thickly wrapped and bound until it was shapeless. The servants all stood about and stared, just as bemused as she was.

'It can't be a diamond,' Thalia murmured. 'Or pearls.'

'Unless it's the biggest diamond in all India.' Clio took the kitchen knife a footman handed her and sliced through the binding ropes, impatiently pushing back the wrappings. As they fell away, a wonder was revealed.

Artemis. The Alabaster Goddess.

She stood there in their small foyer, her bow upraised, her silver-white stone gleaming beyond the light of any diamond. Without her base, she stood almost as tall as Clio.

Clio laid a gentle touch on the intricately carved swirls of her hair, the crescent moon bound there. She was cold and perfect, her serene eyes refusing to divulge any of her long-held secrets.

'It's the Alabaster Goddess,' Thalia breathed in wonder. 'He's given it to you, Clio.'

Had he given it to her? After all they had been through over this one statue, over everything?

The statue was surely the most elaborate gift possible. Was she a sign of farewell? Of contrition, forgiveness?

Clio swung toward the footman, suddenly frantic. 'Was there anything else? A note or message?'

He shook his head. 'Just the statue, *signorina*.'

Clio ran towards the door, hardly noticing the painful twinge in her shoulder or hearing Thalia calling after her. She hurried out to the street, ignoring the startled glances of the people she passed, not stopping until she found her goal. Edward's palazzo.

She stopped at the open gates, out of breath. Not from her mad dash through town, but from what she saw there, servants carrying out trunks and cases. The windows of the house were all open, the curtains stirring in the breeze, adding their sinuous satin whisper to the bustle and dash of the courtyard.

He *was* leaving, she realised in shock. Going away and leaving Artemis to say farewell.

A flash of hot anger burned away the cold shock, and her hands tightened on the wrought-iron bars of the gate. Run away from her, would he? *No!* Not now, not after everything. She wouldn't, couldn't, let him. Couldn't lose him.

That anger chased away all doubts, and her insecurities, too. Only as she stood there, watching him go, did she see the one and only truth that mattered. She loved Edward. He was the only person who had ever seen and understood *her,* as she really was. Because they were cut from the same cloth, two of a kind. It was hardly important that the world would think her a poor excuse for a duchess. She would be *his* duchess, and that was what counted.

If she could just keep him from leaving now!

Clio hurried through the gate, asking the first servant she saw, 'The Duke! Where is he?'

'In his chamber, *signorina*, but I don't…'

She pushed past him, and the butler who tried to stop her at the door, and all the servants carrying their boxes down the stairs. She remembered well where his chamber was, and she didn't stop until she reached it.

Edward sat at his desk, writing. All the antiquities she had seen the night she had broken in were gone, packed away, leaving only the locked box on the dressing table. The one that held the silver bowl and the silken scrap from her old Medusa costume.

He did not even look up from his work, just smiled as if he had been expecting her all along.

'You are looking well today, Clio,' he said.

'Thanks to you. You saved me there, in Lady Riverton's drawing room.'

'It was my fault you were in such a dangerous situation in the first place.'

'No, it was my fault. I insisted on being involved.'

'And now that you have seen how it all ends, would you do it differently?' he asked.

'Certainly not.'

'I didn't think so.' He laid his pen down at last and looked up at her, his arms folded on the desk. 'I have learned a most valuable lesson in all this, my dear.'

'Just one?'

'Oh, no, indeed. But this was the most valuable. You will never be the sort of lady who stays safely at home, out of the way of trouble. If you see a wrong to be righted, you will leap into a fight, come what may. I cannot stop you from that. I can't keep you safe, even by resorting to kidnapping.'

Clio gave a choked laugh. 'It took you this long to decipher that? And here I thought you knew me so well.'

'I do. And that is why I know this—your fierce determination is one of the things I love most about you. If you stayed home embroidering by the fire, you wouldn't be Clio.'

'You—you love me?' she whispered.

'You know I love you. I love everything about you, even that stubbornness that drives me to insanity. I think we have to marry.'

'Why is that?'

'So that when we run into danger again, as we assuredly will, we can save each other. And because I just can't envision my life without you. I have asked you before, Clio, and I ask you again. Will you marry me?'

'Yes!' Clio cried. She threw herself into his lap, kissing him again and again through a storm of laughter and tears. He kissed her, too, holding her so close they could never be parted again. 'Yes, I will marry you. I will make you the most wonderful duchess ever, eventually. I promise. Now, when is the wedding?'

'As soon as I can arrange it, my dear. I told you there were some advantages to being a duke. I'll make the wedding so quick you won't be able to escape me again.'

'Or *you* will not be able to escape *me*! Is that what you were trying to do in leaving Santa Lucia? In sending me the Alabaster Goddess?'

'I am moving to other lodgings. This palazzo has become a bit oppressive, I think. And you can consider Artemis a wedding gift of sorts, if a rather ironic one, considering how fiercely she defended her virginity. But, yes, I am leaving soon. To help your friend Marco find Lady Riverton and the silver.'

'Another adventure, then?'

'But not without you, Clio. Never again without you.'

'I will hold you to that promise,' she said, kissing him again. 'For many, many years to come. All our adventures will be together.'

'Oh, my dear...' he laughed '...when we are together, the world will never, ever be the same.'

* * * * *

0209/04a

MILLS & BOON
Historical

On sale 6th March 2009

Love is the most tempting betrayal of all...

Scotland, 1561

By trying to help the reckless, defiant Mary, Queen of Scots take her rightful place on the throne, Lady Gwenyth Macleod is at perilous odds with Rowan Graham, a laird accomplished in both passion and affairs of state.

The more Gwenyth challenges his intentions, the less he can resist the desire igniting between them. But will Gwenyth's last daring gamble lead her to the ultimate betrayal – or a destiny greater than she could ever imagine?

Available 16th January 2009

M&B

To unmask her secrets, he will
have to unlock her heart!

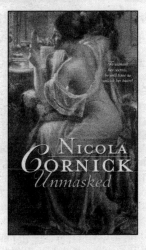

Wickedly handsome Nick Falconer has been
sent to stop a gang of highwaywomen.
But the woman he suspects of leading them
is intoxicatingly beautiful and Nick sets
out to seduce her.

Mari Osbourne's secrets are deeper and
darker than Nick could ever imagine.
Will trusting the one man she wants lead
Mari to the hangman's noose?

Available 20th February 2009

FREE

2 BOOKS AND A SURPRISE GIFT!

We would like to take this opportunity to thank you for reading this Mills & Boon® book by offering you the chance to take TWO more specially selected titles from the Historical series absolutely FREE! We're also making this offer to introduce you to the benefits of the Mills & Boon® Book Club™—

★ **FREE home delivery**
★ **FREE gifts and competitions**
★ **FREE monthly Newsletter**
★ **Books available before they're in the shops**
★ **Exclusive Mills & Boon Book Club offers**

Accepting these FREE books and gift places you under no obligation to buy; you may cancel at any time, even after receiving your free shipment. Simply complete your details below and return the entire page to the address below. You don't even need a stamp!

YES! Please send me 2 free Historical books and a surprise gift. I understand that unless you hear from me, I will receive 4 superb new titles every month for just £3.69 each, postage and packing free. I am under no obligation to purchase any books and may cancel my subscription at any time. The free books and gift will be mine to keep in any case.

H9ZEE

Ms/Mrs/Miss/Mr..Initials ....

BLOCK CAPITALS PLEASE

Surname ....

Address ....

....

....Postcode ....

Send this whole page to:

The Mills & Boon Book Club, FREEPOST CN81, Croydon, CR9 3WZ